YOUR CHILD, MY CHILD

WHOSE CHILD?

EZE NACHO

Published in Britain
By New Generation Publishing, London

ISBN **978-1-909039-64-3**

Cover Design
Ugochukwu Egenamba (Uk Business Aid)

IN THE YEAR OF LONDON OLYMPICS AND PARALYMPICS, HER MAJESTY, THE QUEEN OF ENGLAND'S GOLDEN JUBILEE AND AMERICAN PRESIDENTIAL ELECTION 2012, I BRING YOU, YOUR CHILD, MY CHILD BUT WHOSE CHILD IS IT?

4% of the proceeds from the sale of this book will go to Damilola Taylor Trust, 2% to Healthcare4Africa and another 2% to Children who are in need.

GET WELL SOON FABRICE MUAMBA AND LET'S GO TO WORK!

Dedication

This book is dedicated to my beloved cousin and best friend, Kingsley Ihenacho whose untimely death on 2nd September 2010 left me with the feeling that a part of me has gone forever. The pain I feel about Kingsley's death is a part of the catalysts for this book. Though he died of 'natural causes', his death has given me some level of insight into what might be happening in the lives of those who have lost their loved ones through a stabbing, shooting, strangulation, acts of terrorism, kidnapping and other deliberate acts of fellow human beings. Deaths that are unnecessary and avoidable under 'normal' circumstances.

King Boy, as you were fondly called, may your soul rest in peace. The pain is just too much but our God knows best. Till we meet again to part no more, rest in peace.

Acknowledgements

To the mother of our children 'Baby' for your inspiration. And my wonderful children; Michael, Nadine, Jamie and Jordan for your patience, understanding and encouragement. I thank all of you, for your unwavering support.

To all my friends and critics, well-wishers, colleagues, associates and fans, especially Nikki Plastiras, Bishop David Onuoha, Dr Philip and Mrs Irene Nwachukwu, Maria Eke, Reshna Begum, Mr Senanu Mortty, Rita Ikegwuru, Norma Johnson, Angela Roseline, Afsaneh Motabar, Dr Eugene & Mrs Caroline Mgbemere, Chief B.C. & Lolo Roseline Nwangwu, Mr Lawrence & Mrs Anastasia Ogbonna, Violet Thorpe, Barbara Nicholls, Cllr. Kate Anolue (Mayor of Enfield), Sergeant Shaun Goodchild, Sir Jude & Lady Ezigbo Ibe, Dr G.O.C and Mrs Chidi Duru, Beverley Sykes, Mary Landucci, Sir Emmanuel and Lady Juliet Ngozi Ahanonu, Nze Onyeka Valentine Uzoukwu, Dr Austin and Mrs Tina Okolie, Dr Chino and Mrs Gloria Okwuosa, Sir Jude Nzeako, Fr. Emefiena Ezeani, Rev. Stuart Owen, Michaela Anaka, Anne-Marie Ikegwuru, Olumide Olasehinde Kolade, Chief Freddie Alufuo, Mr Klass, Charles Khiran, Hon. Justice Goddy and Lady Nancy Goddy-Anunihu, George Onuoha PhD, Jide Odusina, Mr Reuben Emelone, Nze Sympathy & Lolo Chioma Nwosu, Mr Ndubuisi Ekomaru, Donnette Julien, Mr Sam Ekenna[1], Mrs Dorinda Harding and Ven. Dr. Amatu Onundu and Mrs Princess Chinyere Christian-Iwuagwu for their professional input, suggestions and contributions. Above all, and as always, the men and women, boys and girls who were happy to discuss some difficult issues with me. I honestly would not have been able to face up to this mammoth task without your contributions. I thank you all indeed!

---

[1] This work was proof-read by Samreader.co.uk

Foreword

It is not always easy to spot behavioural problems in their early stages though they may begin while a child is still a toddler. It is possible some of these could be nipped in the bud at this stage if parents could spot them.

Parents have traditionally been held responsible for their children's behaviours or characters. When youngsters misbehave, the natural tendency is to blame it on parental mismanagement or family disintegration, sometimes rightly so. However, there are times when parents are doing all the right things but the child fails in life. Sometimes parents are abusive or neglecting and still the child develops into a wonderful human being. The implication of this is that parental role alone does not explain the behaviours we see in children. There are often complex reasons behind a child's behaviour.

Behaviour in a child can be as a result of multiple factors or interactions between them, most of which is beyond the control of the parents. These factors may include individual make up, family dynamics, and impairments such as hearing problems and poor vision amongst others, which can frustrate a child into irrational behaviours. Others are environmental factors which can be physical environment like the effect of living in an urban, rural environment or social environment which includes the people around the child, the culture, tradition, religion of the people, technology, media, laws and policies of the society in which they find themselves.

The author, in this book, has given an in-depth insight into these factors whose by-product is the behaviour we see in a child. If the product turns into a well-behaved child, the child becomes a joy and pride, not only to the parents or family but also to the society at large. Everyone enjoys the fruit of good behaviour. If the product turns into a badly behaved child; s/he will constitute a pain and thorn not only in the flesh of the parents and family but also the society at large.

The author has undertaken a very commendable and extensive research into our society of yesteryears and today and has tried to bring to our conscious mind how, why and where things have gone terribly wrong over the years in the terrible situation we find ourselves with some of our children's behaviours today. Following his research, he believes that even though a child biologically belongs to a man and woman (parents), behaviourally, his or her upbringing is a collective responsibility of society as a whole, as parents' role alone is not enough in some cases. Even though in an ideal situation, there will still be some problematic children, he still believes that a collective responsibility from parents, governments, religions, media, cultures and traditions to our children will go a long way to minimise the ills the society suffers today as a result of bad behaviours of our children. His belief in the collective responsibility to our children has led him to observe that there is no question asking *'whose child?'* because it is our child collectively. In this responsibility of a better society for tomorrow, *'your child is my child'* he argues.

Your Child, My Child, Whose Child is a treasure for whoever lays their hands on it. In it lies the understanding of the need for our collective responsibility, as parents, as a society to our children. I strongly, without any reservations, recommend this book to everyone, young and old. I commend the author for a job well done.

Dr Philip Nwachukwu
Psychiatrist
City and Hackney centre for Mental Health.
East Wing, Homerton University Hospital, United Kingdom.

CONTENTS

Foreword...vii
CHAPTER ONE 13
  Food For Thought!... 13
  Introduction... 23
CHAPTER TWO 31
  Human Babies Versus Other Mammals' Babies 31
  Separation of Nature and Nurture 36
  Did Human Beings Really Evolve From Apes And
  Monkeys?... 39
  Why Children Should Be Guided In The Choices They
  Make.. 43
  The Problem With Parenting 51
  Simple Lessons For Parents And Children 81
  A Tribute To An Awesome Father............................... 102
  To All The Children of This World 111
  Hear my little story about cigarette smoking 129
  Bangladeshi Experience 140
  Good Parenting 142
  Bad Parenting 148
  Worst Parenting.. 156
CHAPTER FOUR 161
  Personal Encounters 161
  My Painful Heart Bleeds... 177
CHAPTER FIVE... 187
  Governance.. 187
  The Role Of The Mass Media 218
CHAPTER SIX 225
  The Igbo people 225
  Solutions To Igbo People's Crisis 276
  My Nigerian Child... 283
CHAPTER SEVEN 303
Conclusion 303
References 310
The Author 314

CHAPTER ONE

Food For Thought!

The test of the morality of a society is what it does for its children. - Dietrich Bonheoffer

Nothing misrepresents the capacity and ability of unruly children and people's understanding of the potential capabilities of unruly children more than the result of a survey carried out by Barnardos (a leading children's charity based in the United Kingdom), which stated that 'Almost half of Britons think children are violent and starting to behave like animals' (BBC) Radio 5 live, channel 909 medium wave, Thursday 3rd November 2011). The result of this survey could not be further from the truth. It is either a disservice to animals or an insult to or assault on human capabilities, because animals only attack when threatened or hungry; they have no weapon to deploy or use and their ability to plan is limited. Furthermore, they are seen by human beings as wild and are often avoided, whereas an unruly child's ability to plan evil is unlimited: they can deploy and use weapons and, of course, there are no distinguishing features to alert anyone of a child carrying a weapon or being intent on using it on another human being. So everyone assumes that being a human being is synonymous with being 'considerate' and 'rational'. As a result, a false sense of security is engendered which then, lowers our defenses. These days one doesn't need to provoke or threaten some unruly children before they physically attack you. In some instances just one 'subjectively' defined 'bad' look could be enough.

Though most children and human beings are well behaved, the capacity of one unruly child or adult to cause mayhem is huge, and when they do it can send shock waves across society at large. Whereas all of the wild animals put together can never come close to matching the mayhem that one unruly human being can generate. So if, as a society, we cannot allow anyone to rear a wild animal and unleash it into society, it beggars belief that we allow some parents to hide under the façade of 'it is my business how I bring up my children' to 'nurture' unruly children and unleash them on society, where they then become 'everyone's business' in the end. This is not about percentages, frequency or volume because one incident is bad enough, and it is always and only 'big news' when the story is negative.

Just think! Anders Breivik of Norway single-handedly killed 77 people in 2011; Woo Bom-Kon of South Korea killed 57 people in 1982; Campo Elias Delgado of Colombia, 30 people in 1986; Martin Bryant of Australia, 35 people in 1996; Thomas Hamilton of the United Kingdom, 17 people in 1996; Seung-Hui Cho of the United States of America, 32 people in 2007; and Dr Harold Shipman of the United Kingdom murdered at least 215 of his patients. How about the mayhem, disaster and chaos the few who carried out the evil acts of 9/11 in the USA and 7/7 in the UK caused and how many people they killed and injured? This is to mention just a few incidents and these are just individuals or people destroying fellow human beings. What about Hitler, Saddam and Gaddafi, who used government machinery to destroy their fellow human beings? Assad of Syria is doing the same thing today.

Consider the death of PC David Rathband, who was blinded by Raoul Moat on 4th July 2010. The entire episode brings home the fact that; 'it is not your business how I bring up my child' is a dangerous stance to adopt in view of what we know about 'unruly children'. The far-reaching consequences of one act such as those mentioned above are horrendous. The devastation for and the psychological impact on victims, partners, their children, extended families, communities and society at large can never be fully comprehended; yet there were windows of opportunity that may have been ignored by an individual, family members, associates and community services that could have brought a different outcome for Mr Moat, which would in turn have prevented these shootings and the ongoing suffering of many people. All of these murderers and terrorists were once harmless and innocent babies.

With this in mind, it becomes somewhat obvious that the definition of child abuse or a child in need should not just apply to a child who suffers emotional and/or physical abuse, but should include a child who is deprived of moral values, because nothing else threatens a child's prospects in life and causes that child to threaten the health and safety of others more than a lack of moral values. A child deprived of these is likely to operate outside the 'norms' of the society in which they are born.

It is and should be everyone's responsibility to correct bad behaviour, because the true owner of a gun is not s/he that bought it but s/he that is in possession of it or uses it.

Ignoring bad behaviour is another way of condoning and encouraging it. That baby you are carrying now could tomorrow be someone's partner, neighbour or workmate. That baby you are carrying today could tomorrow be the one carrying a knife or gun or driving with the intention of knocking someone over. At that point, whose business is it? With this in mind, it is crucial to appreciate that the upbringing of your baby should not only be your business, but everyone's business, because 'the child is the father of a man'.

The future belongs to those who can project and prepare for it today. Never create or nurture a 'monster', because the 'monster' you create today could destroy you tomorrow, for evil knows no bounds! It is not just what you told or taught your child that helps make them the 'angel' or 'monster' they become tomorrow, but what you failed to tell or teach your child.

Nature has everything to offer our fellow mammals but very little (in terms of morality or moral values) to offer us (human beings). Therefore nurture accounts for most of the good things human beings do. Leave your baby to the devices of nature and be sent to prison! A baby is not a toy or an accessory; though weak and vulnerable at birth, a baby could have the capacity to inflict the severest of damage on mankind, if not brought up the right way.

Did I just hear 'what is the right way?' Read about 'Good Parenting' on page 142 and see what the right way is. The good intentions/deeds of many count for nothing when compared with one singular heinous act of an individual, hence bad news carries more weight than good, and of course 'the few spoil it for the many'.

Everyone must note and understand that no weapon, gadget or equipment is dangerous, hazardous or harmful on its own; it is only harmful when it comes in contact and used by a human being. Therefore the real weapons are 'human beings'. By the way, who made the weapons? With this in mind, a baby should and must be handled with the utmost care and fed with the right meal; not just food, but sound moral values that are likely to turn the baby into an angel that brings joy to humanity, instead of pain, suffering and sadness. In order words the baby would be turned from agent of 'destruction' to 'construction' if nurtured the right way.

The warning signs should be firmly placed on the agent/s that makes these harmless weapons, gadgets and equipment dangerous. The questions are: has a bullet ever fired itself, has a knife used itself, has an aeroplane flown itself and have you ever seen a stone or stick use itself? The answer to these questions is NO! As human beings, we are confronted by all manner of crises: natural disasters, illnesses, accidents, uprisings, wars and natural deaths that cause us more than enough pain and suffering. Why are we deliberately generating more pain and suffering on ourselves?

Never treat good and bad in equal measure. Though they sit on the opposite side of the spectrum, they are not equal. Good is heavy; not everyone can carry it, and hard work is always required in order to learn how to carry it. Bad is light, very light indeed, and everyone can carry it, often without training. For a child to be good, a lot of hard work is required. Good is solid and bad is liquid that's why bad spreads rapidly and very easy to copy. In all babies, the liquid is already in place; that's why a two-year-old does not require training in order to untidy a room but might require a lifetime to learn how to tidy it. Good is slow and sluggish; bad is rapid and fast. That's why to build is slow but to destroy is fast. A lot of training and preparation go into building, but to destroy it is easy and training may not be required. Using the weed and crop analogy, the weeds are always more than the crops. By this I mean that evil is very attractive and it multiplies very quickly, because often there is no training required and everyone is capable of doing it; it is just a matter of choice but there is no choice in doing good because a lot of good things people do are learned. One cannot do what one hasn't learnt. That is why saving life is good, but not easy – not everyone can save life, but taking life is bad and everyone can destroy life. Think! Why are we then bringing more pain and suffering onto ourselves by deliberately destroying ourselves through stabbings and shootings? How come the bearer of the agent with the potential to destroy the planet and fellow human beings has no manual, training or coaching before becoming a parent?

Our world is in a coma, and in need of the best physicians to diagnose what has gone terribly wrong in the first instance. Being a doctor does not necessarily mean you won't get ill or in need of medical assistance yourself, but it does mean that you play a part in curing other people's illnesses and you help to save lives.

To think negatively is easy, but positive thinking can be very hard. Anything worthwhile is easy to destroy but very difficult to build. Consider the twin tower (World Trade Centre) in New York that took approximately four years each to build whereas their destruction took only minutes. Those who destroyed them, and in the process shattered many lives, were once harmless little babies. It is easy to allow your children to 'get on with it' so that you can get on with other things you consider 'important'; this makes it difficult to spend 'quality' time with your children or to instil life sustaining values into them.

Nothing is as important as spending quality time with your children! Anything you do that never allows you to have quality time with your children cannot be a good thing:
'Your children need your presence more than your presents' (Jesse Jackson). However, your presence alone is as bad as giving only presents and being absent all the time.

Have you told your children how proud you are of them, the standards expected of them and the guiding principles of your family, if you have one? Have you told them how unique they are and why they must not copy the bad behaviour of others? It is better to encourage your child to be a good example to other children. Is your child able to remember any word of wisdom from you? (*See* 'A Tribute to an Awesome Father', page 102). If they can't, then rest assured that you are not doing your job well, and in the process you are creating a crisis for those who will come into contact with your child in the future, as it is very difficult to change an adult personality. A problem that should have been nipped in the bud during childhood becomes deep rooted in adulthood, making it almost impossible to be erased.

Adults, especially parents, need to learn to be 'sensible' not 'reckless' with their perceived 'freedom, choice and liberty' More emphasis on 'responsibility' should accompany the rights we hold dear at all times, due to the impact that a lack of responsibility has on our children and society at large. In most instances, the derailment of children stems from the derailment of parents, as what parents perceive and play out in the name of freedom, choice and liberty is copied by the children as 'normal' behaviour. The only difference is that a parent can control and cover up their tracks but children act as children, even to their own detriment.

Everyone needs to ask and answer the following questions: who am I, what are my values and principles, what do I stand for, is my behaviour likely to create or solve problems, am I a source for good or evil, what sort of family do I come from or want to have, what are the base line values my 'partner to be' must have in order to cohabit or enter into marriage with me and can these values help nurture and mould my children into agents for good?

It goes without saying that if you do not stand firmly for something; you will definitely fall for every and anything!

Hear this and take note! *Though silence is said to be golden, it can also be deadly or futile if it cohabits with or is intertwined with evil. Silence breeds evil and evil multiply when people turn a blind eye or become passive in the face it. If the ills of society are to be corrected, everyone must learn to be proactive in challenging evil. The route to peace is not silence, and silence does not make one a good person but an active participant in acts of evil. Keeping silence in the face of evil is evil in itself, for nothing condones and encourages evil more than silence! Dietrich Bonheoffer echoed the same point when he said,*

'Silence in the face of evil is itself evil: God will not hold us guiltless. Not to speak is to speak. Not to act is to act.' Therefore, where there's a 'doer-active' let there also be a talkative; for 'doer-active' without a talkative encourages the evil doer to do more damage unchecked and uninterrupted, making the passive and silent observer an active participant in the acts committed! Haven't we heard that evil strives when 'good' people stand aside and do nothing? The reality is; the 'good' people who stand aside and do nothing are guiltier, because the evildoer may be influenced by all manner of psychological factors including poly-substance abuse. **Silence can only be 'golden' if it is not co-habiting with evil. One is either part of the solution or they are the problem!**

It would remain doubtful if any parent/s deliberately set out to bring up unruly children. Parent/s cannot give what they do not have; neither can they take what is not on offer. Parents can only give the 'best' they know, often they hand back what they have been given or have taken from their own parents or others through association. This is so because it would be odd for an apple tree to produce a grape. Some well-meaning parents who want to do their best for their children are often unable to do so, due to legislative framework geared towards pleasing the civil libertarians. And often children who want to roam the streets and get up to no good exploit these (see t*he Ordeal of a Father Who Physically Removed His Son from Possible Danger page 166)*. These are children who only want to know what their rights are but have no interest in knowing their responsibilities. In the end some of these children would seek to blame everyone else but themselves when things go wrong. The essence of this book is to come to some level of understanding about why things are the way they are currently with our children and to find a way to break the chain, because one cannot make an omelette without breaking an egg.

When all's said and done, who we are, what we are or what we would become, including all of our achievements is primarily down to 'good or bad fortunes'. As babies do not nominate or elect the families or nations they are born into 'It was undoubtedly chiefly within the family that children learned about the world into which they had been born, and about the roles which they could expect to play' (Cunningham 2005, page 97).

The 'problem' in parenting and children's upbringing is not the issue, though; the real issue is the 'solution', but in order to find the right solution, one must identify (not partly but fully) what the problem really is. As I have previously stated, 'no one can cure cancer with Paracetamol' (Nacho E. 2010). The true soul-searching questions for all parents, as relates to your child and my child, should revolve around asking the following: what have I got or what do I need to offer, what do I need to obtain and what do I need to learn or share with others in order to enhance my own and others' children? For it is, should and must be a collective responsibility if we are to get things right.

*If you cannot see yourself in the other person, something has gone **amiss** in you. This book is not about to change the world but to the individual on whom it has a positive impact, it will seem as though the world has changed.*

Introduction

It is commonly said that children are our future, but they are not only our future, they are also our past as well as our present. Life itself revolves around children because one is never an adult, unless they were once a child. Therefore every human life begins from childhood, as we know it today. Forget about creation, the big bang, evolution or whatever theory there is, depending on one's beliefs.

Throughout history human beings have been known to commit heinous crimes against their fellow human beings, but never in the history of mankind have we seen so many premeditated killings orchestrated by children than in recent years. Children harming or killing children in the past, was done only by accident through play or misadventure. However, irrespective of who is killing who, the fact is that everybody alive today was once a child. Presidents, prime ministers, queens, kings, pope, archbishops, road sweepers, fat cats, terrorists, kidnappers, murderers, gang members, drug barons, those causing us pain and giving us joy, the good, the bad and the ugly were all once children

This fact in itself proves that in the final analysis all human beings are equal, because at the points of arrival and departure we share common similarities irrespective of our status, nationality, creed, gender or colour. The inequality we know and talk about is located only in between points of entry and departure. This is partly illustrated in the film *The Iron Lady*. On arrival, all human beings are harmless, helpless, dependent and very vulnerable.

At birth, human babies are slower to develop (physically and intellectually) compared with other mammals' babies (*see* page 31). In old age, when the wear and tear have taken their toll as we focus on departure, human beings become yet again vulnerable, dependent and helpless, and in death nature puts everyone on a par. As a result, all human beings come in and leave with nothing. That's why all the indispensables, the 'high, powerful and mighty' are located at the graveyards and crematoriums. All the mayhem and crisis are usually generated in between points of arrival and departure when individuals and groups feel invincible and powerful. The fact remains that no one, no group; no nation is 'powerful' without the agreement of others. No one can be taller and shorter than someone at the same time, and of course, it is the losers that make the winners, as one compliments the other.

The importance and power we feel (in between arrival and departure) come from others because no one can feel big without having smaller people around; no nation can classify itself as being powerful without having weak nations around. Here lies the need for us to appreciate one another. But no matter what, as individuals we remain vulnerable and afflicted. Do you, as an individual feel like a president, prime minister or general when you are sitting on the toilet seat, laying on your bed or having a bathe? The answer is likely to be 'no'. Therefore, it is others that make you feel the way you do. The question then is; what is it that happens to human beings – what turns a vulnerable baby into the angel or monster they become later? What is it, we do or fail to do as parents, individuals, peers, communities or society at large that turns vulnerable babies into selfish, self-centred fat cats, those who took us to economic meltdown? As though that was not enough, they are at it again and remain at it, those who are willing to take $/£7 million in bonuses, whilst some people working within the same establishment are struggling to pay for a roof over their heads or to put food on the table for their children. Why do some so-called leaders (who are meant to be servants of the people who put them into power) feel that they own all the people and resources within their jurisdiction to the extent that they resort to killing their own – the people they are meant to protect and serve – because they are told their services are no longer required?

What about those who are ready to take their own lives as well as other peoples' in the name of religion? What about some religious leaders who are charged with protecting the vulnerable, feeding the poor and preaching the message of peace and love according to the Holy Books they profess to defend, who are betraying, exploiting and abusing the vulnerable and preaching the message of hate and violence? What about those producing dangerous sensationalised gadgets, sexually explicit music, videos, films and games full of violence with no interest on the damage done to our children, but only consumed by money and 'fame'?

How about those who have decided to fold their arms (when all are meant to work) and depend on others to pick up the pieces, and those flooding our streets and contaminating our children with illicit drugs, with no consideration for the number of young lives destroyed by drugs, as they are fixated only on the weight of their bank balance? What are the contributing factors that are turning our vulnerable babies into gang members who resort to stabbing and shooting these days in their quest for 'respect'? Children who are being brought up the right way are now perceived as threats by those behaving badly, and they are at risk, to such an extent, some feel, that the only way to feel safe is to join the badly behaved. Conflicts, which teenagers used to resolve through debates, dialogue, communication, argument and, at worst, physical fights in the past, are now being 'resolved' by stabbing and shooting, with no empathy or consideration for the individual stabbed or shot, and without thought for family members and friends, who in most cases, live through the pain and devastation for the rest of their lives. The anguish, frustration and devastation some of the families and friends go through on a daily basis is simply unimaginable, as they reflect on what had happened to their loved ones and what might have been. Some families have been torn apart following such incidents, as parents at times begin to blame one another for what happened to their loved one (see the *Sorrow of a Mother* ... on page 164). Most of these killings stem from parental lifestyle whilst or before becoming pregnant, individuals lifestyle, upbringing, social interaction and societal impact on harmless babies who, through nurture or lack of it were turned into murderers.

The question is, at what point does this needy, vulnerable and helpless baby get to the stage where he/she suddenly feels or believes they are in charge and in some cases own an entire nation and are ready to kill and destroy any opposition? At what point does this vulnerable baby decide that someone else has no right to life and become consumed by their own importance and relevance? What is it we do as parents, peers, groups, communities and society at large that contributes to breeding and nurturing such human beings? Are parents and society at large caught unawares by the explosion of technology?

How much violence and inappropriate material is being made, licensed and purchased for our children in our world today, with designers and producers only interested in profit and nothing else? What must we do to reverse or at the very least keep this trend in check?

It is crucial to bear in mind that a child represents a generation and any child destroyed is not just a loss to a particular person, family or group but to the entire society. When they become a threat, it can affect anyone. For example, a young man who was driving at high speed to escape from a police chase broke through the railway barrier and missed the oncoming train by seconds. Had the train hit his vehicle, it is unlikely that he would have been the only one killed or injured. You, your relative or loved one may have been in that train. So a dangerous child/person poses a threat to all, irrespective of their colour, creed or culture. Why is the human mind always in denial, thinking, 'It can't happen to me'. This type of thing happens to certain types of people and in other places, not around my area'? This is an illusion, as crime is like the air we breathe: it has no boundary, no border and no demarcating lines.

The human brain is wired to naturally pick up bad ideas and behaviour, often with no teaching involved, that's why one does not need to do anything to be useless but the reverse is the case when one embarks on any useful venture. Hard work, repeated teaching, dedication, focus and discipline are required. As a parent, consider how many times you try to get your two-year-old baby to tidy a room and the effort you put into that, then contrast it with the effort (if any) you put in before the same baby turns the room upside down. In order to understand our true human nature, consider that even in our 'sane or rational' state of mind we make mistakes, and contrast this with how difficult it is for us to do any positive thing in our 'insane or irrational' state of mind. Also consider the fact that wrongdoings are associated with being bored and ask why the bored could not do something useful, for example, pick up litter. Positive things often involve persistent teaching and patient learning whereas the reverse is the case when it comes to negative things.

With this in mind, how is it that in our quest to make history, money, dominate, control others and have influence, human beings have turned into the proverbial snail, which sought to extinguish the fire by releasing bodily fluid into the fire, without knowing that it was hastening its own death in the process? How is it that we now promote treating children like adults and expecting children not only to know what is right for them, but to go for it as a matter of 'choice' in the belief that we are making them happy? Yet, as adults, we know that making someone happy does not mean keeping them happy. How is it that we have travelled from one extreme (judging from the story of the watercress girl who, at the age of eight, could not relate to being a child or sharing in the experience of childhood, as narrated by Mayhew (1985) to another extreme where children only know their 'rights' and make their 'choices' with no sense of 'responsibility'? All in the name of 'doing what I like'.

It is not rocket science to appreciate that doing what one likes does not always mean doing what is right, and children doing what they like often means that they choose painless activities full of fun, excitement and pleasure; but it is common knowledge that 'there is no gain without pain'. Most things that give pleasure have very little dividend attached to them. *Your Child, My Child* seeks to address these issues and more.

The world naturally has a lot of hazards confronting human beings, and the natural pain of losing a loved one through an illness such as heart attack, cancer, HIV/AIDS, mental illness, natural disasters or through an accident is always immense, but it is greater, deeper and frustratingly intolerable when the loss is as a result of a deliberate act by another human being, which is illegal and avoidable.

Human beings have done more harm to their fellow human beings than any other creature on this planet, leaving me to conclude that the bushes may be safer now than the streets, so long as one does not meet human beings in the bushes. But the question is, with the cognition and intellectual ability human beings have, if applied correctly, is this supposed to be so?

The 'master key' is located at UPBRINGING, followed by socialisation. *Your Child, My Child* is here to encourage parents to first of all appreciate that they haven't 'got it all' to give. *Your Child, My Child* is also here to help you as a parent to appreciate your strengths and weaknesses and to understand that you cannot give what you don't have. However, the fact that you do not have a strength or skill does not mean the child is not in need of the benefits that the strength or skill might bring them. For example, a parent cannot say, 'I was not taught mathematics and do not understand it, therefore my children do not need mathematics' or 'I don't have the skills or ability to appreciate right from wrong, therefore my children do not need to know what is right or wrong. I also do not need anyone else to teach them, because it is not their business how I bring up my own children.' The riots in United Kingdom (August 2011) and Anders Breivik incident in Norway (July 2011) tell us otherwise and act as a sharp reminder that what may once have been classified as 'one's business', suddenly became 'everyone's business'.

Therefore this book challenges us to be creative in seeking help in order to provide that which our children are in need of but which we do not have. It also helps all parents to explore the base line of what every child should and must have irrespective of their gender, colour, creed or nationality in order to begin the process of turning things around for the better.

Life is like a relay: some of us have been handed dangerous batons. We should first of all acknowledge that and then seek to break the chain and ensure we do not hand such dangerous batons to our offspring.

This book offers some meaningful advice, encouragement and highlights the fact that if we fail to recognise the current trends and take action to reverse or break the cycle, the future will be really bleak for the current and future generations. Consider the current modes and frequency of rioting in our world today and you will see that technology, which has brought much good, has at the same time brought so much evil.

As a person, parent, community and society we need to wake up and smell the coffee. Let all hands be on deck: let's get to work!

CHAPTER TWO

Human Babies Versus Other Mammals' Babies

The intention here is not to make this book too academic, littered with theories on child development and gestation periods of all mammals, in order to show the difference between human babies and other mammal's babies. This is because of the fact that there are already many textbooks written that have dealt with these issues; but most importantly this is because this book is for the 'ordinary' person out there to read, assimilate and, hopefully, understand.

One does not have to study to appreciate through observation that human babies are slower to develop (physically and intellectually) from birth compared with other mammals' babies. Calves, kittens and puppies can walk within hours of their birth and are able to appreciate danger very quickly. Comments from Franklin Park Zoo in Boston Massachusetts reveal that 'a baby gorilla is much stronger and develops more quickly' than a human baby. The comments also confirm that 'within days a baby gorilla can lift its head. From the start, a gorilla's tiny hands can grip with strength, something humans don't acquire for years. By the time it's 6 months old, a gorilla spends all day clinging to its mother's back as she roams the forest in search of food' and at the 'age of 3 a gorilla is basically self-sufficient, foraging for its own food and building its own nest at night'[2]. The reason for this is irrelevant but the lessons from it

---

[2] http://monkeymaddness.com/apes_monkeys/bbm38.htm Accessed 2/4/2011.

are crucial. This shows that nature offers other mammal babies a lot compared to human babies who, rely on nurture before they can even feed. This has always been so and will remain so irrespective of future technological advancements. These other mammals' babies become independent so rapidly, and what makes this even more astonishing is that it is instinctive.

Human babies, on the other hand, can take at least nine to sixteen months before they start to walk. They have no idea of what can be dangerous, as they have no concept of this at birth. Human babies take weeks and months before even recognising who their mothers are. Other mammals' babies walk and not only recognise but run from danger within hours and days. A human baby would lie there for weeks and months, and even if a lion approached, a human baby would not have any sense of danger. In fact a human baby might even put its hands into the lion's mouth or crawl into a burning fire but then cry as a consequence of the pain felt. These facts give a lot of credence to creation and support the fact that the 'chicken came before the egg', because without another adult being looking after the human baby, it is virtually impossible for it to survive. A human baby would not have any recognised language if other human beings did not communicate or interact with it; it would just babble until it became old and dies. A human baby left to the forces of nature would eat its own faeces as food or not eat at all, and would die before it could learn to sit up or crawl, let alone walk. Most of what human babies do is copied; in fact babies still have to be taught how to do properly some of the things they can do naturally. Consider things like eating, urinating and passing human waste, for example; babies still have to be shown and taught how to wipe their bottoms and be potty trained. They have to be shown where to urinate and how to put food in their mouth. Now, if human babies need training in the things they can do naturally, then it would be impossible for them to think about, let alone act in accordance with, unnatural things like morals and values without learning or copying from someone else. These need not only to be activated, but embedded in children from an early age. It takes hard work, patience and repeated teaching to instil morals and values into children as what comes naturally to them and what they can copy easily without much teaching are usually the wrong things. For example, a child finds it easy to eat a ready meal but difficult to put the plate into the sink afterwards, let alone wash it. As a parent, just think how many times you have to remind your child to wash the plate they have just used to eat from. Not washing the plate is the wrong thing because it is unhygienic and the plate needs to be clean for the next meal, but that is what comes easily to the child and it doesn't require teaching to reject washing the plate. Washing the plate is the right thing to do because it is hygienic and it keeps the hands and plate clean in readiness for the next meal, but this doesn't come easily or naturally. Therefore, it requires persistent teaching, with patience and loads of reminders. Playing on the play station is easy, fun and has little benefit. Therefore very little teaching is involved before your child 'goes to town' with it and very soon becomes your master in the games. I am still struggling to find a parent who tells me that they had to persistently remind their child to go and play on the play station. Compare this to the number of times parents complain of reminding their child to do their homework, which is the right and good thing to do.

Children have to be taught to see themselves in someone else; they have to be taught how to tidy up, cook and look after themselves as well as others. They have to be taught how to love themselves, love others and above all, love God with all their heart, soul and strength, depending on their religious beliefs. They have to be taught that every action brings about a reaction and that there is no right, choice or freedom without responsibility. They must and should be made to know that the easy, fun and lovely things they naturally enjoy may lead them nowhere. As a result, they must learn the words 'living a structured' life, with time to play, eat and work hard. They must be made to appreciate those who bring hard work and structure into their life, not just those that bring fun and sweet things. Explaining these things to them would help them begin to appreciate what you are trying to do with them. Inform them that it is only those with their best interest at heart that will bring structure into their lives, and insist on them allocating time for study, chores, moral instruction and, of course, play. Inform them that in order to do these things, discipline, focus, determination and commitment are the key words. None of their friends will tell them this and it is highly unlikely they will get it from the society we live in today. Try as much as possible to live by example; because your child is likely to copy you because, children are 'copy cats'. Having copied, then their personality may make them advance, reduce or maintain whatever behaviour they have copied. Human beings are clearly different from all other mammals and are a different species to our fellow primates. Below is my contention.

In all the studies of feral children (neglected children who live in a wild, lawless or anti-social way; some of them have been known to live with animals) I have read, whether factual or otherwise, one thing is universally clear: human babies as earlier stated are 'copy cats'. These studies illustrate the power and significance of nurturing in human beings, as each child behaved like the adult animal caregiver. The baby brought up by a wolf behaved like wolves, the one reared by a monkey behaved like monkeys and the one brought up by a dog behaved like dogs.

Another interesting aspect of these studies is the revelation that the formative age of a child is critical to its development, as a child has a limited period to have a language, and if that period lapses without the child having a language, it becomes practically impossible for that baby to learn, understand and use a recognisable language. According to Dr Candland, the author of *Feral Children and Clever Animals*, there are certain common elements in all the children he studied. He states that 'the child had no recognisable speech, the child did not like to eat cooked food, the child walked on all fours and quite properly, people would say this is a wild child' [3]

---

[3] http://video.nationalgeographic.com/video/national-geographic-channel/specials-1/science-technology/ngc-feral-children/ Accessed 2/3/2011.

Separation of Nature and Nurture

All human beings alive are nurtured, because none of us can survive by nature alone. That is why prison awaits any parent who employs only nature to bring up their child. The fact us that it is impossible to nurture every aspect of a child's life. Being that nurture is necessary for our survival, the issue becomes whether we are properly or badly nurtured. Having said that, in this topic, any mention of 'nurture' implies 'properly nurtured'.

Nature has no role to play in any orchestrated human activity; being born, dying, sleeping, eating and playing are not orchestrated human activities because everyone can do them and training is not required. They are natural and the forces of nature take care of all these. Important as they are to human beings, they are not what distinguish us from other animals rather they are what we have in common with most of them.

Nurture is solely responsible for all orchestrated human activities such as brushing teeth, making beds, saying good morning, bathing, reading and cooking. These activities are not easy; they don't come naturally and training is required. That's why no child, irrespective of culture, colour, nationality or creed wakes up to brush their teeth, say good morning, make their bed or arrange their room without being taught. On the other hand nurture does not teach any child to play, sleep or eat.

From many people's perspective, it may be difficult to separate what is nature from what is nurture when it comes to human behaviour. However, it is evidently clear that everyone is different; as even twins brought up by the same parent/s (even if they look identical) are likely to have individual traits, that is, individual personalities. For example, siblings brought up by the same parents with similar experience do not grow up behaving the same way, as parents' behaviour can differ from child to child. Furthermore, it is not certain that because you come from the same womb your associations and interactions outside your household or within it will always be the same. Out of one hundred individuals who have siblings with whom I explored this, ninety-five per cent of them agreed this to be true. Science has proven that everyone carries different deoxyribonucleic acid (DNA). However, it would remain arguable whether any of us is particularly born to kill, rather we (as human beings) are all potential killers, put in the right conditions. Wouldn't you do something to stop or resist someone who is trying to strangle you, for instance? Therefore nature makes us potential killers, but how we are nurtured can increase or decrease our potential to kill or harm others.

Nature and nurture play significant, important and differing roles in human beings. Without nature human beings would not exist and the absence of nurture makes it impossible for human beings to survive. Though nature is primarily responsible for our arrival and departure, for our sleeping and waking up, and forms the basis of our existence, its role after that (in terms of human orchestrated activities) is usually negative because no human baby is likely to survive without someone or something nurturing it. Nature is primarily responsible for most 'wrong' and 'useless' things human beings do, because it offers us mainly fun, play, self-centredness and a negative fixation on differences and lack of boundaries. Nature forces human beings to be dis-inhibited, irrational, thoughtless, instinctive and reactive. Nature points us to 'the only way' that's why as human beings we are excited about revenge, taking advantage and cheating for 'gain'. Examine your natural emotions when someone has wronged you, for example, another driver cuts in front of your vehicle, what sort of things go through your mind? Human beings are naturally emotional and emotion is irrational. This is why seeking revenge excites human beings. The revenge we seek is not usually in equal measure but one seeks to add extra to the actual did done, in order to be satisfied, hence victims do not pass sentences. Even the modern day Christianity preaches revenge with slogans like 'back to sender' 'defeat of enemy' and 'not my portion', though the Author of our faith (JESUS CHRIST) tells us not to repay evil with evil and commands all Christians (His followers) to Love and Prayer for their enemies. He (CHRIST) commands us to 'turn the other cheek' and promises us that vengeance is 'mine'. He urges us to allow for the 'wrath of God', yet our human nature makes it difficult for us not to get excited about revenge. If Christians struggle with this, how about people whose religion actively supports and encourages revenge, non-believers and non-believers who have no morals coupled with the abuse of illicit substances? A thorough understanding of what nature offers human being is critical otherwise, it would be difficult to appreciate the importance of nurture. No one can forgive without being properly nurtured. Human beings also feel a sense of surprise and warmth towards the few who genuinely forgive others who have wronged them. This is part of the reasons; Nelson Mandela is an icon around the world today. He went against human nature, by pursuing peace, unity and reconciliation instead of revenge in spite of all he went through.

Nurture points us 'the other way' and helps human beings to be rational, patient, proactive, disciplined, reflective, projective, considerate, inhibitive, less-instinctive and focus on similarities. It compels us to see 'beyond our nose'. Above all, nurture helps us to empathise with others. It is nurture that provides us with these vital elements that distinguish us from our fellow primates and other animals, and places us in charge of all other creatures on this planet. In other words, nurture is what really makes us fully-fledged HUMAN BEINGS. The things nature gives us require no training, hard work or discipline to achieve, because they are mostly 'can dos'. The things nurture offers us have to be learnt because they are 'can't dos'. This is why nature remains superior to nurture.

Did Human Beings Really Evolve From Apes And Monkeys?

It is and will remain my contention that we may have been cousins with apes and monkeys, but we are definitely not from the same womb; neither did we graduate from them. Archaeologists, Anthropologists and indeed scientists in general, have done great work to resolve a lot of myths surrounding human life and our environment. However, in their quest to display superiority in knowledge amongst their peers, to make history and control human thoughts, they have at times gone beyond the realms of their ability. As John Watson (the architect of behaviourism) claimed, 'Give me a dozen healthy infants, well-formed, and my own specified world to bring them up in and I'll guarantee to take any one at random and train him to become any type of specialist I might select – doctor, lawyer, artist, merchant-chief and, yes, even beggar-man and thief, regardless of his talents, penchants, tendencies, abilities, vocations, and race of his ancestors'. *Mr. Watson later confessed, in the book, behaviourism (1930),* 'I am going beyond my facts and I admit it, but so have the advocates of the contrary and they have been doing it for many thousands of years' (page 82). *If one was to dig up two skulls belonging to a goat and a sheep buried over thirty years ago, and present them to ten scientists for analysis, one would find that there would be differing outcomes. There is likely to be one that would say that the two skulls are from the same breed. The truth is, one skull belonged to a goat and the other to a sheep. Yes, they may look the same and come from the same family, as classified by human beings, but they are different species and would never cross over. The sheep would not start eating yam as it is not their usual food, whereas it is normal for goats.*

No matter how we compare human beings, their fellow primates and other mammals, human beings remain unique when it comes to brain activities. We can bring or force our fellow primates and other mammals into our world, but no mammal out there can bring human beings into theirs. We can study, understand and write down our findings about other mammals, but it would remain a mystery whether other mammals could do that. Above all, no other mammal out there can make, deploy or use weapons except human beings.

Just as pussycats are in the same family as lions, they can never cross over. Lions are born, live and die as lions; pussycats are born, live and die as pussycats. In the same way we are born, live and die as human beings, and apes (no matter how great) are born, live and die as apes. If we truly evolved from apes and monkeys, why on earth did the process stop? Can anyone show us where the next generation of apes and monkeys that are about to graduate into human beings are because; at the last count we still have apes and monkeys alive with us today. If there were no apes and monkeys alive today, then this theory can have some basis. It is highly unlikely that anyone has seen, observed or lived through the transformation of an ape into human being. It is possible that, human beings and apes shared the same ancestors so long as goats and sheep shared same ancestral background. My contention is: just like lions and pussycats, goats and sheep, there is no crossing over with apes and human beings. Though we are classified as being in the same subfamily (Hominidae) as African apes, the studies and classifications remain ours, and until we compare notes with African apes or any of our primates, my contention would remain that over the years we, as human beings, have 'evolved' due to climate change, dietary intake, science and technology, but we have always remained HUMAN BEINGS. Just as there are similarities when comparing a goat with a sheep, so we share similarities with our fellow primates, but we are the species of HUMAN BEINGS; and as it was, it is now and so will remain and never change!

On these basis, having known the facts that nurture is key to a child's proper upbringing against nature; It is crucial to inform those (especially men) who argue that in the female of the species in the 'animal kingdom' is mainly responsible for the feeding and upbringing of their offspring, that: having absorbed what is written above, it is clear that nature plays a predominant role in relation to other mammals' babies, as most of the things they do are instinctive, for example walking, or knowing where to find their food. But most importantly, they do not have to be served cooked meals, have nappies and clothing changed, be potty trained, be taken to school, go to work, bathe or taught how to tidy up. With this in mind, couples should be equal partners in the upbringing of their babies because human babies need to be taught most of the things they do and the responsibility is too huge to be left to one parent. In some cultures boys are not allowed to participate in domestic chores, let alone go into the kitchen, and some parents display how rich they are by flooding their houses with maids, in the weird belief that their children taking part in domestic chores amounts to 'suffering'. They put all the emphasis on buying expensive things for their children and sending them to the 'best' schools. These children are usually the ones likely to create problems for those they come into contact with in married life (see Bad parenting and the worst parenting from page 148), as their parent/s inculcated few morals, ethics or values in them. They grow up without 'real' life experience; in other words they are likely to think that the tooth fairy and Father Christmas are real, even in adulthood. Frightening enough as this may be, they may go on to replicate the same thing with their own children because one can only give what they have.

Why Children Should Be Guided In The Choices They Make

Having performed as a master of ceremony at many Christenings and birthday parties; having entertained and been entertained by the children there, I learnt a lot from my interaction with children. I learnt that children are really amazing, and that though they are not a homogenous group, they have lots in common irrespective of their colour, creed, race or culture. Over the last two years, I embarked on a quest to try to find out more about what children liked or preferred. I knew that I would be writing about children and how they are parented in this 'internet age'. I had always believed, through my upbringing (*See* 'A Tribute to an Awesome Father', page 102), that given a choice, a child would choose all the 'fun things', easy and sweet things that, overall, do not have much dividend or benefit apart from momentary pleasure. For example, the things children prefer, like eating, sleeping and playing as mentioned above, are so common that other mammals do them. At the same time, given the choice, children would avoid the things that appear difficult, that is, things that require hard work, concentration, determination and discipline. The things I have classified as 'orchestrated human activities' which separate us from other mammals/animals sustain us as human beings and bring dividend in the long run. However they often require persistent training, repetition and guidance, hence the need for parental guidance. This is why, when you ask a child to point at his/her friend, s/he is likely to point at someone who brings fun and excitement. Important as these are to children and without underestimating the value of what they learn from playing, their overindulgence in these activities is likely to harm their prospects in life. But ask the same child to point at someone they do not like and almost inevitably it will be someone who tries to provide them with structure in order to make them focus on the important things that would benefit them in the long run. Here lies the reason why, in some families today, where parents have failed to give their children good moral instruction to appreciate these things as early as possible, the children have been encouraged by the parents' action or inaction to divide their parents into 'good' and 'bad' parents, depending on who brings fun and who brings structure. As a result, parents have, to their cost, encouraged such madness without having an understanding themselves of what they are doing to their children, and it is often this same parent, who encourages the 'divide and rule' approach, that accuses and blames everyone but themselves when things go horribly wrong later on.

During the last two years, a total of 300 children aged between seven and ten years of age took part in my survey without knowing why I was posing the questions. *I got their attention by promising them that if they kept quiet and took part in my 'fun' game, I would lift an adult up with my teeth without touching the person with my hands. This always got them excited and ensured their participation and concentration. However, I always told them that my promise would be fulfilled at the end of the 'fun' game.*

I would tell them the ground rules for every question I asked, there would be two options and each child would be entitled to choose only one option by a show of hands. Then I told them to imagine I had a chocolate in my left hand and an apple in my right hand. I asked them which one they would choose. A total of 250 went for the chocolate and only 50 raised their hands for the apple. Then I said: imagine I had a fun fair in my left hand and a library in my right hand. The entire 300 hands went up for the fun fair, with no one opting for the library. I asked for their response if I had a McDonalds meal in my left hand and food prepared at home in my right; again the entire 300 hands went up for McDonalds. Finally, I asked them to answer again in response to me holding a PSP game boy in my left hand and a lovely storybook in my right; unsurprisingly, a total of 281 went for the PSP and only 19 went for the storybook. This illustrates the mind-set of children and the choices they can make. Children are more likely to go for anything fun, sweet and exciting. As parents, observe your children at home, carry out some experiments yourself and you will see why nurture is the key to your baby's development, physically, intellectually and morally. Check out your nine-year-old; place a game boy and a baby's simple mathematics book in front of him/her. Without a doubt, your nine-year-old would soon work out all the functions of the game boy and even teach you how to use it, but with the simple mathematics book you would have to explain its contents and teach them repeatedly before your nine-year-old understands. Everyone is aware that the word 'yes' is the opposite of 'no'. Therefore, it is fair to suggest that although there is a difference in meaning and significance, the two are equal in terms of value. However, because 'no' is often used in a 'negative' context and 'yes' in a positive context, your baby is likely to pick up 'no' without much teaching and claim ownership of that word. You are likely to repeatedly teach your baby the word 'yes', which has more of a positive connotation, and remind them to say it before they claim ownership of it. Human beings find wrong things easy to pick up, because often there is no teaching involved. This could certainly be said of hanging out on the street, verbally or physically abusing someone and disappearing from your family home when it pleases you and going to an unknown destination without regard for the impact of your behaviour on your partner and children. Doing your own thing as and when it pleases you in a family environment is easy and cheap. It doesn't require training and everyone can do it because it is a 'can do'. 'Can dos' are not usually the right things to do, whereas doing the right things is not always easy but is highly beneficial. There is no teaching involved in stabbing or shooting someone, justifying your actions and behaviour without rationale or blaming others and absolving yourself of all responsibility when you have orchestrated a crisis. These actions are all easy. Defending, supporting or being silent about the behaviour of wrongdoers is to condone them, since you too are capable of doing the same things as them because it is easy and no teaching is required. Abusing drugs and alcohol is easy: there is no teaching involved. Sleeping or playing all day, partying all night, eating ready meals, doing nothing, impregnation and giving birth (once pregnant like any other animal out there), playing with gadgets, joining a gang and living in your own 'little world' without consideration of others are all easy, with no teaching involved, and all these come naturally to human beings. The opposite of any of these would involve hard work and being taught with patience. The teaching and persistence are hard when one is dealing with a baby. It is even harder when dealing with an already formed adult, whose parents did not do their work. It becomes almost an impossibility if that adult does not see anything wrong in their behaviour. NEVER WASTE YOUR BREATH TEACHING HE OR SHE THAT KNOWS NOT BUT DOES NOT KNOW OR BELIEVE THAT THEY KNOW NOT, for it is easier to change the stripes of a zebra than seek to change an adult personality, especially when that adult sees nothing wrong in their behaviour.

Every parent must realise that babies learn by association and through interaction. It is not natural for babies to do what is 'right' until they have been taught what is right. Thinking that a baby's brain will just produce the 'positives' is as good as expecting a baby born in England to start speaking French without having heard anyone speak French to them. A 'normal' baby has all the genes in them to do almost everything and anything. However, it is usually only the negative genes that are active, and the positive ones have to be activated. For example, leave your mobile and healthy baby in a well-arranged room, without saying anything, and you will observe the baby will rip up books, dismantle things and pull things down to the floor automatically. Leave the same baby in a cluttered room and see if the baby starts arranging it or just adding to the clutter. This is what babies do, and there's nothing wrong with it because babies have to explore the world they have come into, but what could be wrong is the adult's reactions to and actions in response to what the baby does.

Ladies and gentlemen, babies will dismantle things automatically without being taught how to do it because that's what nature offers them. Though it is not wrong, dismantling things and ripping up books cannot be considered a good thing from a 'normal' person's perspective. One is left to wonder why nature did not automatically offer the baby the sense to arrange instead of untidy the room. A significant amount of hard work, time and patience is needed to teach your baby/child how to arrange a room, which of course is the right thing to do. Sometimes it can take a lifetime to teach someone how to keep his or her environment clean, but to clutter it up comes very easily. To destroy is easy and less time-consuming, but to build is difficult and more time-consuming.

As a child, I found it easy to hit my younger sibling whenever I perceived any behaviour I deemed inappropriate. It was easy and instinctive, and although it was the wrong thing to do, I did not need anyone to teach me how to it. This was the pattern until my mother got me to pinch myself hard (which I struggled to do and got a smack for my reluctance) to make me realise the pain I was inflicting on my younger sibling. This is so with most children, and if their wrong behaviour is not corrected and nipped in the bud, a child is likely to take the same behaviour into adulthood, and is likely to pass such behaviour on or condone it when their own children exhibit similar threats. Some children, mainly young boys, struggle at school because education requires discipline, concentration, determination and patience if one is to succeed, and that is why it is not easy. As a result, some of these boys give up in school and play truant, often because many of these young boys have no male role models around to guide them. Unfortunately, the role models they see are the hip-hop rap artists, footballers earning fat wages, superstar athletes, lead gangsters and drug dealers. They delude themselves that they will become one of these characters 'soon' (see the story of a man who was excluded from school on page 172). They very easily reassure themselves of becoming one of these, forgetting that 'the thought is easy but the reality is not'. Therefore they do what comes naturally to them, which is easy and leads nowhere other than into trouble. They cause trouble at school because they have no discipline to cope with the requirements and demands of education. They leave or are excluded from school. They start wasting away at home watching screens, listening to violent hip hop music, roaming the streets, hooking up with drug dealers and seeking out gangs to become members. Boys like this usually replicate the behaviour of their parents or others close to them. In such households there is usually no discipline, no family ethics (right or wrong), mother and father often leave the household without notification of where they are going, and therefore the children follow suit in the belief that it is 'normal'. 'Things have fallen apart and the centre cannot hold' (Orjiako. 2009). These observations indicate that the derailment of children often stems from the derailment of parents.

CHAPTER THREE

The Problem With Parenting

Modern parenting is the most important and demanding job in this world, in view of the pressing demands of keeping a home (high cost of living), the flooding of our streets with adulterated illicit drugs, peer pressure, the culture of wants outstripping needs, impact of mass media and highly sensationalised images on the screens, easily accessible and affordable alcohol, the breakdown of families and, along with this, the breakdown of moral values. Equally important is the impact of this modern sophisticated technological age that has caught parents and society unawares, coupled with too much right, choice, freedom and liberty without responsibility. These facts are not yet fully acknowledged, understood or appreciated. It is important to keep in mind that easy things haven't got much profit or dividend attached to them and they are the 'can dos'. This is not only because everyone can do easy things, it is because one doesn't often require training, discipline, dedication and focus to do easy things. Those who live an easy, carefree life usually have nothing positive to show for their existence and in the end usually live and die in a lonely way. They get momentary satisfaction and pleasure but later regret and sadness follow. Always keep in mind that how one feels today is more important than how one felt yesterday, and that 'nothing good comes easy'. To do good things or the right things one must work hard. Those who make hard things easy are generally called 'geniuses' or 'talented people' and they get great rewards from their exploits. Unfortunately, no such talent is linked to parenting because one has no experience of parenting until one becomes a parent. There is a common saying that 'there's no best way to parent a child' but, there are right and wrong ways to parent a child, (see 'Good, bad and worst parenting' starting from page 142). A person only needs the skills of a parent at the moment they become one, and then 'once a parent, always a parent'. There are no standard criteria for becoming a parent apart from the fact that there is an expectation that one should be 'of age', that is be an adult, to parent a child. However, in our world today we have not only seen adults in 'children mode' having children, but eleven- to twelve-year-olds having children. The youngest mother in the United Kingdom is eleven years old, whilst the world record holder is a Peruvian girl who had a baby at the age of five (Wikipedia). There is no designated college for parenting; therefore there is nothing out there to prepare one for the role/responsibility of being a parent. It is a role that is even more important in this modern age: a role that has become too important, due to us being in a sophisticated technological age that is geared towards sensationalising children, and where there has been an explosion of civil libertarian agenda, decay of family and moral values, a climate of wants outstripping needs (capitalism gone mad), intensive peer pressure and an influx of dangerous street drugs. These combinations have made the job of even the best parents difficult, let alone parents without parenting experience and skills. These combinations have turned what was an 'innocent childhood' into something every reasonable person struggles to define.

The law may limit the number of children one can have in some countries, but no man-made law prevents one from being a parent; rather, in some places, such as Europe for example, it is a human rights issue, as Article 8 of the European Convention on Human Rights refers to the rights of every citizen to 'private and family life'. Currently, in the Western world particularly, the upbringing of a child is primarily the responsibility of the child's parent/s or caregiver. The parent or caregiver in some cases is also faced with huge demands to meet their wants, not just their needs. Some 'well-meaning' parents are also constrained by the government, who on the one hand want parents to parent but on the other hand have tied their hands from parenting their children (see the ordeal of a father who physically removed his son from possible danger on page 166).

Though everyone may not see them as equal, marriage and cohabitation are the two vital components that are likely to bring one to the parenting stage, although one can become a parent without being married or cohabiting. Marriage and cohabitation are two of the best and worthwhile things life has on offer. This is why they are not easy, and prove very hard and difficult to manage. Everyone knows the value of gold and oil but one can never find either on the surface: one must dig deep. No one has ever obtained a doctoral degree by dancing all night: they must dig deep and study hard. The same applies to marriage, which is worth more than all these. Now, if one must dig deep for these 'less important' things, then think about the most important thing life has on offer 'marriage'. One must really work hard in order to get marriage and cohabitation right. Marriage and cohabitation are good, right and proper things to do, and they carry high dividends at the end of them when couples get it right from the start. Good things don't come cheap or easy. Hard work, patience and dedication are required. Couples, who both understand this from the start and put in the hard work, while not expecting it to be a 'bed of roses', are more likely to succeed in their union. When only one partner understands this and the other is pulling in the opposite direction, crisis awaits because 'it takes two to tango'. If both partners lack an understanding of what they have embarked upon then severe crisis awaits. Those couples who think that love sustains marriage and cohabitation struggle to carry on with it when they realise that love may bring couples together but what sustains marriage and cohabitation is, UNDERSTANDING! Those who got into it carelessly want to take it easy or cut corners always get it wrong, especially when children are involved. They are usually the ones that run for a quick exit through separation and divorce once they are not finding it as easy as they thought it would be. Living a single person's lifestyle may be easier when you are young, but wait until old age or you run into a crisis on your own. You will find that your immediate problem will eclipse all the enjoyment of the past. Yes, a youthful single person's lifestyle may seem less pressurised and full of fun and enjoyment compared to the life of a parent with children. However, there is usually a smaller dividend at the end of it, and when the challenges of life (which are continual) hit a single person, regrets usually follow as they struggle on their own and are likely to develop psychological problems. All one needs to remember, as a single person, is the possible nightmare that could happen when an illness strikes: just a fall and all you need is someone to make that all-important call when you cannot reach the telephone. The single person may have had the 'time of their life' the previous day, yet today they are faced with the true challenges of life.

As an approved mental health professional, I have first-hand experience of how loneliness can not only cause but also worsen people's psychological problems, as friends are more likely to desert an individual with a mental disorder. However, one's family members are hopefully there through thick and thin, offering their support and aiding recovery.

It is not a natural process to cohabit or get married; it is only a natural process to be pregnant once the 'deed is done', but giving birth is natural once one is pregnant. When it comes to the moral values associated with the upbringing of a child, nature has very little or no role at all to play in the matter. Only the hard work put in by nurturing the child yields the required dividend. Though each child has his/her own personality, nature cannot do much for any child in terms of sound upbringing, and prison awaits any parent that depends on nature solely to bring up their child. Every parent needs to realise that babies have no clue on arrival. The way human hair and nails can grow out of control is the way children's behaviour can get out of control if not kept in check by parents. If the duty to tidy up the hair falls on a child who has not been trained to cut hair, then it is likely the child will leave a lot of mess and/or sustain injury in the process. This is exactly what happens when parents neglect their duty and leave their children to bring themselves up. How the child turns out usually determines the success or failure of a parent. It also determines the joy or sadness of a parent. Children are not and should not be seen as part of one's accessories. They should come with warning signs saying 'treat with the utmost care, regard and sensitivity'. Those who persevere and get the hard work done in the right manner go on to bring up sound, considerate and reasonable children, and they reap the benefits that come with this. A word of caution: never go into marriage or cohabitation with the intention of having a child if you are dependent on nature to do your work, otherwise you are likely to inflict untold damage, not only on the child, but on yourself and society at large. For that little, vulnerable and helpless baby you have in your hands today will tomorrow have the capacity to either make the world a better place or a frightening place to be, depending on what you and I do; or what you and I fail to do, as parent/s and as a society.

Many parents sing from different hymn sheets, and nothing confuses and damages a child like sending mixed messages. Children thrive on clarity, structure and set boundaries, and they do not see it as demanding if they are taught like this from day one. They only rebel against set boundaries if introduced when they have already changed from liquid to solid, resulting in some parents being afraid of their children as they rebel against what they are not used to. Everyone knows how difficult change is for human beings even if the change is positive in the long run. That's why your child rebels when you introduce something they are not used to, which disrupts their usual norms.

Any parent/s who is ill-equipped and did not get proper parenting themselves is likely to view their child as a 'friend' or believe that dressing up the child in expensive outfits and buying them gadgets amounts to training. Such parent/s would find it difficult to set boundaries for their child, because setting boundaries is not compatible with friendship but an integral part of parenting. They are likely to believe that good parenting equals making the child happy at all times. They would never consider all the things that make their children happy and ask whether those things provide any real benefit in the long run for them and their children. They are the type of parents who give, give, give without guidance or explanation, giving their children a false sense of security and damaging their children's innate will to survive, which every 'normal' human being has, but it does need to be activated. Their children are then likely to think that the world owes them their living, and will continue to make demands from their parents well into their 30s (*see* page 140). These children are usually the ones that run into trouble when eventually nature forces them to start fending for themselves, as they look for an easy way out, having not had the discipline or acquired the skills to survive independently. They are then easily attracted to dealing in drugs, thieving and gambling, and are ready to do anything in the name of a 'quick fix' because most of these 'bad' things do not require training. The parent/s of such children are usually those who condone anything their children do, no matter how wrong, for fear of making their children unhappy. I have heard such a parent say, 'Some people are born to take risks,' in the presence of their children, as they are not willing, able and ready to condemn what their children do. Furthermore, the parents' interest is usually solely in money, so their children can take a gamble and hit the jackpot and then the parents' celebration will begin. Such parent/s will claim responsibility for inspiring their child to take risks but will blame someone else if the gamble goes wrong and shy away from taking any responsibility. They take the credit when it goes 'well', but will find somewhere else to lay the blame when things fall apart and they fail. They are happy and willing to take commendation for the success of their children but would not want to be associated with the failures of their children. These attitudes confirm that 'blame is linked to failure' (Nacho, 2010 page xix)

Some of these parent/s extend their un-reasonability to when they become mother or father in-law, as they support their children in whatever evil they do to their partners (see Story of Ms S page 161) They depend on others and make unrealistic demands of others, especially their in-laws, but would never ask whether they or their children in a similar position have ever or would give the same as they are demanding of their in-laws. No matter what someone does for them, such parents will never appreciate it; rather, they will minimise it and will continue to put pressure on the giver, illustrating the adage that 'only the willing horse gets flogged and only those present at church get the wrath of the preacher'. They forget they were once an in-law to other people too and would not ask how much they had done or what their own children in similar circumstances are doing for their own in-laws. Such parents, as well as their children, have no regard for and give no consideration to fair play and the possible consequences of their actions. They are always ready to defend their children against any teacher, person in authority or member of the public, irrespective of the evidence against their children. Once the act is done by their children, no matter how bad, then the act becomes 'OK' or there will be justification of it and blame placed on others, absolving themselves and the children of any responsibility for their actions. There is no limit to irresponsibility when it comes to such parent/s.

The height of such negation of responsibility can be seen in relation to mental health, where some parents advice their children who are mentally unwell to stop taking their medication, replace the medication with something else like holy water and/or olive oil and reassure their children by saying, 'It is well,' or 'there's nothing wrong with you.' Now, when something goes horribly wrong, for example a child commits homicide because of a relapse of the illness due to non-compliance with medical instructions, the same parent/s then blame others, and in some cases look for ways to make money by seeking to sue the local authorities responsible for their child's care. This is so obscene it beggars belief. These parents must be taught that if there is any money that results from such tragedies then the families of the victims are the ones deserving of it, and I wonder why (if it is obvious that the cessation of taking medication was as a result of advice given by a parent/s to a vulnerable adult) such parent/s are not held equally responsible for their child's actions, because such incidents may not have occurred bur for their advice or action which influenced their vulnerable adult child.

Some couples wait until it is too late before correcting the behaviour of their children when they are babies, condoning everything the child does with the excuse that 's/he is only a child, they will learn when they grow up.' They forget, or lack the understanding that babies come in liquid form and are likely to go into any shape presented to them very quickly, but once they firm up and become solid, they have to be broken (which would amount to abuse) in order to try a different shape. They do not realise that though babies may not communicate verbally, but their ears hear information and instruction from the day of delivery (even whilst in the womb). They do not know that the formative age of a child begins from the day the child is born to five years of age, and anything one fails to inculcate in a child before then would require a battle to inculcate, at a later date, if at all possible.

Here are a few examples I have seen in public places where some children have been left to their own devices, whilst their parent/s got on with their own business. Just imagine a farmer leaving his crops to grow on their own without tending to them. What would the harvest bring?

As I undertook one of my duties as a master of ceremony at a wedding reception, I called the newly wedded couple to cut the cake. As the couple made their way for the cutting of the cake, a boy of about five years of age went straight to the seats vacated by the couple, stood on one of the seats and then jumped up and down on it. His parents were there and had to be prompted before the father came and carried the child out. Seconds later, the boy was at it again. It took some strong, 'diplomatic' words for the father to realise that the behaviour of the child was not acceptable. If this child could display such behaviour in a public place, one can only imagine what the child had been allowed to get up to at home.

At one of the local churches I attend, a boy has the habit of running around in the church during communion. This boy climbs the pulpit while his mother walks around with no care in the world. At times the lay reader tries to stop this behaviour, but the boy's mother remains indifferent. It is obvious that the boy's father does not attend this particular church or may not even be on the scene. Consider a boy who is growing up in this way and imagine what he could be getting up to at home and what he will be like as a teenager or an adult.'

One day I went shopping at one of the Tesco supermarkets. As I was about to drive off, I noticed two children aged about nine and five years old respectively sitting in a car beside mine. Their father had left his car keys with the children and the nine-year-old started the vehicle and was revving the engine. There were other onlookers in the car park, unwilling to do anything but visibly shocked. I became worried, dialled 999 and requested the police, as the law demands that no one should take the law into their own hands. That child could have engaged the gear, and one can only imagine what the possible outcome would have been. Had we laws on the side of those trying to correct bad behaviour and prevent crime, perhaps the onlookers and I would have done something different. But as it was that child could have done lasting damage to himself and/or others, before the arrival of the police.

Hear this, as seen by one of our AMHP (approved mental health professional) trainees (Jan Holloway). Jan was on the train with a mother and her young daughter. Jan observed that at each stop the little girl would jump out of the train and hop back in before the doors shut and her mother did not give a jot about what her daughter was doing. Jan bravely said to the mother, 'Look, your daughter is putting herself in danger by doing that.' To Jan's surprise, the mother responded, 'Mind your own business. She's my child and she can do what she likes.'

One can only imagine what such children get away with in the privacy of their own homes, judging from what they are allowed to do in public and how this behaviour gradually becomes normal for these children. In my work as an AMHP I often notice that some young people detained under the Mental Health Act 1983 (as amended by the 2007 Mental Health Act) suffer from narcissistic threats, not because they are genetically predisposed to these, but because of how they were brought up. Their parents allowed the world to revolve around them, and they got what they wanted, when and how they wanted it. When they become part of the real world they cannot cope, because in the real world one does not always get what one wants or when they want it. These children derail as a result of having formed bad behaviour that went unchallenged during childhood. These are the likely by-products of parents letting their children get away with anything. They are likely to pose a danger to themselves and others as they become frustrated with the real world. Remember, when a child becomes unruly and dangerous they will not only be threatening their own health and safety or that of their parents, they will be a threat to everyone, including YOU! Unfortunately, that child is then highly likely to reproduce a generation like themselves, as they can only hand over what they have received. Remember some examples already listed in this book. However, it is not only the way such badly brought up parents replicate the treatment they had from their parents that is a problem, but how they see challenging their partners as an achievement, in the presence of the children. At times that's all their own parents wish for and want to see. While good parents are working hard, gaining promotion for their hard work, working together at home, with all their energy geared towards the upbringing of their offspring in the right way, these badly brought up parents will be busy challenging themselves and using and preparing their children as witnesses to their impending hearings.

Some of these parents are brought up to have no regard for boundaries or cannot even recognise boundaries in the first instance, as they go 'walkabout' with no accountability or understanding of the impact it has on their children, who view them as their role models. Consider a mother or father leaving their children for five days with only a telephone, and on the day of disappearance saying, 'I will be away training for six days,' with no indication as to where this training is taking place, what the training is about or who they are training with. Such parents forget that their children who are watching and copying, are likely to deem such behaviour to be 'normal,' and therefore are likely to behave that way in their own relationships later. For such parents, once their own parent/s are in the loop of what they are up to, then that makes everything fine.

These parents go on to become 'lazy' parents, as their own parents were; they are ready to do everything in the home, because 'It is quicker and I want my child to be happy doing what he/she chooses/likes' (see 'Why children should be guided in the choices they make' on page 43). They do not teach their children anything useful, let alone morals and values. Their children will only eat ready meals or takeaway food at home, as their parents will not devote any time to teaching them how to cook or tidy up. Such children are always busy playing with their gadgets, and their gadgets become more important to them than interaction with human beings. In some cases some parents buy their under-aged children inappropriate games full of shooting and violence, with no clue as to what that could mean to a child. They justify this on the basis that 'It makes my child happy' and 'It keeps my child busy so I can get on with other things I want to do.' These children grow up wasting too much money on takeaway food and shortening their lives by eating unhealthy food. They can also grow up with no human feelings, as their interactions were mainly with gadgets, not their fellow human beings. This can make a child see and value only themselves and their gadgets and no one else. Visit some homes and see for yourselves that these children may be in the same living room but will not notice your arrival, let alone greet you. Even when you greet them, notice how quickly and snappily they say, 'Hi,' and refocus on their gadgets. Such parents struggle to understand that they are doing the wrong thing. They are usually quick to say, 'It is not your business how I am bringing up my child,' if you try to suggest ways of encouraging the child. They will not see anything useful in what you have said, but would interpret what you have said to mean that they are parenting badly. Of course they are, in the actual sense, but they are only giving what they received from their own parents, unfortunately. They have no idea that their children will get away with murder, and in many cases they do, with such parents around. Such parents are the type that claim (when things go horribly wrong), 'I never told my child to do that,' but they cannot say what they told their child to do.

Now, if in adulthood you make the terrible mistake of marrying or cohabiting with a person brought up by such parents, without asking the appropriate questions below, you will experience 'hell on earth', as your partner and parent-in-law 'from hell' descend on you, sharing the attitude that 'everything my child, and everything my parent does is right'. You will soon notice that the umbilical cord is still in place, because your partner can only relate to and trust the parent who justifies everything they do and vice versa. This parent-in-law from hell is likely to be the person deciding what happens in your home; they will bring ideas, and sometimes materials, into your home that are not compatible with your family life and hand them over to your partner without your knowledge. No matter what you do to please them, you will never succeed as long as you are challenging things you notice could destroy your children, as you try to break the chain. You will be perceived as the 'number one enemy' and you are likely to hear your partner refer to their parent as 'my family' and be ready to utilise or waste resources meant for your children's upbringing on your parent-in-law from hell. Such a parent-in-law will continue to make your partner believe that their real home is still the one they departed from, and this will apply no matter how old your partner is. Because of the way they were brought up, they are likely to still view whatever their parents say (no matter how wrong) as true, and always see themselves as a baby because the umbilical cord has not been psychologically cut. Such a parent-in-law will hold differing views on one issue and will say the one he or she wants you to hear, but then in secret tell your partner the other fabricated version, designed to damage your family and further their 'importance'. You will notice them feeding each other with lies and fabricated stories as they reaffirm their loyalty to each other. What can be most shocking is the unrealistic, deluded view such a parent can have, as they may cite their own marriage as an example of a good marriage, with no insight into how bad and damaged their own products have become. The real measure of success and/or failure of a union is solely based on how successful and well behaved the children are. Try pointing them to this fact and see their negative or irrational reaction, as they prefer to delude themselves and are not ready to stop and think. If you are well brought up yourself and believe in family life, you will then be fighting a running battle to protect your children from picking from the 'dirty basket' in an attempt to break the circle. The time you and your partner should have utilised focusing on the upbringing of the children, nurturing them and exposing them to your particular culture will then be wasted on arguing and trying to prevent such a distorted lifestyle from affecting your children. You will also notice (if your partner has other siblings) a pattern of crisis in those siblings' life as well, unless they have been influenced by other factors. This will lead you to conclude that it is a 'system' problem or failure, not an individual one, and you must and should give your all to help instigate a turnaround of this situation. This might still prove impossible but, nonetheless, try until all is exhausted.

This type of situation is more difficult if you are the father, because no matter how bad a mother is, she is still likely to be preferred by a child than a 'brilliant' father; don't ask why, because the answer is located somewhere in between nature and nurture. Little children cannot perceive any wrongdoing by their mothers: no matter how bad, 'mum is mum'. They may only begin to understand when they grow up. This is why children without mothers or mother figures are more likely to develop psychological problems in later life. Only when the child grows up would they begin to make informed decisions or analysis of both parents in terms of who had their best interest at heart. This should not really be the case, because parents bring different things and attributes to their children. In the same way parents should not favour a particular child over the others, as all the children are individuals and should be treated equally. However, the father in this position would have to work out a strategy to ensure that his desired outcome is achieved. This involves a lot of sacrifice, patience and focus. There is nobody and nothing else in this world worthy of your sacrifice than God, who must come first, and then the children, who are your primary responsibility, should come second. Therefore, as a father you must find a way to encourage your children's mother to be present in their lives; otherwise they may suffer some psychological problems if their mother becomes absent when they are too young. However such fathers should find ways to ensure that the children have a balanced view of life, as their mother is likely to be manifesting some bad habits the children might interpret as the norms. Mothers in the reverse situation, where the father is making life 'hell' should seek to have full custody of the children, whilst the fathers visit occasionally. The same principle should apply with the mother viewing the children's father, as part of the weeds that are likely to damage the crops. Whatever you do ensure that you point out the good attributes of your partner because no one is totally good or bad; but highlight those things that you believe might damage the children or cause them problem in adulthood. The mothers in this situation should aim to take full control of the children because, a sound mother is very capable of bringing up reasonable and sound children (so are sound fathers) but to a lesser degree, for an 'obvious' reason. It is obvious in that no father has ever had a link with their child, nine months before their birth as mothers do. Fathers are strangers to their babies until they arrive in this world on the day of delivery. Mothers have a link with their babies from the day of conception. That's part of the reasons why, to a child, a 'horrible mother' is preferable to the 'most wonderful' father, until they get to the age of understanding.

The problem with parenting often stems from the reasons people have for getting married or cohabiting and the fact that people are often unprepared to face the realities of living together and taking responsibility for bringing up children. People often go into these unions with the preconceived idea that living together will be easy and all about LOVE, because they usually see couples happy on the day of marriage and happy on the streets. The truth about marriage and cohabitation is: it is hard work. I repeat – it is very difficult because it is a good thing! No good thing comes easy and hard work is required when dealing with difficult things. If it is easy, it won't be worthwhile or useful. People who are unprepared or have the intention of only experiencing 'happiness or fun galore' usually run from it once the realities of living together and bringing up children become real.

In my experience both as a marriage counsellor and as a person, the reasons for becoming a couple play a major role in the success or failure of the union, and this has a serious bearing on the upbringing of any child within such a union. People have gone into marriages and cohabitation for all sorts of reasons, for example, 'My mates are getting married; I am under pressure from my parents to give them grandchildren; I must marry him or her before someone else takes him or her from me; he/she is gorgeous and very rich; his or her parents have loads of money; we've gone too far now, I don't want to disappoint him or her; it is love at first sight; or time is running out for me.' Whilst these types of things may be part of the reasons, they should not be the sole or main reasons for getting married or cohabiting. People often do not ask the important questions, such as 'Am I ready to get married or cohabit? Am I adult enough; have I broken the umbilical cord tying me to my parents; have I had enough of being single or are there things I still want to do as a single person that are not compatible with married life, like leaving your partner and children for days without disclosing your whereabouts? This person I want to live with, is h/she compatible with me, do we share the same or similar values, and if not, is either one of us willing, able and ready to compromise; and am I marrying or cohabiting on emotional and sentimental grounds only? Most importantly, do I know anything about the background of the person I am intending to share my life with?' This last question is very necessary because people generally repeat what they picked up from their parents, though there will always be exceptions to the rule due to other influences. These should and must be the questions one needs to ask and answer before marrying or cohabiting with someone. Marriage or cohabitation must be a deliberate act; otherwise it will be built on dodgy ground. Marriage or cohabitation should not occur accidentally; if it does, the union will suffer many problems and will probably not survive. The children born into such a union bear the brunt of the suffering. Some people have claimed that children are resilient! Yes, children are usually resilient when they are little, because children are able to adapt and say to each parent what they believe the parent wants to hear, in order not to upset them. However, having carried out countless Mental Health Act assessments, I can convincingly say that the consequences of a broken home are felt in later years. Eighty percent of young people/adults I have assessed under the Mental Health Act in nearly a decade, came from broken families, though the cause of some breakdowns are not deliberate, as death at times plays a part in disorganising families. When people marry for the wrong reasons or rush into marriage and cohabitation, they suddenly realise they have made a mistake. However, before this realisation a child may have been born, and instead of channelling all their energy and effort as a united unit into building the family and training and nurturing the child, the couple resort to challenging each other, creating competition, arguments and fights, and in some cases preparing their child as a witness to an impending crisis relating to the breakdown of the relationship. The 'sane' parent may carry on in the belief that one day the partner could learn (not change, because they must learn before they can change). The union may limp along, and more children be born, but the couple lose sight of their primary responsibility and compete against each other, seeking to get the children on their side in case of any future court case. I have heard a parent say to the other parent, 'My son would stand as a witness,' when their crisis begins. This is usually a parent who has put all their energy into fighting the partner and nothing towards the sound upbringing of their child.

The foundation of a union needs to be right and solid, and once it is right then the by-product is likely to be right too. But if the foundation is wrong, then the opposite is likely to be the case. People who fail to ask the right questions before moving in together are more than likely to get into trouble in their union, and in turn are likely to sow the wrong seeds in their children. Remember that once a bad seed is sown it can easily lead to one becoming a 'damaged adult', and the proceeds from that 'damage' are not quantifiable and cannot be estimated and this in turn can become a generational issue, because a mango tree is not capable of producing an orange.

Those who go into marriage and cohabitation for the wrong reasons often see their dreams shattered and turned into a nightmare, the nightmare usually occurring when children are involved. The cost of separation and divorce, the impact on the extended families, the psychological damage to the partners and, most importantly, their children are usually incalculable. Their infatuations and dreams soon come tumbling down and reality sets in. At this stage couples find it difficult to credit their partners with anything good, and one begins to wonder how they got together in the first instance as couples. They struggle to see anything positive in their partners and create unhappiness within themselves. They see their children as witnesses in future conflicts, and go out of their way to buy their children over for that purpose, thus destroying the children in the process without realising it.

As stated earlier, a parent is like a restaurant owner whose cooking would make an impact on members of the public. The food would either nourish or poison them. Therefore the restaurant owner cannot say, 'It is not anyone's business how I prepare the food.' In the same way, that little baby of yours could tomorrow be someone else's son-in-law, daughter-in-law, next-door neighbour, the one carrying a knife or gun or driving a car under the influence of drugs or alcohol, endangering others' lives. At that point, whose business is it? In the light of this, every parent must see himself or herself as a farmer. When a farmer sows his or her crops, they immediately work towards harvesting by tending the crops. They are aware that the weeds have the same right as their crops to grow on the farm. However, in order to give their crops the best opportunity to survive, the farmer ensures that the weeds are taken out on a regular basis. They also feed their crops with manure, fertiliser and other things that are needed, in preparation for a good harvest. Farmers who fail to take these measures usually suffer the consequences of neglecting the crops, as they will not have a good harvest. This confirms the adage 'you reap what you sow' or 'you get back what you put in'. However the major difference is that; in the case of farmers, the consequences of not tending their crops may only affect them. But when it comes to a parent, the consequences of not nurturing your child the right way could affect anyone. A case in point is the carnage in France on Monday 19th March 2012, when three children and an adult were shot and killed outside a Jewish school. This incident left a mother to bury her husband and two children. This has also left her little girl without a father and two brothers. These were not natural deaths or deaths by accident but rather, deaths by deliberate act of a human being who was once an innocent baby. This is how, what was once a parent's own 'business' turns into a nightmare for other people and becomes everyone's business.

Good parenting starts by marrying or cohabiting for the right reasons, as stated above, with clear objectives and an understanding that the union you have embarked on is likely to produce life itself, children. A good parent must understand the seriousness of having children, which is the most important thing in life, and plan their tactics well in advance. Even in football, which is of course far less important than having a child, a lot of planning is done before a match. Parents-to-be MUST see what they are embarking upon as a 'Project' and that every project requires preparation and planning. No matter what you do and whether you like it or not, preparation (planning) is involved and you either prepare to succeed or prepare to fail! Agree with your partner what you stand for, in the knowledge that if you stand for nothing you will fall for any and everything. In other words, define your beliefs and be deep rooted in them (if they are good/right beliefs) otherwise you become like waves, tossed about by any wind that blows in your direction. You MUST define your relationship too, and set some guiding principles. It is these guiding principles that will shape your child. Ensure your guiding principles revolve around love for oneself and love for others, respect for oneself and others, consideration for others, and the ability to challenge bad behaviour and say what good behaviour should be and the benefits (*See* 'A Tribute to an Awesome Father', page 102). Never preach any word or condone any word of hate, because your child may grow up to either understand through interaction and cognition that you were wrong, or develop a deep-rooted belief based on what you said or failed to correct. Once it turns into a belief, you won't be able to legislate, what that child would do with such belief. Remember Anders Breivik of Norway; he made it clear that 'one person with a belief is equal to a force of 99 who have only interests' according to Mill J (1861). Remember at all times that keeping quiet when a child says or does a bad thing is as good as condoning it, and that you have contributed to any harm caused by that child to him/herself or someone else just by keeping silent in the face of evil; for 'a person may cause evil to others not only by his or her action but by his/her inaction, and in either case h/she is justly accountable to them for the injury' (Mill J).

Good parents must work in partnership and complement each other, be ready to support and fill in for the other whenever the need arises, look out for each other and make communication key to their union. You must have the understanding that your baby, on arrival, will do what all babies do under normal circumstances: 'seek to control'; this will very quickly move on to, 'seek to divide and rule' if you, as parents, fail to understand and prepare yourselves for this. The first thing to do is to make a wilful decision that both of you must sing from the same hymn sheet and provide a united front at all times, in order to ensure stability and the kind of focus your children want and need. Remember, you are like a farmer about to sow your seed on the farm. Remember all the preparations the farmer has to make.

You should make sure, when cohabiting, that you develop your 'family mission statement' with your partner, according to Covey S (1997), the author of The Seven Habits of Highly Effective Families. *Can I add that the mission statement needs to be a positive not negative one*?

Be sure that prior to getting pregnant you deal with any bad habits that are likely to adversely affect your unborn baby in the womb, for example alcohol and/or illicit drug abuse. When your baby arrives, it is ready to hear you, though it will not respond because everything is new to it. Begin to talk to your baby. At home, make sure you give plenty of care, love and attention to your baby, but at the same time watch out for its controlling side to appear and be prepared, with your partner, to deal with it. Begin to teach your baby independence and responsibility as soon as possible; remember, whilst your baby is still struggling to sit up, other mammals' babies born on the same day as your baby have long since established their independence, as indicated previously. What you do or fail to do will eventually contribute to and determine how your baby responds. Keep in mind that your baby arrived in a liquid form, awaiting the shape you want to give it, and is naturally ready to go its own shape if none is provided. Never let your baby develop its own 'natural' shape because it would be the 'wrong' shape. Remember how many times, as a parent you prompt your children to get things done in the right manner and how the forces of nature automatically pull them to doing the opposite. Compare how many times you say to your child, 'Go and wash the plate you used to eat; tidy up your room; come and join me in the kitchen; go and do your home work,' and then contrast this with the number of times you have to remind the same child to go and eat or play. Children do not automatically do what is 'right' without being taught how to do it or observing the right thing being done around them. They are programmed to automatically do what is 'wrong' from an adult's perspective. That's why a two-year-old left alone in a room will not require any coaching to scatter things around and rip to shreds any paper on sight, but it may take a lifetime to teach the same child how to arrange that room. You are there as a parent for a reason.

Once you have fed your baby, make sure they are dry and do not have a high temperature, then put the baby in their cot or a secure place, put on gentle music and tell the baby in a lovely 'baby-like' soft voice that they should stay there whilst you attend to other things in the home, keep listening out for your baby to show any signs of discomfort and be ready to attend to the baby. The baby is likely to cry when you go to the kitchen or somewhere else in the house; attend to the baby to be sure they are not in any discomfort, and reaffirm that you need to get on with other things once you are sure they are only seeking attention. When this is repeated over time, your baby will get the message that you are not to be dictated to, though sometimes you can deliberately allow the baby to get its own way. Both parents must do the same thing, otherwise you are making room for the 'divide and rule' problem, which damages the family and renders the children useless, as they play one parent against the other. The same rule must apply when sending the baby to a nanny or someone to look after. Talk to the baby, do not worry if they appear not to be listening or responding, tell him or her where you are taking them and when you will come to collect them. Be consistent and explain any inconsistencies to the child. Children do better and feel more reassured when clear boundaries are set for them, and this point cannot be overemphasised. Don't play 'hide and seek' with your baby on these serious issues. You can play hide and seek within an appropriate play context when your baby understands that that's what you are doing. Having said all this, one of the best gifts to give to your child is teaching him or her how to SHARE and WAIT.

By sharing, your child learns about human interaction and the ability to see themselves in someone else, helping them to avoid the dangerous phenomenon of 'me, myself and I', which can lead them to having no consideration for anyone else. By sharing, a child begins to appreciate that life is not only about them but that the other person has needs too, and by sharing we gain more through the act of giving. The act of sharing eliminates the 'me, myself and I' phenomenon. This phenomenon is the root cause of greed and selfishness in our world. It is at the centre of the economic meltdown in our world today which threatens the stability of the world. The people responsible for this are as dangerous as those stabbing and shooting on the streets. With increased numbers of depressed people, increased suicide rates, a high number of repossessions and people's livelihood under persistent financial pressure. The level of damage and deaths these brand of individuals have brought to society at large is incalculable. However, these individuals did not just turn out they way they did for no reason. Some parents think that once their children dress well, attend the best schools and have a first class degree, training is complete. Well, if one has such thoughts, they are likely to breed and unleash a crisis into society, as we have all seen. How else does one explain the fact that an individual is willing to collect $/£7 million in bonuses, while some people in the same company are struggling to survive?

It is also the habit of not sharing, having only the ability to receive but not to give, that creates those who fold their arms and wait for the state and others to fund all aspects of their lives, despite having no disability preventing them from earning their living. These individuals create mayhem of their own and, in some developing countries, put much demand on their siblings and extended families. These individuals are willing and ready to kill in order to please those sponsoring them. Some of them in the contrary are willing to arrange for armed criminals to visit their own relatives, who they believe are rich, in the name of 'grab and share' without regard as to whether their relatives lose their lives in the operation or not.

By waiting, children learn how to be patient, which is a virtue. Remember the saying 'good things happen to those who wait'. Therefore, every parent (irrespective of how rich they are) needs to teach his or her child how to wait. Impatience is one of the contributing factors in the damage seen in most children and adults who suffer from mental disorder. Those who haven't learnt to wait can easily develop a narcissistic personality, expecting the whole world to revolve around them and respond according to their wishes, needs and demands. Well, it is a well known fact that this is impossible, as most things human beings do in life involve waiting, including the pursuit of pleasure. Giving a child everything they want is in itself the easiest and most effective way to destroy the child (*See* 'A Tribute to an Awesome Father', page 102), let alone giving on demand. If your child makes a request, take time to discuss that request, and if it is not something that requires immediate action and you have no time, tell your child to wait for the appropriate time to discuss their request. Let the child present their need and state the reasons for their request. Also, let the child tell you how they would benefit from having what they say they need. Sometimes you will get the response, 'but my friend Victor has it.' Right! This is where your parenting skill comes to hand and the child is ready to learn. Remember, the child is simply acting as a child, but you, as an adult and as a parent, must act like a parent. The preferred reply to, 'But my friend Victor has it' should be, 'But your name is John, not Victor, and Victor hasn't got everything you have, has he?' Let the child respond. But whatever the child goes on to say on this particular matter, as a parent you must and should convey the message that John is an individual, special in his own way. Encourage John to see the benefits of who he is, and instil the habit of John not wanting to copy others, but the belief that others should copy John. When this is repeated, over time, John is likely to develop some level of contentment and pride in the values he has been taught. Make John aware that Victor's parents have different names to yours as well. A good parent, after doing this, would conclude that the child's request is not need-based but want-based, and is therefore likely to turn the request down. Even the child might begin to appreciate that the request is unnecessary. You as a parent, may not have given what the child has requested, but you have in the process given the child more, as this conversation could help him towards becoming a well-rounded individual. Having said that, should the parent decide to go ahead and grant the request, the parent must and should make certain that the child is aware that the gadget, or whatever it is that has been requested, is on loan. The parent needs to understand what is contained in that gadget and set rules regarding all gadgets, and the child should be made aware that the gadgets would be withdrawn if they violate the rules. Never buy a gadget for your child if you are not sure of what the content is or whether it is age appropriate. The fact that your child is unhappy does not mean that you as a parent should do what is wrong to make the child happy today and therefore cause permanent damage to the child and others tomorrow. A child operates better within a structure, and a lack of structure confuses a child. This could lead to the child making up right and wrong as they go along, meaning that once they can make out what they perceive as 'justification', they commit the act. Sometimes we hear 'I stabbed him because he did not show me respect,' or 'I became bad because my father or mother did not show me love.' Parents and adults generally who ask, 'Whose right or wrong are we talking about?' are responsible for confusing children. There is wrong and there is right. Whatever you know you wouldn't like done to you, you must refrain from doing unto others, and I repeat, 'If it is a crime, let the law deal with it. If it is a sin let God deal with it', but if you can prevent a crime from happening, please do so, for it is a civic responsibility. Parents must wake up and be parents first before becoming friends with their children later in life. Love and nurture your child from day one, for tomorrow may be too late!

Simple Lessons For Parents And Children

As a parent in this modern age, do not be ashamed to acknowledge your weaknesses. Seek and accept help/support in parenting your child. Do not be reluctant to give suggestions or advice when it is obvious that a parent is struggling with their child. The strength one person possesses may be someone else's weakness. Little things you may take for granted may be the part of the jigsaw missing for someone else, therefore sharing is required. Remember your child is not just yours alone. In other words, just like the restaurant owner you are preparing food not only for your consumption but also for other people's consumption. None of us is perfect in the game of parenting, and perfection is not needed, but we all have something different to offer which should be shared. Show some genuine interest in that baby and s/he will definitely interact with you or the likes of you in future whether you like it or not. Parenting may be an exclusive business reserved for parents; however, nurturing a child should and must be the collective responsibility of all who come into contact with that child. Never allow a bad act, which a child is entitled to display as part of its exploration, to become a pattern of behaviour in that child. Never deliberately sow a bad seed in that child because it could turn into something you never expected, and anything can come from it when that seed germinates and becomes a tree with a deep root. The effects can be huge and very likely to affect YOU, the person who sowed that seed. Remember Anders Breivik of Norway: without knowing about his mind-set or background, one obvious thing to note is that the thoughts he had did not start the day before he killed approximately seventy-seven of his 'own' people; his real anger was against Muslims and people he deemed to be aliens. Furthermore, it is obvious that he did not have those thoughts as a baby. A bad seed sown in a child or picked up by a child which is not moderated or removed as early as possible can cause real problems, including mental disorder, for that child in adulthood, because in some instances they seek to change the world in the weird belief they have 'special power and on an assignment'. This belief is difficult to change in adulthood. Just consider the difficulty one faces trying to pull down a tree and compare it with the relative ease of nipping a germinated seed from its bud. That is exactly what happens when we allow our children to carry on behaving badly. The bad behaviour becomes deep rooted and difficult to uproot in adulthood. However, the most frightening aspect of it is the fact that the tree will not only be difficult to uproot but will bear many fruits, and the fruits cannot be anything other than those of the tree which produced it, unless there are some modifications from other factors, which is unnatural because a mango tree can only produce mangos.

If your child does not first consider your feelings as a parent before considering the law or enforcers of the law when they are in the process of doing something wrong, then you need to query your role/duty as a parent.

Parents are like farmers: if you fail to tend your crops, the weeds will tend them for you and your dreams (if you have any) would be shattered on harvest day! For one will usually reap what one has sown.

As stated earlier, life is best described as a relay race with everyone holding a baton. The only question is, what kind of baton is it you are handing over? It does not matter whether you are holding a baton or not, you must hand something over, because it is not only what you do or say but what you fail to do or say that matters. How many times have we heard parents say, 'I never told my child to say or do that', but by keeping quiet or turning a blind eye whilst the child indulged in these bad activities, you have encouraged him or her unwittingly and have reinforced such behaviour, and to a child this means that the behaviour is acceptable to 'my parent'. The best and most worthwhile gift to give to children is to help them love, value, respect and dignify themselves, but that is just the first half of the job. The second half is to get them to see themselves in others by loving, valuing and respecting others, irrespective of their gender, colour, race, creed, sexual orientation or disability. Help your children to see themselves in others. Many parents have achieved both, and today have well-rounded children who do not find it difficult to put themselves into someone else's shoes in order to feel what they are feeling. These children have grown up knowing how to put not only their own needs but also other people's needs into consideration. Some parents achieve only stage one and, through that, manage to produce selfish, greedy, self-centred, 'me, myself and I' kinds of individuals, some of whom have gone on to become 'fat cats' willing to collect £7 million in bonuses whilst some people in the same establishment are struggling to pay their bills, feed their children or even hold to on to their jobs. This is the by-product of academia without moral values. Academic excellence without sound moral values can only be described as, having a beautiful church full of demons. The killings are not only happening on our streets but in the boardrooms, and it is this that has led to the current economic meltdown in our society today, condemning people to depression or suicide. In my work as an approved mental health professional, I have seen my workload double as a result of the economic downturn.

Some parents have not managed to teach their children anything useful because, their own parents taught them nothing; as such, they haven't got anything inside them to hand over. Some of these parents were not brought up with any moral values and some abused drugs and alcohol before or during pregnancy, which affected their unborn children, who become 'damaged from the womb' (*see* interview with a neonatal nurse on page 174). Some of these children grow with no comprehension of issues relating to life, and they are unable to reflect and project. Therefore they grow up to be 'empty', and they cannot see themselves, let alone others. In this situation, some of them go on to develop cravings for illicit substances and are at times introduced to drugs and alcohol by their addicted parents. Nothing is more futile and dangerous; and threatening to mankind than an individual with no moral values who, is also involved in poly-substance abuse. This is the most deadly combination, and this is the combination that produces some acts that 'rational' human beings find extremely difficult to understand. For example, the story of the nineteen-year-old pregnant woman from Wales who was just two weeks from giving birth but was stabbed to death and her flat set on fire (Sky News, 2011) or the incident where armed robbers in Nigeria forced passengers they had robbed to lie on the road and then watched them crushed to death by an oncoming vehicle (*see* My painful heart bleeds on page 177). Someone with this combination can only respond to what comes naturally to them without the ability to rationalise the impact of their actions on others, irrespective of whether they are educated or not, making them more dangerous than all the wild animals put together. People who are lacking in morals and abusing poly-substances become 'psychotic' momentarily whenever they are high on these substances. Some go on to develop 'drug induced psychosis'. This goes a long way to show that mental heath problem on its own is not directly associated with violence or dangerousness. According to Walsh et all, 'people with mental illness are more dangerous to themselves than they are to others; 90 percent of people who die through suicide in the United Kingdom are experiencing mental distress' and 'the fear of random unprovoked attacks on strangers by people with mental health problem is unjustified. This has been highlighted by a US finding that patients with psychosis who are living in the community are 14 times more likely to be victims of a violent crime than to be arrested for such a crime' (pages 233-238). In most cases where a mental health client has committed a violent crime, it is often associated with drug and/or alcohol abuse. Parents have a duty to make their children aware of these facts as early as possible. According to Cassin, (1999) 'I am also convinced that the first and most influential step in preventing drug problems is to affirm and impart values to children during their formative years (which is generally accepted to be from 0 to 5 years), which will enable them to make the right choices about drugs when the time comes' (page 2).

Parents also need to be aware that due to the level of violence children see these days through technological gadgets, they are now more likely to re-enact them once under the influence of these substances. Therefore, keeping a close eye on and helping your child to learn how to separate fiction from fact is crucial. It is also advisable that as a parent your actions are not based on the demands of your child, but instead you should evaluate what your child is asking for before responding. Make your child aware from the beginning that unless it is an emergency, you will need time to think through the request s/he makes. This would instil one of the very important values in your child: 'patience in waiting'; and this is the 'real' world you are introducing to your child, as most things we do and get in life involve waiting. In addition, you will not be in a rush and make the mistake of giving your child something that is not age appropriate and which could damage them in the long run, without you realising the part you may have played in the process. Not understanding the contents of the gadgets your child is using and the kinds of 'friends' they have is key to the crisis on our streets today. The question is: as a farmer, who is tending your crops, is it you or the weeds? Never wait until the child is a year or two old before you start. YOUR WORK STARTS FROM DAY ONE. *The ultimate aim is to bring up your child as 'a parent to be not as a child to remain'*

As a parent, remember that every child needs identity, guidance, direction, care and love, and where these are lacking in a family environment they seek them outside. Some, in their quest for a viable option, will join gangs, and the gangs then provide them with an identity, an emblem and some level of meaning to their lives. Gangs have always existed, but in different forms. Those we have now in our inner cities have become very threatening, challenging and deadly. Even some well-behaved children sometimes feel they run the risk of 'standing out' and becoming a victim if they do not join. This is even more the case when parents have failed to meet the needs of their children (see the account of a probation officer on page 168). Parents and society as a whole are at the point of losing control if rapid action is not taken. This is why the way we bring up children in this 'highly technological age' really needs a proper examination. A lot of parents have no idea what is in the games they buy for their children. Some of these games contain images that are not age appropriate, for example sexually explicit materials, violence and horror images that children get accustomed to and believe to be normal. Some games and internet sites contain information on how to join gangs. Some children find it hard to differentiate what is real from what is fiction, even some parents who were not brought up properly struggle to separate fiction from fact or reality, let alone their children. As a parent, you are busy with 'life activities' and not necessarily aware that the gadget you have bought for your child has enabled strange, dangerous and deadly visitors you would never have allowed to associate with your child to come into your home and constantly interact with your child, teaching them what you never would have taught or wanted them to learn. Suddenly you begin to wonder why your child's behaviour has changed. Some parents who have lost their children through violence or whose children were perpetrators never knew their children were involved in gangs. Some of these children would attend church or the mosque and do activities with their parents but they were living another life at the same time, as society empowers them to keep their own secrets, and yet expect you to parent. At times if you want to do the right things to keep your children in check you are termed 'a control freak'. To all the parents who are keen on knowing what their children are up to and helping in shaping them into becoming useful, law abiding citizens, I say this to you;

If the meaning of 'control freak' is knowing what your child is doing, who they are with, the type of family values the children they interact with have, and setting boundaries for them, then every parent is encouraged to be a 'control freak'. Please, please, please be a control freak! This does not mean you cannot take a step back and allow your child to explore and learn from his/her own mistakes, but you must and should set the parameters first; this is not a gambling game. Remember you cannot toy with a loaded gun; let alone being the agent that makes a loaded gun dangerous.

This point can never be over emphasised. As a parent, you must view your role as that of a farmer, and tend to your crops, remembering at all times that the weeds have the same right as your crops to grow in the farm. You must and should tend to your crops, not for one week or one month but until harvest. Once harvested and your crops are sold or given to someone else to keep, you will be causing a disaster if you continue to tend to that crop. This is what a lot of grandparents who interfere in their adult children's marriages or partnerships fail to realise. They do not realise the bias and poison they sow in their children's families, and the impact it has on the little children being brought up within such families; who might not have a clue where the crisis is coming from. When couples have difficulties (which is normal) in any relationship, it is not the job of grandparents to sort out, rather couples must seek the input of an 'independent', preferably a paid marriage counsellor, who can objectively explore things with them and develop meaningful strategies to remedy the situation. Where a parent sees their own parent as counsellor and allows them to meddle in the affairs of their immediate family, disaster awaits and children in that family usually bear the brunt of the disaster.

A child is more likely to be spoilt and damaged if brought up by a grandparent. Grandparents have a different role to play in your children's life, based on genuine affection and love. They are likely to be reluctant to discipline their grandchildren, as they are likely to see that as parental responsibility. Grandparents are likely to allow your children get away with things they would not have allowed you to get away with. Subconsciously, they know it is not their place to discipline their grandchildren; in fact at times they will not tell you what the child did wrong, so you won't be annoyed, or they will minimise it and reassure you that they have dealt with it. To bring up your family correctly, the umbilical cord has to be cut prior to getting into a committed relationship. If you are still consulting with your parent and not your partner before making a decision on issues relating to your immediate family, then you are an adult in a 'child's mood' and should be living with your parents. If you are only out to please your parents and negate the needs of your immediate family, then something is wrong with not only you but also your parents, who cannot see the crisis being generated by you and them to the detriment of your children and immediate family.

How many times have we heard that one of the reasons for the spate of stabbings in our society today is that the victim is judged by the perpetrator not to have shown respect to that perpetrator? The word 'respect' is more likely to have been understood by your child if you and your partner concentrated on bringing your children up, rather than having a primary focus on your parents, who have already lived their own lives. The reality is that if one has enough respect for oneself that should always weigh more than that expected from someone else. It is difficult to comprehend how the perpetrator gets 'respect' either from facing life in prison in front of a high court judge or from the victim who is already dead. The truth is that anyone who stabs or kills someone for such a 'weird' reason is insecure, lacking in self-worth and above all a coward! Animals have no understanding of the word 'respect', but won't kill for such a reason; they only kill in order to feed, or when threatened. If someone were really in need of respect as a rational being, it would be more realisable if they won a boxing or wrestling match against the person they craved respect from, for example, so that at least that individual would be alive to offer 'respect' after having lost the fight.

Some people say that, hypothetically speaking, they would only consider killing someone if, after a 'successful' business transaction, the person refuses to give them their own share of the money. Others say they would commit suicide if they could not see any way out of their hardship or if they felt that life was not offering them any satisfaction. Each time I hear this, I realise that a lot of parents out there do not give their children 'moral instructions', and that our schools, too, are failing in this aspect of education today. It is a parent's responsibility to make their children aware that under no circumstances should they harm or kill anyone. It is also the job of a parent to inculcate the belief that suicide is not an option, as no one knows what he or she is letting himself or herself into. Every child and adult must know that there is nothing to be gained if you kill someone. On the contrary, you lose 'big time' and the loss is permanent when you kill someone deliberately. The respect you want from the individual you have murdered, you've permanently ensured the person cannot give you; the money the person owes you, you have also ensured you will never get back, as no one has seen a dead person handing back what they owed; and you are not able to say to the dead, 'Didn't I tell you I will deal with you?' You have not only destroyed a life but many lives, as the victim's relatives and friends are condemned to everlasting pain. Furthermore, you could have lost some money if you had hired people to do the killing for you. You also lose in the sense that you have killed someone and there is a saying (even if you are not caught at or linked to the crime) that 'the guilty is always afraid'. Even if you are not afraid, to date no one has died and come back to tell us that heaven and hell are not real. So one's final destination after committing murder is not clearly defined; you might escape 'human' justice but you will not escape 'natural' justice. You will never know whether the person you killed or paid money to be assassinated would be the one to deal with you when you answer your own call. Why would you send your 'enemy' to a place you would eventually go, without guarantying what advantage or disadvantage your enemy may have over you? It is also for this reason that suicide cannot be an option, as no one has committed suicide and then come back to tell us, 'I really ended it, and I am enjoying it now.' You also lose because, if you are caught, you are likely to be spending the rest of your life in prison or be killed as a consequence of your actions, depending on the country in which you committed the crime.

It is the job of a parent to instruct and remind their children that if they let the person owing them money stay alive, one day they may have a change of heart and pay them. Since life is complex, the person owing them may run out of money but fortunes could favour the child later, and the debtor would be alive to witness their success and feel the pain of regret. The best way to get respect from someone is to work hard and accomplish some achievements or prove 'them wrong'. When you do so, your spirit and whole being will be satisfied and you will not need anyone to tell you who you are or 'respect' you, because you will have more than enough respect for yourself. The best way to silence your critics or adversaries is by your noble achievements, so they stay alive and 'eat' their own words. Never in life is it said that the dead person showed respect to the person responsible for their death. When I heard a man say to his wife, 'Bet me, you would die before me,' I thought to myself, 'What a stupid and thoughtless statement.' It was obvious that this man was not thinking right at the time. If he had been, he would have known that there would never be any way he and his wife would be alive together to see the eventual outcome, because if his wishes were realised, he would not be able to say to his dead wife, 'Didn't I tell you?' He may choose to say this to his dead wife but it is a certainty that he would have no response from her. There would be no such response as 'Yes, my husband, you were right' coming from the dead. On the other hand, if the husband got it wrong and died before the wife, the poor wife would not have the pleasure/opportunity of telling him that he was wrong. 'My dear husband, I thought we had a bet that I would go before you, how come...' This is an indication that many wrong things human beings do, is because of their 'poor' cognition (thought process).

Parents need to educate their children and condemn suicide in all its forms. Though most suicide is linked to 'poor' mental state, it is also linked to 'poor judgement'. If you have not given yourself life then you are not meant to take your own life. Why hasten your death when you are bound to die anyway? It is not only the fact that no one has died and come back, but it is also the fact that nothing is as constant as change, which means that no matter how bad things are now, they are subject to change. Why take this irreversible route? The usual belief of someone contemplating suicide is expressed by saying, 'I have had enough; life is not worth it; I want to end it; everything and everyone is against me; I can't live like this; I can't live with the shame.' These feelings, and all the other things that frustrate the mind, leading to acts of suicide, need not make one take that final step. It should be considered that the only realistic guarantee is that no one has ever taken their life and come back to life to tell us that 'the spirit does or does not live on; oh, it is better on the other side; I enjoyed it' or 'the suffering continued and even worsened; I regretted my actions' or 'I truly ended it, for all my pains were gone.' No one can categorically say what really happens following someone's death. All we have are different theories based on the different beliefs of those alive, including scientists, but unfortunately science has no factual link to spiritualism, as all scientific views on 'life after death' are abstract and mere suppositions. Never has a scientist told us exactly where the wind took off from and where it rested, and until science is able to do that, my take is that science cannot be factual about what happens to the spirit in death. The only thing science offers when it comes to death is that life stops, but science cannot provide proof about whether or not life carries on spiritually, therefore it cannot deal with this question. Only the dead can shed light on it, but the dead have very little or nothing to do with the living, unfortunately.

If you are desperate to die, be patient, for death will surely come, and in your patience there is every chance things would improve for the better. Change must surely occur whether it is intended or not; the question is whether it is a positive or negative change. Nothing you have done, no situation you are in and no condition you find yourself in is worthy of taking your own life, as at your final destination you would only find many other people who have been or are currently in the same or a worse situation than you. If it is an illness (physical or mental) let the clinicians deal with it; if you have suffered a bereavement or loss of any kind, let counselling be your answer; if it is a crime, let the law deal with it; and if it is a sin, let God deal with it. You won't be the first or the last person in the same situation, and even those condemning you may also be afflicted, but as nature's rules demand, sadly they may want to play 'holier than thou'. Seek help. There's an escape; don't pursue suicide, because there is nothing to gain but all to lose. The earlier parents inculcate the reality that no one truly knows what happens in death into their children the better.

If, as a parent, you have no words of wisdom to give to your child, it is very likely you are not bringing that child up in the right way. If you cannot remember any words of wisdom from your own parents, it is also an indication that you may not have been brought up properly. Start seeking help, for there's help out there! Don't be shy, ashamed, or silent and try to cover up and depend on luck because that is more dangerous than driving at high speed whilst blindfolded. Be proactive and remember that you are not on your own; there are many other parents in the same boat as you. And 'group therapy' does work.

Every parent and child must keep in mind that one does not need to do anything to be useless, so you don't need to waste energy or pay to be useless, as there's no cost attached. On the other hand, everything that has value requires hard work, focus and commitment, and can often be very expensive. Therefore, to achieve anything good, discipline is required, and discipline is not a word children like, especially children who have been allowed to develop a pattern of life estranged from hard work and dedication. To have a balanced life one must experience good and bad times, enjoy riches and understand poverty. Having everything the way you want it or being made to feel happy by always getting whatever you want gives you a false sense of security, because that's not what the real world offers. Everything that makes a child useful is usually difficult and time-consuming to learn, for example, cooking, studying and tidying up. Some parents, who want to feel that they are parenting and who also want to save time, do the cooking, serve their children and tidy up as well. There's nothing wrong in doing so sometimes, but the children benefit more when they are informed of the benefits of cooking not only for themselves but also for others. This offers them choice in adulthood and will not only save them money but help them to eat healthily. Buying and eating takeaway food all the time is expensive and unhealthy. Being able to cook is also a source of support for future partners: a lot of adults who cannot cook or tidy up put too much pressure on their partners to do this for them. This is one of the reasons why men suffer the most when they separate from their partners. Seventy percent of all the men surveyed highlighted this point: that their partners leaving them made them very vulnerable because they depended on them for all the domestic chores. Some turned to drinking and drug use, as they could not cope.

Children, from an early age, usually like to participate in the kitchen, but some parents who are short-sighted do not encourage them to do so because it can be time-consuming and requires patience. *Parents must focus on the long-term gain for all, not the short-term pain for the few.* Parents must know that a child who is not taught how to cook and clean is likely to struggle in life and negatively affect others who come into contact with them. The overall cost is huge; but when you sacrifice time and get your children to be self-sufficient, you have set them up for life and they are likely to bring happiness to those they come in contact with; moreover, they have the skills to pass on to their own children. When your children show interest in coming into the kitchen, give them simple tasks and take your time to teach them. Soon they will perfect the act and enjoy doing it independently. Guess what? Remind them to do the same with their own kids and that circle will have started and be carried on. As children are slow to walk, talk and run, so they are slow in comprehending good things, so be patient and keep repeating yourself. It is priceless when your message gets through, never give up or give in – it might not please them at the time but they will soon realise the investment you have made. Even if they do not thank you, you will never regret helping them to be able to survive and be independent. Give your children 'moral' instructions, for example what to do if they see an old person struggling with a heavy load, and getting them to 'pinch' themselves in order to appreciate how others feel when pinched. Speak to your children from the day they are born; don't wait until they are two or three before correcting them because you will have left it too late. Get your children to place more value on human interaction than interaction with gadgets, for if they place more value on gadgets than on their fellow human beings, they are likely to kill for gadgets. These things do not come naturally! Remember, babies still require training and guidance for the things they can do naturally, as stated earlier. Ensure your children value themselves, you as parents and their siblings and get them to appreciate that that is how other families value their members, too. In doing so, you have enabled your children to learn how to show empathy. Never think sending your children to school and making them academically efficient is the only training they require, for parents who think that way encourage a 'me, myself and I' attitude in their children, and such children are likely to grow up to be selfish and make selfish decisions in the boardrooms that affect others negatively. Once this 'me, myself and I' attitude is developed, it is easy for your children to either fold their arms and feel the world owes them a living or go on to become 'fat cats': either way they are unlikely to become well-rounded individuals.

As a parent you should realise that given the choice every child, especially boys, would choose the easy way out: play and fun. The people children like most are those with a good sense of fun and play – they usually see these people as friends, because friendship is an equal relationship and in most cases it is based on common interests. A friend is not equipped to rebuke or discipline another friend. Those who preach discipline and commitment are not always in the good books of children. We have to beware of things that are easy and only offer excitement, enjoyment and fun, because these are often for 'momentary' satisfaction and can be very costly overall. This point cannot be overemphasised. Whenever life seems really simplistic, exciting and easy, watch out! We have heard it numerous times: 'no pain, no gain'. Nothing good comes easily; if it's easy it may not be good enough. If it is cheap, there is a reason why it is cheap. Most things that offer us value usually present huge challenges to us, because if not, the value would be lost because everyone can afford them. To have what others do not have one must do what others could not do or are not doing.

Some parents believe that being a good parent means that their children always need to be happy, or that to be a good parent one has to be friends with one's children. Any parent who thinks this way is in a 'dangerous' territory. Your children cannot be your friends. Children are born and friends are made. One cannot discipline or set boundaries for one's friends, but setting boundaries and discipline are key to parenting.

Do your work as a parent. It is the most important job in this world. It is a full-time, 24-hour, 7-day-a-week job. You may have breaks, but no holidays or time off on long-term sick leave. Observe, monitor and focus on your children. If you notice anything untoward, seek to deal with it with your child. If your child does not respond positively, don't stop but persist and bring out the issue, because 'a problem shared is likely to be a problem solved'. Your friend or the relative you are discussing the problem with may have been in or is currently in the same boat. If not in the same boat, they are likely to be going through a different kind of difficulty in their own homes. If you are the person with whom the problem is shared, do your best to help, support and encourage. Never hide the problem, thinking of the shame, or in the belief that you are washing dirty linen in public. It is better to suffer the 'shame' momentarily than live with shame or guilt for the rest of your life. Never leave any stone unturned in trying to support and turn around your child. Let your child know that it is LOVE that is driving you, as you do not want them to go the wrong way, get into trouble or become a source of pain for others, which is so easy to do. There is no guarantee that things will turn out as expected due to so many other influences on your child. However, if things go wrong it wouldn't then be because you did not do your job. You will have done yourself a big favour because the guilt would not haunt you, or will haunt you less. Furthermore, your child will always remember that you did your job, as it is likely that what they had got wrong was something you had previously warned them against. As for mistakes, we have all made and will continue to make them as parents; they form part of our human make-up, and there is no such thing as perfect parenting. According to Edwin Bliss, 'Perfection, fortunately is not the only alternative to mediocrity. A more sensible alternative is excellence. Striving for excellence is stimulating and rewarding, striving for perfection in practically anything is both neurotic and futile.' Having said that, mistakes that are habitual are not mistakes but deliberate wrongdoings.

I could not help but feel sad when a young man told me, 'Sir I have heard a little of what your father taught you about life, and I feel inspired by it. I wish I had had a dad like that. All my dad kept telling us when we were growing up was how lucky we were to have him around,' meaning that his father had not left them for another woman. How depressing! Every child is entitled to, and in need of, a family that is loving, caring and supportive. If, as a parent, you have not provided such a family, your child is likely to seek an alternative, which is more often a 'gang'. The 'gang' usually starts as supportive, protective and caring towards your child, but can evolve into anything due to internal or external influences and pressures.

Please talk to your children from birth; they are ready to listen to you even from the womb. Do not worry when they do not respond in speech; they can hear you and they are listening to you. Sing and play gentle music to them. As quickly as possible begin to teach them independence; teach them how to value themselves and the things you have bought for them. When they have learnt these, they are likely to value you and your things and are likely to transfer these values to how they treat other people. Show your children love, teach them respect and watch them reciprocate these. Don't take your eyes off the ball, thinking it is a day's job; it is a lifetime job, or at least lasts until they establish full independence. Remember they are not fully independent until they can pay their own way and take absolute care of their own issues and needs. Independence comes not with age but with deeds. For I have seen thirteen-year-olds who are more independent than thirty-year-olds. Good luck, and remember this: how you feel today, as a parent and as an individual is more important than how you have felt in all the days and years of your past, including yesterday. Therefore aim to feel good, happy and reassured in your old age, in your last days. It is the hard work you put in today that will secure the happiness you crave for tomorrow. Some of the things that offer you excitement and fun today are likely to bring pain and suffering tomorrow, for example, choosing to live a single or carefree life into old age or selfish separation with no meaningful or positive contribution practically and financially to the upbringing and nurturing of your children. These are easy; these are 'can dos' and no effort is required to accomplish them because there's no huge dividend at the end of these, rather the cost at the end might be huge, and it usually translates into 'gain now, pain later'. In contrast, marriage, cohabitation, the 'we, not me' approach in family life, dedication to nurturing your offspring and commitment to your union are not easy, because they are the right, good and proper things to do, and good things are not usually easy to accomplish. Those who work hard and go through the pain of bringing their children up the right way enjoy the dividend in old age. I have worked in an older people's home, where nature has assembled the high, powerful and mighty and then levels them by forcing them against their will to become needy, helpless, vulnerable and dependent. The only difference noted between them was the joy and excitement some of them had when their children came to visit. One cannot help but feel sad for those who have children but are abandoned, especially when they see their fellow residents enjoying family interaction, which can be very therapeutic indeed. There may be no guarantees, but one stands a better chance of enjoying one's old age when one inculcates morals and values into one's children, not just academic skills and the desire to look good in designer's wares.

A Tribute To An Awesome Father

I thank God for choosing my parents, especially my father, the late Prince Japheth Abanobi Ihenacho, and my mother, the late Mrs Christiana Nnenna Ihenacho, without whom I would possibly not have been part of this world. I particularly thank God when I remember what my father told me he went through before he was allowed to marry my mother, in those 'good old days'.

My maternal grandparents, especially my maternal grandfather, swore that my father could only marry my mother 'over his dead body'. This was because my maternal grandfather was very poor, and my mother, being the 'prettiest girl' in Umunachi Obowo, was his only 'insurance', because she was likely to attract a rich man. As a result, he had already committed himself by accepting an initial deposit (part of the dowry) from another man, whose son was very rich, for my mother's hand in marriage. My father went to hell and back. He was lucky because my mother genuinely loved and had a lot of respect for him, a young, elegant teacher working in the local school that my mother attended. Some of the sufferings my father reported he endured, I find hard to imagine, given the modern world we live in today. He was made to sleep outside in the dark (interacting with all the dangerous elements like the snakes) because my maternal grandfather refused to let him into his house. Even my grandfather, the then Warrant Chief of Ogwa Community, had to leave his Kingdom for Obowo in order to influence matters, and offers were made to my maternal grandfather to triple the deposit he had already collected on my mother's account, but being a principled man, my maternal grandfather apologised respectfully but refused. One would have thought that my maternal grandfather would have jumped at such an offer (as many people would do today), so that his daughter would be married into a well-known family in Igbo land, but that wasn't the case. Despite his poverty, he remained principled. My grandfather was so infuriated at being turned down – possibly for the first time – that he told my father to withdraw his interest in my mother. My grandfather offered to ensure that no matter what my father saw in my mother, he would make sure he got another woman who had more.

My father took all this in, but was not going to relent in his effort to secure my mother's hand in marriage. My father stubbornly continued to camp outside my mother's home, pleading to be given a chance. He mounted so much pressure that my maternal grandfather consulted with elders in his community and they came up with a plan. The plan was one that they believed would not only stop my father, but would also humiliate and disgrace him. Since it was the season for their town wrestling festival, they came up with the plan to set my father up in a 'winner takes all' contest, putting him up against the best wrestler in Obowo. They told my father that if he won, my mother would be his, but if he lost, that would be the end of the matter. My maternal grandfather, being a principled man, ensured that the man he collected money from agreed to the plan, and he offered to refund the money in the 'unlikely' event of my father winning the fight. However, the man was so convinced that my father would lose, that he told my maternal grandfather that the money he gave him was non-refundable, as he could not see how an 'ordinary' teacher could face up to, let alone defeat their best wrestler. My father was surprised and shocked at hearing this, but was prepared to take any chance on offer, in the name of love. His excitement grew and he travelled back home to inform my grandfather. My maternal grandfather and his folks toasted themselves at having come up with the master plan that would end the saga, which was what they wanted.

However, unbeknown to them, my father was not just an 'ordinary' teacher as they thought, but also a skilled wrestler. He had mastered the skill of wrestling at his maternal home (Idem Ogwa). The news of what was going to happen was spread by the local town crier, and when the day of reckoning came, the entire Umunachi Obowo community gathered. The delegation sent by my grandfather to give moral support to my father, having seen how determined and unrelenting he was, arrived in Obowo and was welcomed by my maternal grandfather and his people. To everyone's amazement, my father, the teacher, took to the stage against all the odds to wrestle with the local warrior, who was already out and dancing to the sound of wrestling drums and basking in the support of the local crowd, who were cheering him as their hero. My father told me that he was very worried and nervous, but quietly confident. He was driven and motivated not only by the embarrassment of losing, but mainly the passion, love and affection he felt for my mother, who could not attend the event for obvious reasons: My mother said that she could not attend because she was downcast in the belief that my father would lose. She said she could not envisage how my father could defeat their local wrestling champion. She said, she was so afraid and sad, she could not eat. All she did was cry in the belief that she had lost my father for good. My father told me that, it was not just a wrestling match, but a fight for his life, because losing meant losing my mother and losing my mother meant losing everything, meaning as he put it 'the end of my life'. As soon as the referee gave the signal for the fight to commence, my father told me that he pounced on the local hero at the roaring of the crowd, and within minutes my father said, he lifted the warrior up and threw him to the floor. With that action my father was declared the winner. The watching crowd was stunned. My maternal grandfather and his people were shocked, dumb-founded and could not believe what they had witnessed, according to my father. The delegates sent by my grandfather were elated and couldn't contain their joy, as they took over the arena in celebration carrying my father shoulder high in jubilation. My father told me, he could not contain his excitement, and was in tears as he was declared the winner. From that day, all restrictions preventing him from marrying my mother were lifted and he became a hero in Umunachi, Obowo. I keep wondering if I would have been part of this world had my father lost that fight, as my mother would have been forced to marry someone else for money not love. I remember asking my father what he would have really done had he lost the fight, and he smiled and said 'I don't know my son, I never wanted to contemplate that but I know for sure, life would have been empty,' and at that point he became a bit emotional. It was as if he couldn't see any other thing in life beyond my mother, and my father loved her so much she ended up becoming his ninth child, competing with us for my father's love at every stage.

My mother always believed and trusted in my father's judgement. They addressed each other as JC and CJ (Japheth Christiana) and (Christiana Japheth). But my mother often called my father *onye nkuzi* (teacher). I wish and hope that such love, passion and affection can be obtainable in today's world. My father transferred the same level of affection to all his children but less so with my senior brother. However he was ready at all times to put his life on the line for our sake. I miss him so much. He was always there, willing, ready and able to deal with whatever it was, but in the same breath ready to admonish me if I had got it wrong, because he believed in 'calling a spade a spade' and always quoted the adage 'spare the rod and spoil the child'.

I pray to God to give me the strength, dedication and wisdom to one day write about my wonderful, brilliant and awesome father – teacher, wrestler, artist, expert motorbike rider, musician, composer, conductor and choirmaster – who translated his teachings into music in order to make his students remember and understand. A man who never believed the 'hype', and the only person I'm convinced understood and believed in me. In all his dealings with me (even the name he called me 'Eze ka ibe ya' meaning 'king above his contemporaries') there was the indication that he saw something special in me. I have just on reflection realised that but I renounce the name he called me because I am not a king. Eze though means king but it is taken from my full name Ezenwa. I am always filled with emotion each time I remember my father. He shouted at times and rebuked and disciplined me – but all in the name of love, as he never wanted me to derail or to come into harm's way. I understood that, even though at the time I didn't quite like the telling off I got from him. He told me that it was only those who had my best interests at heart who would tell me what I was doing wrong, and that sometimes the truth hurts. Everything he told me, I grew up to realise, was true. He was an upright man, at all times making things clear and making me aware of right and wrong. He maintained a steady stance on things; he would not say one thing one day and another the next day, or say one thing to one person and the opposite to someone else. He was not perfect, as no one is perfect, but he called it as he saw it. He remains (even in death) the best thing that ever happened to me. He denied me a lot of what I wanted as a child and he explained why. He told me that a child who gets all he or she wants is running the risk of becoming useless, and a parent who gives everything a child asks for is responsible for making that child useless, and is not worthy of being a parent. I tried to find out what he meant, and he explained that a child could ask for anything but it is the job of a parent to ascertain what the child really needs. He went further and said that a child can jump into the fire because he or she has little or no understanding of the consequences, but a parent should understand and must do whatever it takes to prevent that child from jumping into the fire, even if that child cries endlessly. My father said that he always viewed with pity parents who think that bringing up children only revolves around buying expensive things and dressing up the children for 'parades'. He maintained that the 'have nots' are the ones with the right ingredients to aspire to have, and 'the haves' are the most likely to lose what they have, especially if they did not have to do anything to acquire it. He went further and explained 'Those born with silver spoons in their mouths are more likely not to have the skills and discipline to work hard and are likely to use shovels in wasting the wealth their parents toiled to acquire with spoons.' On the other hand, he said 'Those born with nothing usually fight and develop skills for survival and are more likely to attain a height people never envisaged.' My father was a TRUE teacher indeed.

Though my father has been gone for so long – and forever – it seems like only yesterday, and I still miss him dearly. I wish I had had more time with him. I was only fourteen years of age when he died, but he gave me all I have today in the short period I had with him. Not the perishables like money, a house, etc. – he had none of those things to give – but he taught me values, morals, discipline and respect for others and for myself. He once told me, '*Nwam* (my child), each time you look for someone to blame for anything in your life, it means that in that thing you have failed.' He went on to qualify this by saying, 'Blame is linked to failure because people rarely ascribe success to others, and when they do it is usually as a secondary consideration. People will always take the credit first for their successes.' This made me always look within myself, in good and in bad situations. A lot of people today spend their time searching for answers and blaming others when things go wrong in their lives. They absolve themselves of every responsibility, never seeing what they may have done wrong or how they have contributed to their bad situation. In that frame of mind, they can never see what they can do to turn things around, because they are chasing shadows. The same people will take credit for any success, perhaps even coming up with some 'crazy' ideas about their contributions to any success they see from someone close to them, as well as their own success.

My father always encouraged me to be 'a star'. I was very young and couldn't understand. He knew I couldn't understand, and in his usual way explained: 'I want you to be a star, my son.' Pointing to the sky, he made me look up, and said, 'You see the stars, they are up there; they do not say a word, they don't say what they are, but people look at them and know they are stars. Any star that ever says, "Here I am, I am a star!" is not even a "fake" star, let alone a real star.' He concluded by saying, 'Let your behaviour, deeds and attributes say who you are. Be sure and certain of who you are, but let others make the call, because empty vessels make the most noise.' He then sounded a word of caution, and said, 'Even if people judge you wrongly – because some people will – don't worry, remain who you are – "a star". Do not change so long as you are on steady ground. You can't really control what others do, think or say, but your thoughts, behaviour and speech you can control. Just be yourself. Respect and show humility, but fear no one, for whatever happens, all that a man can do is temporary and every man is subject to death. Fear is for God alone, as he remains in control of the world he created in spite of all odds.' My father was the first person I heard say 'everything that glitters is not gold' and 'parenting a child is not just about what a parent says or does but what a parent fails to do or say to a child'. He affirmed that it is bad to ignore a child who does or says the wrong thing. Furthermore, he said that it is even worse when one parent says one thing on an issue and the other parent says another or appears indifferent. My father said that nothing confuses a child more than this, and that the child is likely to play one parent against the other, and before too long everyone will start looking for someone else to blame when things turn nasty.

These words are not only food for thought but also food for life. They stand the test of time. No amount of money or possessions can afford them; they are too expensive to buy because they are priceless. Any child who is not taught these things from an early age, I consider a deprived child, and therefore, by my definition, a child in need.

In the short period I had with my father, he invested a lot in me and the evidence shows that better returns are usually achieved when real-life ethics are embedded in children. Therefore I appeal to all parents, wherever you are, please invest in your children. Teach them morals and life-sustaining values; show them you care. No matter the situation, never run away from your responsibilities unless your life is at stake. Remember that when it goes wrong, it is not only you who will feel the pain, but society suffers as well. The success of a parent is not judged by his/her bank balance or material wealth, but by the success and behaviour of his/her children, and that is also what determines the pride or shame of a parent. To my beloved father, 'Sir Mmoyi', as he was fondly called, rest in perfect peace until we meet again. Meanwhile, I can't stop missing you! I wish you were still alive to see the fruit of your labour.

To All The Children of This World

There are three crucial things for every child to note, understand and remember.

1. You never asked to be born, your parents were not nominated by anyone to give birth to you and you did not make any request to be born into any particular family, community or nation. So, like everyone, it was just sheer luck or misfortune where you found yourself. As such, we all started as babies of this world. That's why, on arrival (at birth), no baby is able to identify its parents or the nation they are born into. For example, if you were born in China to a Chinese parent and at birth an American parent took you to America, you will grow up not ever knowing your true parents are Chinese and you were born in China unless you saw documentation or someone stated the facts to you.

2. It costs little or nothing to be useless and one doesn't need to do anything to be useless. However, when one becomes useless, the consequences become too costly to the individual, family and society at large. On the contrary, it costs a lot to be useful and a lot of hard work, dedication and discipline are required, but when one becomes useful, the benefit for the individual, family and society is huge.

3. Every child is special, unique and born for a purpose. Therefore never wish to be someone else but copy any good thing seen in someone else to enhance your uniqueness and strive to be the best you can be.

Every child needs to know that it is only natural and automatic for play and fun to have a dominant role in every 'normal' child's life, and play can be extremely beneficial to a child's learning and development. It is a well-documented fact that human beings learn a lot through play. However, children need to be aware that playing all the time can also have a detrimental impact on their lives, and any adult allowing or offering a child only play, fun and excitement is not necessarily their 'best' friend because they have very little benefit from this overall. Those who offer you, as a child, these things may not have the intention to harm you deliberately, but may not be fully aware that offering you only these, means that you are not being prepared well for adulthood. As a result, they have unintentionally set you up to fail because you might not be able to face up to real life challenges, which surely will come your way. Therefore you are likely to become a burden on others and a great source of discomfort to people you come into contact with in adulthood. Only people who have your best interest at heart and want you to succeed in life will tell you what you are doing wrong. You might not like it at the time, because in most cases doing what is right usually involves hard work and doing the wrong thing doesn't, as it can provide momentary pleasure or satisfaction, but can be futile and costly in the long run. It is usually your parents or relatives who are likely to tell you what you are doing wrong, because they want to see you succeed in life.

Those who bring structure, boundaries, discipline and focus into your life are the ones that have your best interest at heart, and they are your true 'best' friends. They are the ones preparing you for an independent life, good grades at school, a good career and the ability to afford what you want and to provide for others. When an adult says to you, in order that you concentrate on important things, it is time to stop playing, it is time do your chores, it is time to study, it is time for some moral instructions or to stop using your gadgets, if you are abusing them, that adult has your best interest at heart. You must remember at all times that you don't need to do anything to be useless. As a child, try and make 'moderation' your watchword. That means, try to do everything in moderation. Don't let any particular thing take over your life: not play, not hard work and obviously not doing anything at all.

As a child, watch out also for all the 'can dos', that is, all the things you can do; you will find that most of them are usually easy and often the wrong and less profitable things. Concentrate on the 'can't dos', that is, all the things you cannot do; usually they will present more difficulty and challenges, but often they are the right and useful things that bring dividends in the long run. Everything useful has a cost attached to it and requires us to work hard before we can have it, otherwise everyone would have them and the value would be lost. Remember, for one to have what others don't have, one must do what others can't do. Any path that leads to a good thing and/or life is usually littered with hazards. Look at the expensive things of this life; can anyone find gold or oil on the surface of the earth? No! One has to dig really deep to find them. To have an 'A star' one has to put in the work. But what does it take to fail? Consider how easy it is for you as a child to wake up in the morning and begin to watch television, play with your gadgets and eat some kind of convenience food for breakfast, and then compare this to how hard it is for you to wake up in the morning, make your bed, tidy up your room and cook your breakfast yourself. And then compare which option comes more naturally and easily and which one is more difficult and requires nurturing. Finally consider which is more beneficial in the long run. The easy part you find you are likely to do without prompts from anyone or repeated reminders. The difficult part is likely to require training and regular prompts from parents and loved ones. Your friends cannot prompt you to do the difficult ones because friendship is an equal partnership, which offers no partner the authority or power to impose structure or set boundaries for the other. Therefore your parent/s have to be your parents and may decide to be your friend(s) when you are an independent adult. You choose your friends, but you cannot choose your parents, and if your parents are not setting boundaries and providing structure for you then they are quite simply failing you as a child. However, be careful not to blame others, because blame is linked to failure. When one seeks to blame someone else, it usually turns out that they have failed in that thing or area themselves (see the story of two Bangladeshi men below). The same person would not credit anyone for any success in their life, but if they must it is usually as a secondary consideration. It is not right to say, 'I fight all the time because my mother did not show me enough love' or 'I abuse my child because I was abused by my parents'; these cannot be reasons or excuses for doing the wrong thing but are rather a sign of failure, because the person saying these things would also take the credit first if it relates to a success story. Abuse is an awful crime against humanity; however, many people who were abused remember how bad they felt and ensure they never put anyone through what they went through themselves. Think right and produce good; think wrong and produce evil; and think nothing at all and you are more likely to produce evil because you become like a wave tossed about by any wind that comes your way, as wrong things can be eye-catching, easier to follow and more in tune with our natural/animalistic instinct.

There is a 'kick' associated with doing bad things; that's why human beings are more likely to do the wrong things when they are idle, hence the saying 'an idle mind is a devil's workshop'. Therefore, link your brain to your eyes not your heart and fist. It is your eyes that make the first connection to something and after that you have a decision to make: either switch on the brain or switch on your heart. If you choose to switch on your brain, you are likely to be rational and act in the right manner, but if you choose to switch on your heart you are more than likely to engage your fist, as your emotion drives you to act in an irrational manner.

Doing what you want, when and how you want may provide you with excitement and pleasure now, but the bitter side of today's pleasure lies ahead and its impact at times is more far-reaching than anyone could imagine! It is truly expensive to be good and very cheap to be bad. Being good should not be optional but standard, but it cannot be over emphasised that a lot of hard work is required in order to achieve this. *Doing what is good, what is not easy and what others cannot do or find difficult to do leads to having what others don't have.*

When you are a child, learn to share, learn to respect, love and appreciate not only yourself but others also. Take your education seriously. Learn to cook, clean up, iron, shop and look after yourself. If your parent/s do not want you to do any of these things because they think they are too rich or for any other reason, remind them that you want to be self-sufficient and have the ability to exercise choice in future, and that this is the best time to prepare yourself for adulthood and independent living, so you can avoid being a burden to others. Remind them that you need to be able to cook for yourself because you want to have some choice in this aspect of life and be able to save some money and have good health. Cooking your meals means you can control what you eat and not depend on restaurants (which can be both very expensive and very unhealthy). Remind them also that you will be responsible for the next generation, so you want to learn in order to teach your own children. You only want to employ a cleaner or someone to do the chores as a matter of choice, not because you are incapable. If you cannot clean, so you employ a cleaner, what happens if you run out of money? Are you going to live in dirt? Tell them that you do not want to be like the thirty-year-old man in Bangladesh (see below) when you become an adult. Remind them also that they, as your parents, are unlikely to be around for the rest of your life to provide all your needs and those of your offspring. *Therefore the best way to face up to the challenges of life is by developing the appropriate skills needed for independent living, for disaster awaits if one is in the air, inside the cockpit, alone but with no skill to pilot the aircraft. That's what happens when one grows into adulthood without the skills required to live an independent life.* In my work as an approved mental health professional I have assessed and detained many adults whose mental relapse stemmed primarily from the fact that they couldn't cope with life once they lost the person who was doing their day-to-day chores. This is why it is crucial to equip yourself in childhood and demand to be equipped so you do not feel 'lost' when the true challenges of life confront you. Work hard and remember that the end will justify the means. There's no need to remind you to have fun and play because you will do that anyway as a child. Play is what nature offers everyone and it serves it own 'useful' purpose. The key is moderation, because too much of anything, including drinking too much water, for example, is harmful.

Remember to be thoughtful at all times. Before you make demands of your parents ask yourself, 'do I really need this?' or 'do I want this because Andrew or Stephanie my friend has it?' If the answer is yes, then consider the things you have that Andrew or Stephanie do not have or their individual circumstances and see if they are exactly the same as yours. Have you done everything Andrew or Stephanie have done? Remember that your own name is James, not Andrew or Stephanie, and it is likely your parents' name is different from that of their parents, meaning that there are two different circumstances at play. Therefore never try to be someone else, for everybody has his or her own issues to contend with. *Behind a beautiful door may lay untold pain and sorrow. There is a reason why you are you! All you need to copy is good behaviour and useful acts to enhance your being so as to be the best you can be, but don't desire to be Andrew if your name is James.* If your role model is a musician on drugs or a footballer who uses bad language, for example, focus on their music or football skills or any other good aspects of their life, but don't copy the bad aspects because you are unique, special and born for a purpose. You don't have to take drugs or use bad language in order to sing or play football. In fact taking illicit drugs not only destroys your pocket but also ultimately destroys your life (see below). Michael

Jackson, Amy Winehouse and Whitney Houston started off without drugs and produced beautiful music. Thierry Henry, Lionel Messi and David Beckham are all great football players and did not have to swear in order to play good football. Never give up or give in. Work hard, use your brain not just your sight or fist, *think before you act and ensure at all times that your reaction plays second fiddle and does not take centre stage to the action that pre-empted it.*

Remember, if you do not have the means, you do not have the need unless you have a genuine way to find the means. Learn to be patient, save up before you buy and forget about 'buy now, pay later'. This is part of what has led to our financial nightmare and caused a lot of people who could not afford to 'pay later' to fall into depression. Life is a marathon not a sprint. In other words, life is a process not an event and prizes are never given out or won at the beginning or in the middle but at the end of the marathon. Be wise! Tell your parent, 'Mum or dad, I would like to have this or that but only if you have the money. Please don't borrow or buy now and pay later for my sake. I am happy to wait.' In fact, when you wait you are likely to have a better item, because new things are always coming out and the one you have bought today might not be what you need in six months time. 'Good things happen to those who wait; the patient dog eats the fattest bone'. When and if you get a gift or present from your parents, be thankful, because there are many children out there without anyone to buy them presents; there are others who have parents who cannot even afford to put food on the table, let alone buy presents for their children, and there are also plenty of rich parents whose children cannot enjoy the presents because of ill-health. There are a lot of rich parents who are desperate to have children and be able to offer gifts to them, and also some who have had children who died during pregnancy or soon after birth. Furthermore, you had no control over where you ended up as a baby, so you could easily have been one of those children going without presents. So, count yourself lucky, be grateful and thankful and spare a thought for those who are not so privileged. As human beings, we have brains not fists to use!

If, as a child, you use the only time (which is limited in childhood) designed for you to equip yourself with knowledge, skill and the moral values for a 'better life' in adulthood to seek pleasure, which is unlimited, then in adulthood you are likely to find that you have failed to equip yourself with the right knowledge and that you cannot exercise choice in the unlimited pleasures of this world. This will either lead you to an unfulfilled life or criminal activity as you strive to make ends meet in a desperate attempt to gamble your way out of trouble. Therefore, focus and use the limited time life offers you to prepare yourself for the unlimited pleasures of this world. Don't miss this opportunity, so that you don't miss out on the good life and the best things you crave for. You either have them now (temporary) and lose them later (permanent) or lose them now (temporary) and have them later (permanent). Remember, how you feel today will always be more important and relevant to how you felt yesterday. The choice is yours. If, as a child, you have fun all the time, stop and think, something is not right, because there is a time to play and a time to work.

Consider this: my parents were 'poor teachers' and had eight children. I am the fourth, and there were gaps of two years between each child from the first to the fifth. Therefore I was fourteen years of age and my oldest sibling was twenty when my father died. I could never remember celebrating my birthday, let alone having a birthday present. The only time I remember having a Christmas outfit made for all of us was when we had to work very hard by collecting and selling massive heaps of sand used for building houses. The money was only enough to pay for the outfits; there were no shoes to go with them, let alone shoes to match. But I saw loads of children from the townships with all sorts of new clothes and the latest brands of outfits and toys. However, my father had made me understand that 'all that glitters is not gold.' I have no memory of anyone buying me a new pair of shoes. I remember getting a pair of used trainers from a cousin in the extended family, whom I saw wearing them when we were playing football. You can guess what I was wearing: I was barefooted. I begged him for the trainers (because I thought he was wasting and damaging them, when someone could wear them to church) and said, 'If only I could have that pair of trainers, I would wear them to church, not use them for football.' He was very kind, and surprised me when he said I could have them after the game. I felt on top of the world and wore them to every 'important' event. To the best of my knowledge and belief, I had bought my first new pair of shoes. The only new footwear I had from my parents as a child were sandals for school, and I will not waste your time describing how many times I had to visit the shoe repairer for alterations and repairs. Perhaps this is the reason why I overcompensate now by having a lot of clothes and shoes, or at least this is how psychologists may interpret it. This is why I believe that it is the wisdom, not the material things, gained in childhood that defines one in adulthood.

When you make monetary demands of your parents, consider that they may not have the means to afford them. Try and reason with your parents, and if satisfying the demands would force your parents to borrow money and be in debt, then be creative and see if there are other ways to cope without the particular thing you are craving for; see if you can defer getting it. Ensure your parents are not living above their means simply because they have to meet your demands, be grateful when they satisfy your needs and do not take anything for granted.

Learn to see yourself in others. Pinch yourself; if it is painful then rest assured that any other person pinched would feel the same. Take a look at your parents and siblings; would you like to see something bad happen to them, see someone hurt them or take their life? If someone did that to you, how would you feel? How you feel is likely to be the same for any other person who suffers a similar fate. What you mean to your family is likely to be what another child means to their family, and what your family means to you is what the other child's family means to them. As a child, make time to have proper 'human interactions'. Pause your gadget if you have a visitor, go and greet the visitor, have some interaction with the visitor and begin to see yourself in someone else. Value those that earn the money and provide gadgets more than the money or gadgets they provide. Never place gadgets or money above human life, because life is priceless and gives birth to money and gadgets. Therefore, it is better to destroy the golden egg than destroy the hen that lays it. Ensure you are not interacting only with your gadgets. Never let your reaction take centre stage over the action that pre-empted it, as stated earlier, otherwise 'the fly will cease to be the issue and the harmer used in killing it becomes the issue'. When you are in the wrong, say you are sorry genuinely. Never allow a case to develop when you are at fault. Learn the lessons of the past in order not to repeat the mistakes of the past. For those who fail to learn historic lessons end up repeating history. However, never carry anger over to a new day. Remember at all times that humility is never a sign of weakness.

Always look out for those less privileged than you, and think about what assistance you can give. In every situation you find yourself, consider what you can do which could alleviate someone else's problem. Offer to assist if you know you can when you see someone in difficulty. If anyone, including your parent(s), tells you to hate someone because of how they look, their religion, their gender or their sexual orientation, tell the person that 'hating someone means hating myself'. Those who tell you to hate others for these reasons are sowing a bad seed in you; they are propelled by natural instincts, which make them focus a lot on differences, and though they may be adult in age, their mindset is like that of a child. It is only little children who are likely not to understand that no nation and no individual can survive on their own. But when people are nurtured in the right way they will both see and appreciate the similarities in all human beings, which are a great source of strength, as we need each other in order to survive. If anyone including your parent/s tells you that you should look down on anyone or you are superior to anyone one, be smart enough to remind the person that, you cannot be 'taller and shorter' than someone at the same time. Remind them also that it is the shorter person that made you feel tall, therefore you need to appreciate and respect the person through whom, you placed a value on yourself. People who were brought up with such ridiculous mindset are primarily responsible for the carnage our world is witnessing. Therefore whatever gift, whatever advantage you have over someone else; think positively and use it for service. Never use it to oppress.

If, as a child, you cannot recall any words of wisdom your parents taught you (*See* 'a tribute to an awesome father', page 102), then it is likely you are in need of something. This does not mean that your parents do not love you or do not want to say the right things to you. This could mean that your parents were not taught these things, so they cannot give what they do not have. Therefore encourage your parent(s), because one is never too old to learn. Challenge yourself too; ask questions at school make friends with those who you see are well behaved and doing well at school, begin to put structure into your life and ensure that you have a timetable. Play, but make time for other important things. Remember that anything that's easy, cheap or free may not have many dividends, so pay attention to the things you perceive to be difficult and find ways to make difficult things easy. Then you are en route to successful and productive adulthood. Don't run away from difficult things or give up on them, but be patient and work hard at them. Persevere with anything that you are doing that is hard. There's a reason why it is hard, and that reason must be a good thing, because if it is not hard everyone would be able to do it, and whatever everyone can do has no dividend attached to it and is devalued because no one will pay for a show they can perform themselves! Work hard and begin to make difficult things easy and second nature. However, whatever you do, enjoy your childhood and don't be in a hurry to get to adulthood, because when you get there, trust me, you are likely to feel that 'it could be greener on the other side'. Hear this little story of mine. As a child, I was desperate to become an adult so I could do things the way I wanted to do them and begin to make my own decisions. When I was in primary school, I thought to myself, 'If I get to secondary school, things will get better.' I went to secondary school and did not appreciate what 'things getting better' meant, so I thought it would happen when I went to university. Well, I went to university, and thought things would surely get better when I finished and started working. I started working and suddenly realised I was still waiting for things to get better. I then thought that once I married things would greatly improve. I entered into 'traditional marriage' and began to notice my neighbours a lot more, having been 'blind' before that, then had children and felt the 'real' pressure of life, as I came to terms with my responsibility as a parent. The thoughts and worries of being a parent have never left me and, funnily enough, I am now banking on, 'Oh, when the children reach eighteen or when they become adults and get married, then I can rest and things will surely get better', but a little bird whispered in my ear and said, 'My dear friend, the rest will only come when you are resting in peace'. The truth is, I have come to realise that though it is good to live in hope, my best days were in my childhood when I had no responsibility and was under the protection of my parents. I have now learnt to enjoy the moment and not defer it, as the future is not guaranteed to make things better and is not ours to control or see. So make the most of your childhood and do not rush into adulthood because you have only one chance of being a child, but once an adult always an adult, and there is no turning back.

As children, and even as adults, the biggest problem is that we are never told the 'real' truth about marriage and poly-substance (drug and alcohol) misuse until we are either already married or addicted to something, and then it is often too late and it is not possible to reverse the situation. We are not told that although marriage can be difficult, those who understand it and work hard at it end up making it easy and enjoying the rewards of their hard work later. Those who thought it was meant to be all fun and a 'bed of roses' end up not working hard at it and becoming disappointed, as what they conceived of in their dreams very quickly turns into a 'nightmare' (read more on page 51 about *The Problem with Parenting*).

When it comes to poly-substance misuse, we are never told how controlling and powerful alcohol and illicit drugs are; all we hear of is how 'horrible' they are. They are controlling and powerful because anything that has the potential to take over one's life must be powerful (though sometimes 'wonderful') for the individual involved, because people struggle to give them up, irrespective of the huge financial cost, the damage to one's health and the possible life of crime that come with them.

It is difficult to give up using these substances because from the point of view of the addicted user there is usually nothing to replace the cravings. The user will hang on to their habit in spite of the huge cost (financially and health-wise) and its capacity to force one into all manner of criminal activities, including robbery and homicide, in order to feed it. The user, once addicted, is likely to see drugs and/or alcohol as the most important things in their life, and the more their life is affected by their poly-substance misuse, for example family break up or the loss of their job and health (physical and/or mental), the more they hold onto drugs and alcohol.

There are three types of crime associated with drug/alcohol misuse:

1. Those crimes associated with the effects of drug/alcohol on the user's thought process and behaviour, for example, violence.

2. Those crimes associated with the income needed to fund the user's habit, for example stealing.

3. Those crimes associated with the people involved with both users and dealers, for example violence related to the production and sale of drugs.

These crimes are frequent and sometimes involve fatality, including homicide/suicide, as the substances cloud the user's judgement. However, to the addicted user, the need to satisfy the craving and feed the habit will far outweigh any other need. This is the power and control that illicit drugs and alcohol can have on human beings. Anything that can play such a dominant role in one's life can only be described as a 'can't do without' thing. Therefore, before making anything a 'can't do without' thing, you must (not should) understand all aspects of that thing first and be clear that that's what you want to do before getting into it. Therefore I want to give you the absolute truth about poly-substance misuse.

Just as Cassin (1999) stated in his book, 'People will tell you all sorts of thing about drugs. You will hear frightening exaggerations, half-truths and sometimes even downright lies.' One of these misconceptions is that illicit drug use is 'bad' or 'horrible'. There is some truth in this, but this is not how the individual using the drug sees it: to them it may be the most valuable and important thing in their life, so this becomes a half-truth. Cassin went on to say, 'it is useful to keep in mind that drugs themselves are neither good nor bad, helpful nor harmful. All the dangers or benefits are in the way they are used. Societies as far back as 3,000 BC have used opium. Every civilisation uses drugs to a greater or lesser extent. Some of these drugs are accepted and some are taboo. In our society, alcohol and tobacco are socially and culturally accepted, while the coca leaf that makes cocaine is accepted in South American countries. The central issue is not the presence or absence of drugs but how they are used' (page 3) and of course, when they are used.

As a child, there are three major things to avoid, and avoiding them means you are more likely to succeed in life than those who embrace them. These are:

Playing all the time.
Poly-substance abuse.
Emotional relationship at too young an age.

Enough has been said already about playing all the time, and the summary is that one is likely to achieve less in life if one played all the time, compared to someone who had structure in his or her life. Therefore let's take a look at the other two items listed above. The other two are critical because they both have the capacity to consume an individual's life. Irrespective of how good they are claimed to be or the benefits people claim they get from them, every child must, not just should, avoid them. Nothing has the capacity to ruin a child's prospects in life more than these two. This is not only because of their addictive, destructive and controlling nature but also because of the financial cost to the individual caught up in them. This is a very 'deep pit' every child must know about and avoid because once one enters into it by mistake, getting out of it can be very difficult, and is in most cases an impossible task.

Hear my little story about cigarette smoking

Remember my parents were teachers and strict ones too. As a child, we couldn't even roll paper up into the form of a cigarette without getting flogged or rebuked. However, I had always admired my uncles and adults who I saw smoking. I liked the sort of 'carefree' persona I saw in them as a child: it was really 'cool' from my perspective. I was determined to become a smoker whenever I gained some level of independence. As a child, I usually got fixated on things, may be I still do, and that is why, once I have resolved to do something, I pursue it to completion. I gained my first freedom when I left the seminary to go to a technical college and lived as a boarding student. By that time my father had died. One evening I went out with my mates, some of whom were smokers. I had to present myself as one of them and pretend I was a seasoned smoker. With the little money I had, I bought two 'sticks' of Benson & Hedges and, in my excitement, coupled with the need to show myself as being on the same level or even a more sophisticated smoker than my mates, I lit up and aggressively inhaled. The impact was instant, and I choked and then fainted. My mates became concerned and embarked on a first aid mission they were never trained for. One of them, I gathered, went and brought a bucket of cold water with a towel. As I regained consciousness, I noticed a damp towel resting on my forehead as I lay on the floor. I felt so ashamed and embarrassed recalling what had just happened, but I was even more embarrassed at my failure to show I was 'one of the boys' who ought to be an expert cigarette smoker. My friends began to use my misadventure to ridicule me, and I had many fights because of that. I became afraid of smoking, but my love for smokers and quest to smoke hadn't gone. I was scared, but in my mind I was working out a strategy to take it easy and gradually start to smoke. I wasn't going to give up, for it was a 'childhood dream'. I decided to take my time, as I was also hampered due to lack of resources. I never touched cigarettes again until I came to England in 1989.

When I arrived in England, I met someone who became a very good friend. His name is Ifeanyi Okpara and he became the 'perfect friend' because he wasn't only kind to me, he smoked as well. I very quickly joined in, but was very cautious; as I did not want to suffer the embarrassment I had suffered in college. I took it easy and never allowed the smoke to go anywhere other than in my mouth. I gradually began to gently release the smoke through my nose, but didn't quite enjoy the experience as I felt I was going to choke. Eventually, I persuaded my friend that we should both stop smoking. My primary reason for persuading him was not because I had given up on my desire to become a smoker, but because I was afraid of choking and also smoking was costing me a lot of money. The strong desire to become a smoker was still there, but somehow I didn't feel I was in the right place or that it was the right time to give it a 'real go'. Since then (1990–1992), I once in a while get offered a cigarette, which I smoke rather cautiously but never get hooked. I would always hear how addictive cigarettes, alcohol and illicit drugs can be, but my new challenge was never to get addicted to cigarettes, which, fortunately or unfortunately, were the only things I was interested in. I convinced myself that I had grown beyond addiction because I only smoked when offered a cigarette, but never went into shops to buy them for myself. I often requested a stick from my good friend and colleague (Raul Bustillos) when we both worked for Barking and Dagenham Council. Whenever he was on a cigarette break, I always went outside with him, not just for a cigarette but also to share some philosophical and ideological views on many issues. He would often say to me, 'Eze, you will one day get addicted to cigarettes,' but I would be quick in reminding him that though being a smoker was my ultimate goal, I had now grown beyond addiction. I strongly believed this, as I never bought cigarettes myself! I was convinced I would not get addicted. Even though I wanted to, so I could fulfil that childhood dream, I never felt it would happen for me. I wasn't bothered about all the health concerns or financial implications at that stage; I just wanted to become a 'proper' smoker. In my inner heart I knew this was a silly mission because I saw many people struggling to quit, but I was going to do that in old age. I would always use statements like, 'life is about people coming in and going out' to justify my weird stance. Many of my colleagues and friends who knew how desperate I was in trying to become a smoker thought I was crazy. I thought that, too, but I had insight.

The fact that I wasn't getting addicted led me not to fully appreciate what addiction meant for other people, including clients I worked with. Though I had always remained professional in my job, deep in my heart I used to have limited patience for clients who refused to heed advice to reduce or stop abusing illicit drugs and alcohol due to their adverse impact on prescribed medication, which ultimately caused a relapse in their mental state. Now I feel disappointed when I see young men and women, who have been diagnosed with drug-induced psychosis, brought into hospital under a section of the Mental Health Act and then rapidly get better because of the absence of illicit drugs whilst on admission as detained patients. I feel disappointed when they fail to recognise the overall impact of poly-substance abuse on their lives generally. In a lot of cases, as professionals, we see and know that so many clients could live a decent and normal life if they stopped abusing drugs and/or alcohol. I never fully appreciated the 'demon' in these substances until my episode with cigarette smoking.

When I left Barking and Dagenham Council for Haringey Council and later Waltham Forest Council, the opportunity to smoke became limited as I only had occasional, not regular, offers of a stick or two. This could have been because in these boroughs workers are stingy with their cigarettes or because they had all quit smoking. In 2008, I left Waltham Forest when I set up a limited company and started working via a locum agency as an approved social worker (ASW) and then later as an approved mental health professional. My first posting was in Slough, and I had to travel there on a daily basis from Edmonton, where I lived at the time. The traffic on the A10 and the M25 was daunting and horrendous, and I always arrived at work and returned home tired and stressed out.

One day I was in so much traffic on the M25 that I was late for work and missed an early morning appointment. I was really annoyed and frustrated, but a colleague told me not to worry too much about it. He then said, 'Well, Eze, you are not a smoker. I find that when I am in traffic and I light up, I relax.' 'Oh!' I thought to myself in excitement at hearing this, 'I can now have a real go at being a smoker.' It was music to my ears, and during my break I bought a packet of ten menthol cigarettes; as I was driving back home that day I lit up and found what my colleague said was true, psychologically: I felt very 'relaxed'. From that day onwards, I always associated my smoking with driving, and I gradually began to notice the addictive nature of cigarette smoking, as I went from a packet of ten to a packet of twenty, and from five sticks to ten a day. I got so excited that I had cracked it, but at the same time began to feel really bad, as I was no longer in control of the smoking. I felt real pain in my heart knowing that I was wasting resources that could have been spent on my family, destroying my health and falling from the dizzy height of being the best critic of those who are addicts of anything. I also lived in fear of my children knowing that I had suddenly turned into a smoker, and was wasting petrol driving around aimlessly in order to smoke. But most importantly, I felt terrible that what I considered as my 'strong will' had deserted me. Each time I was about to run out of cigarettes, my mind was set on getting a replacement packet. I challenged myself on a regular basis, trying to impose my will, but each time I said 'This one is my last packet,' it never was. It felt like I was being swept away in a flood of water. Even shopkeepers could see me struggling, as I would go into the shop and moan and moan before buying a packet. Quitting cigarette smoking was on my New Year's resolutions list every year, but I could not feel good when leaving for work if I didn't have a packet to smoke.

The pain of not being able to stop was simply too much to bear. I started to regret pushing myself too hard to start. A lot of my colleagues and friends tried to encourage me, and their advice can be summarised in two different types of comments.

Some would say, 'Stop it; it's not quite like you to smoke, give it up,' and they would tell me how they managed to stop. Others would say, 'Enjoy it; when the time to stop comes you will know and no one will need to tell you, so stop beating yourself up about it.' The latter comment was more consoling and the former was more encouraging and challenging, but I was still in pain! At times I would not smoke for a few days, and a good friend of mine gave me an electric cigarette, which helped, but as soon as I met up with a colleague smoking, I got back onto it and then bought another packet, with the same usual promise that 'This will definitely be my last one.' I managed to conquer my cigarette smoking when I eventually remembered the 'inherent' gift I possess. I remembered that I became a smoker primarily because I was so determined from childhood to become one; then I thought to myself that I was very determined to stop and couldn't see why the same principle would not be applicable. The only hiccup was the fact that doing the wrong thing is usually easy, but getting things right is much more difficult. However, remembering my determined spirit was my breakthrough: I just simply knew I had to work harder. This is why, even in relationships, if both parties go back to 'first principles' when things go wrong, that is, not focussing on what has gone wrong but remembering the reason/s for coming together in the first instance, many relationships would not break down irretrievably. As soon as this came to mind, I parted company with cigarettes by never again buying any when I went into shops, and since 16th June 2012 this has been so and I intend not change that. Never to buy cigarette with my money!

Now, let us consider the true implications of addiction and what it could mean for you as a child.

On average I used to smoke three packets of twenty menthol cigarettes every week, but the smoking was directly linked to driving and the work environment. I never smoked when I was at home and rarely smoked at weekends. No one would have classified me as a heavy smoker because a heavy smoker would smoke at least a packet of twenty daily. Having said that, let us consider how much of my resources went up in smoke and look at the implications.

A packet of twenty menthol cigarettes cost a little under £6, but for argument and modesty's sake let's work with £5 per packet. Therefore, at a minimum cost of £5 per packet, this means that I was spending at least £15 every week on cigarettes. In one year I burnt at least £780, and if I smoked for 30 years I would spend £23,400. Remember, this is just for an 'average' smoker like me. For those who smoke a packet of twenty a day, in a year they would have spent £1,820 and in 30 years, they would have lit up £54,600 in flames. This is frightening considering the damage to one's health and the 'useful' things that could be done with such a large amount of money, if it was saved instead. The money could buy most things one needs in life here and anywhere in the world. It would buy extra tuition for the children and aid other children who are less privileged.

Now, the smoking habit did not really get me into trouble, because when I became addicted to it, I was in a position to fund it. What do you think would have happened if I had become addicted to it when I was a child and had no income to fund it? It is highly likely that I or anyone in my position could have been forced either to steal or do something bad to get the money to feed the habit. One does not need to be a genius to work that out. Here the subject matter is just 'tobacco', which is legal in most countries. The same goes for alcohol, and talking of alcohol, I was lucky my father destroyed my appetite for alcohol from childhood. As a result I never acquired the taste and would never drink alcohol on its own, unless it is sweet, such as Baileys. It is not just about how expensive cigarettes and alcohol are; also relevant are the damage smoking does to one's health and the nuisance, suffering and pain caused to others, especially loved ones, when one becomes dependent on them. In the case of other illicit substances (including alcohol), for example cannabis, heroin and LSD, it is not just about how expensive they are but also about the damaging effects they have on the individuals abusing them and on society at large. The truth is, there are variations in feedback from users, but there are some certainties about these substances and they are:

Most, if not all, psychiatrists interviewed on this issue agree that these substances can cause or worsen a mental health problem.
They are very expensive.
They affect the limbic system and the autonomic nervous system (the parts of the brain that control emotions). According to Sumner (2009) 'emotion involves the entire nervous system, of course. But there are two parts of the nervous system that are especially significant: The limbic system and the autonomic nervous system'.
They interact with prescribed medications, lessening or nullifying their potency.
They can be addictive and one can become dependent on them.
They have the capacity to take over one's life and become the most important thing in a user's life.

In countries where they are illegal, the black market factor comes into play and, according to Cassin (1999) 'to increase income to the supplier, these drugs are frequently increased in volume by adding sugar, laxatives or cheaper drugs. This means that you can never be sure of the strength of the drug, which can result in overdose or poisoning'. This can also result in the relapse of one's mental state.

Speaking to a very good colleague of mine, who subscribes to the universal doctrine of peace and love and who is a drug, mental and spiritual health specialist (Ras Congo), I gained a better insight into why drug abuse is linked to most crimes in society today. RAS CONGO stated, 'an average user of crack cocaine can easily spend £300 per week and an average cannabis user between £30 and £50 per week.' This simply means that in one year an average cocaine user would have spent at least £15,600, whilst a cannabis user would have spent at the very least £1,560. You can calculate for yourself what these figures become in thirty years for a user, and ask: how many people are users and how many can really afford it? Once one becomes addicted to these substances, one becomes dedicated to them and dependent on them. It becomes a health problem as some users begin to struggle with giving up, just like my struggle to give up cigarette smoking. In my work experience, I have met many users who understand the damage that can be caused and live in pain because they have become 'slaves' to these substances. They understand the terrible implications of abusing drugs or alcohol but have lost the will to reverse the trend. As a result the cravings and habit have to be fed on a regular basis. Forget about the benefit or the cost attached to these substances; the truth is that if you get involved in using any of these substances as a child or young adult when you cannot afford it, you are more than likely to live a life of crime and achieve very little or nothing in your life. You are more than likely to bring pain to yourself, your family and wider society, more than all the wild animals put together, because you are a human being with a capacity to plan and execute evil, as indicated earlier. Therefore, if you must experiment with any of these substances, please, please, please wait until you can afford it, in order to limit the potential distress, damage and harm to others, if not to yourself. The reason I say this is that 'the economics of drugs and alcohol may change from time to time but the cost to one's health, dignity, self-esteem, loved ones, family and society at large is always the same, and it is THE COSTLIEST PRICE OF ALL TO PAY' (RAS CONGO). Many who have experimented with drugs have not suffered an immediate, negative outcome. Some have died from one experiment with drugs and some have developed drug-induced psychosis. Most of the street drugs are mixed with many other substances for profit reasons; they are not 'pure' and can have a devastating impact on one's system. How many times have I assessed young 'prospective' people who suddenly become catatonic (mute) or behave in a bizarre way while their parents are in shock as their children become unrecognisable to them? Some would become so confused and psychotic they would mistake their parent for someone else. Parents are even more shocked when they find out that drugs were the primary cause of their children's bizarre behaviour. The most frustrating side of these episodes is the hidden side of the impact, as one single act kick-starts the nightmare of the destabilisation of the family. As parents go on a 'guilt trip', feeling anxious about their other children and their need to persistently keep an eye on the affected child, there is no guaranteed end in sight; there is a loss of friendships, a reduced ability to socialise and many other adverse impacts on family life just because of one incident. Those bringing illicit drugs onto our streets should be made to visit psychiatric units and see the mayhem they are generating. Please, please and please again, don't touch drugs and/or alcohol during your childhood!

Every child needs to know that entering into an emotional relationship at a very young age can hamper a child's progress in life. Emotional relationships are a wonderful life heritage. However, they can be damaging if entered into at the wrong time. Even a platonic relationship can affect a child's dedication to studies or commitment to learning, let alone an emotional relationship. Just like drugs and alcohol, an emotional relationship can overwhelm an adult, let alone a child. It can limit one's concentration in the classroom and dominate a child's focus at home, as the time for learning useful academic, domestic and life-sustaining skills is instead dedicated to emotional union. As a child, it is very useful to have and keep good friends. However, ensure they are platonic and concentrate on working and playing with your friends, leaving emotional relationships (which can be wonderful) to when you are sure of where you are going with life.

In summary, if there is nothing else you remember from this chapter, please remember these: whatever you would not want anyone else to do to you or your loved ones, make sure you do not do it to someone else or their loved ones. Avoid illicit substances including alcohol and tobacco, emotional relationships and playing all the time at all cost, in young age.

Bangladeshi Experience

I will turn now to the contrasting stories of two Bangladeshi men: One was brought up getting everything he wanted from his parents but the other was taught how to become independent and learnt to do things for himself.

The first one was a thirty-year-old man, born and bred in Bangladesh to a fairly rich family, who was sent to private nursery, primary and secondary schools and a private college. His parents pampered him, he had whatever he wanted and he had played a lot with his friends. He left college without good grades and ended up opening up a business, which his parents borrowed money to fund. He ran the business down and accrued a lot of debt, including rent, as he loitered with his friends. His landlord decided to sell the property, which meant that he needed to relocate the business and settle his rents. He ran to his parents, demanding they raise the money for not only settling the rent, but for relocation and expansion of the business. The money he was requesting was equivalent to £5,000.00. His parents were unable to raise the money, and reminded him that they were still struggling to offset the money they borrowed to help him open the business he desired. He demanded that they contact relatives abroad, and though his parents tried to obtain money from them, they did not get any as some relatives were aware of the failings of both the parents and this grown man. The thirty-year-old man became very disappointed and annoyed with his parents and asked them, 'Why did you have me, if you cannot provide for my needs?'

The other man, aged twenty-five years of age, was brought up in London. He was taught discipline and independence from an early age. This young man was able to study as well as work and saved enough money to contribute to his travel and study in Egypt. He is currently an Oxford University undergraduate and has developed an internet web-based teaching business called 'Al-Arabiya', which teaches Arabic as a foreign language to students' abroad. He has recruited four teachers from Egypt to run the course. These two cases contrast starkly: if one fails to prepare, then automatically one prepares to fail. If one prepares, one is likely to succeed and if one fails to prepare, failure will be the likely outcome.

Good Parenting

There is no best way but there is a wrong way to parent a child. These qualities below are what is required for good parenting, irrespective of whether it is a two-parent or a one-parent family. It is better for a child to have one parent who can offer this than have two parents who 'sing from different hymn sheets' on an issue and end up, confusing and ruining the child's life.

Good parents are those parents who work together as a team with the primary aim of bringing up individuals who are well rounded academically, socially, emotionally, morally and physically. In a one-parent situation the working together means being consistent in your words and actions and ensuring that when you say don't to your baby, you mean don't, and when you say do, you mean do. This does not mean you can't change your mind, but when you do you do so with an explanation, so the child is clear as to why you changed your mind. That way your child is likely not to be confused.

Such parent/s provide an adequate structure and set boundaries, which their children really want. They sing from the same hymn sheet, and there is not a situation where one parent gives the child what the other parent had turned down, or says yes where the other parent said no. They teach and inculcate in their children moral values for themselves and for others. Now, when someone values him or herself and transfers that value to someone else they will never harm that other person, or at the very least they will think twice before they do wrong or harm to them. The biblical saying, 'love thy neighbour as yourself' comes to mind, and if one were capable of living by this, harming one's neighbour would not be easy, as it would mean harming yourself. These types of parents not only teach their children how to love, value and respect themselves, but they also ensure their children accord the same to others. Such parents show themselves and their children affection. 'Affection in this world is able to work wonders if we have the divine patience to co-operate with it. Affection tames a pet in the house... It is affection that binds one to submit to another, that binds a brave heart to a coward, a higher being to a lower creature, a noble to a slave, a man to an animal, and even an enemy to a bitter foe. The essence of human life is nothing but affection' (Candland, 1993, page 62). These parents realise that children brought up with affection have 'consideration' as their watchword, and they would rather feel pain before they inflict pain on another person. They would feel the anguish, sorrow and hurt of others who are in pain because their heart is filled with affection, empathy and consideration. These qualities are not within human beings naturally. They do not just get into a child. THEY HAVE TO BE INCULCATED AND EMBEDDED INTO A CHILD. THESE PARENTS REALISE IT AND ENSURE THEY ACTIVATE SUCH FEELINGS IN THEIR CHILDREN. Such parents never teach hatred or allow their children to subscribe to any negative teaching; rather they challenge and correct any wrong utterance from their children, leaving them with the correct call on things. They realise that keeping quiet when a child has expressed a wrong view is reinforcing that wrong view for the child, highlighting what happens when silence cohabits with evil. They keep a close eye on their crops and rid them of weeds and supply them with fertilizer that will aid them to grow to their full potential. They also teach their children to live within their means and not try to be like 'John' if their name is 'Andrew' (i.e. save up before you buy; do not buy before you find the money). These parents are the ones that give us the saints and the unsung heroes/heroines of this world. They teach their children life-sustaining values and independent living skills from an early age. Men have been known to fare badly after separation or divorce, and one of the contributing factors is that bad parents do not often teach boys how to cook, tidy up and serve others. Therefore these boys grow up to become a total burden on their partners, and when their partners can no longer cope and decide to leave, these men are more likely to become depressed and turn to drugs and alcohol as they are not able to maintain independence. Good parents realise this and equip their children for a life after theirs, and their children bring joy and happiness to the people they come into contact with because they are always considerate in their approach. Children brought up by such parents usually consider their parents before they think about committing an offence or think about the law enforcement agencies. This is because they would not want to disappoint their parents. Good parents understand that sowing a bad seed in a child can destroy not only the child but others. Consider Anders Breivik of Norway, who had such a bad seed of hatred against Muslims (without knowing how, when or where he gathered such hatred) that in the end he killed those considered to be his own. Evil is like wind: it can blow in any direction and has no set boundary. Good parents never sow seeds of hatred because they understand that creating and nurturing a monster can put the creator, as well as others, at risk. As stated earlier, the true owner of the gun is not the person that purchased it, rather the person in possession of it. So why keep a gun? Good parent/s treat their children with equality, love and fairness. They never have favourites or show favouritism when it comes to their children. They understand the impact of discrimination on their children. Good parent/s seek to weed out any seed of discrimination from their children and would never have smacking or non-smacking as a rule because they understand that children are not homogeneous but individuals. They never view their children as peers or friends, but understand that as parents they have a responsibility to put boundaries and structure in place, so their children can strive.

Hear this sad and shameful story of mine and see why parent/s must not single out any of their children for ridicule or praise, for example 'you are my best or worst child'.

Growing up, I noticed that my parents had favourites. My mother did not hide her love for and closeness to my oldest two siblings, especially my elder brother who, in Igbo tradition, was an incarnate of her dead grandfather, Nwagwu. As far as my mother was concerned, my older brother could 'get away with murder'. She would keep some wrong things he did from my father, to ensure he was not punished. My father had his favourites and I noticed his love for my middle sister and me. On reflection, I think he loved me most because as a child I came up with a 'few surprises' and he kept wondering what I would turn into. One of the things that rendered my father speechless (a man who would not stand for any challenge or sign of contempt – a strict disciplinarian) was when I was between the ages of nine and ten; I asked him a question that he couldn't answer and he couldn't make out how I came up with the question. At that time, I had become fed up with my father saying, 'If not for all of you (referring to the eight of us), I would have done this, that and the other.' I spent a lot of time feeling sad and sorry that I was responsible for making my parents' lives difficult, but I then suddenly had a thought in my head, wondering whether we came to him via the mailing system or whether someone else gave birth to us and took us to him to bring up. I waited, knowing full well that it wouldn't be long before the same line would emerge again. As I thought, it happened on that fateful day when he summoned all of us to remind us of everything he would have achieved if not for us. Scratching my head, I said in a quiet tone, *mpameh, onwere onye muru anyi, kpota anyi nga ka izua*? This means, 'dear father, did anyone else give birth to us and brought us here for you to bring up?' My father was visibly shocked and also speechless! My father, who was a brilliant communicator, turned to my mother, but neither could provide a response. It was like a knockout punch. He dismissed us and never referred to or used that line again. He saw me do a few more things that baffled him, like lifting people up with my teeth without touching them. I overheard him say to my mother one day, 'CJ, there is something about this your son Ezenwa; I am wondering what he would turn into,' and my mother replied, 'I don't know; isn't he your son?'

My father did not hide his dislike for my older brother and made it clear that he was a 'never-do-well' child. He held him responsible for everything that went wrong in the household. If anything went missing, my father would start looking for him and nothing would persuade him that my older brother was not responsible for the missing item, unless my father or someone else found the item. This position my father adopted was dangerous, as it not only made my brother believe he was bad and act like a bad, useless and ne'er-do-well son who had been written off, but it encouraged me to play a 'fast one' on everyone. I became very crafty and thought to myself that whenever my older brother was not around I would do everything to perfection and ensure nothing went missing, but when he was at home then I would help myself to things and he would be held responsible. And that's what happened. I am still and will forever feel sad and sorry for those acts and have rendered my unreserved apology to my older brother for all the telling offs and floggings he got from my father on my account. Parents must learn and know that children can be very clever and interpret or act on things in so many ways. Therefore, they need to appreciate all the possible implications of their words and actions on their children. Having favourites when the children are not adults is very dangerous and can cause animosity between the children in adulthood. If a parent must have favourites this should only happen when the children are adults and one can do it then based on which child lived up to the 'mission statement' of the family.

When the children are young, praise has to be given to encourage them, for the child praised will then repeat the act that you praised, and this will encourage others to copy the particular good deed that brought the praise. But never single out any of your children as the 'bad' one. Even if you feel that way, don't let the rest know about it. Nothing demoralises the one singled out as bad more than this, and it also encourages others (who are like me, as a child) to exploit the situation.

Good parents recognise this and ensure that it does not happen. They ensure that their children interact with human beings more than they interact with gadgets. They make sure the gadgets their children use are not only age appropriate but advantageous for their learning and development. They also make their children appreciate that all gadgets are on loan and can be withdrawn when they abuse them. These parents organise themselves in such a way that their children feel their presence wherever they go and know their parent's stance on most things. They never throw money at things or see money as the answer to all the issues surrounding their children, even if they are millionaires. These parents understand that making their children happy all the time, in the long term does not mean keeping them happy.

Bad Parenting

Bad parents are those who teach their children how to love themselves alone. They never teach them to share or consider other people. They make their children realise they sing from different hymn sheets as they criticise each other in the presence of their children, and when one disagrees with a child's request the other overrules this and fulfils that request. They are usually in competition for their children's love and their children exploit this. These parents are usually very single-minded, and at times will give their children the best education the world has to offer without inculcating morals and life-sustaining values, in their delusional belief that education is all that their children need. These parents forget that academic achievements and dressing up children as if they were in a parade are different from moral values, which are crucial as otherwise children would become and look like a 'beautiful church full of demons'. Some of such parent/s spend time to tell their children how superior they are compared to others without appreciating that there is nothing called superiority, if there was no inferiority. Hence the need to value, respect and appreciate inferiority, if people are truly not born as equals.

These are parents that have given birth to some of the 'fat cats', who only believe in 'me,
myself and I'; no one else matters as far as they are concerned. Some of their children grew up to become top politicians and bankers, who are only academically prudent but lacking in moral judgement. They were put in positions where they have been and still are making decisions affecting the lives of many. They became fixated on their bonuses and offered loans and mortgages to people they knew could not afford to pay them back, resulting in the financial crisis which everyone is paying a huge price for now. Some of their children are the ones producing highly sexualised, violent and sensational music and gadgets to the children of this world. With that 'me, myself and I' approach, they are careless about the negative impact they are having on children and are more interested in how much money they are making.

These are also the type of parents who are likely to produce children who grow up to depend on others to provide for their needs. They fold their arms in the belief that the world owes them a living because they do everything for their children and spoil them by not allowing them to learn how to fend for themselves. They surround their children with maids and give them everything they ask for in the name of making and keeping them 'happy'. Some of them swear and exhibit their vices in front of their children without care or regard for the impact of their behaviour on their children or how their children might perceive and interpret their behaviour. When one tries to tell some of them not to use foul language in front of the children, they try to justify their position by saying, 'The kids already know these things.' They have no clue that parenting is nothing to do with what the kids think, say, do or learn from others but is to do with correcting any bad behaviour and helping to shape the kids into 'reasonable' and well-adjusted individuals. These parents produce the individuals that cause misery to this world.

At times you see some of these parents in public places trying to correct their children's bad behaviour, as they feel embarrassed. They forget that when a good foundation is laid for children at home, one does not need to go about chasing one's children on the streets, as children will respond positively and behave well in public (in most instances) automatically if good parenting is taking place at home. These are parents who embrace freedom, liberty and choice without responsibility and who turn themselves into 'loose cannons' with no regard as to how their behaviour impacts on their children. They take pleasure in, and get excited by, life outside their homes, misplacing their loyalty and commitment by protecting the needs of their own parents, friends and associates outside, and negating the needs of their immediate family (children and partner) which ought to be paramount. They act and dance to the tune of people outside the home and display to a gallery that has no bearing on the needs of their immediate family and has no trophies to offer. These parents seek and pursue a single person's lifestyle whilst pretending to be in a union with their partners. They forget that a single person's lifestyle might seem easier due to some degree of freedom and less accountability, but it can also be difficult when the challenges of life kick in. When something is worthwhile and valuable and has a huge dividend at the end of it, serious hard work and sacrifice are needed. Such bad parents struggle to understand this phenomenon and prefer immediate satisfaction to delayed gratification. In the name of liberty, choice and freedom, they will disappear for hours, days and weeks from their homes, and their partners and children will never know where they have been. They are usually quick to use emotional and sentimental statements that are not very easy to quantify or qualify to try and justify their actions and, at times, in order to draw sympathy, they will cry. They often have no awareness that they are the ones inflicting emotional abuse on their partner and children, as no one knows what they will do next. Once they set their plans in motion with whosoever is outside the home, they look for ways to create a crisis in their home in order to satisfy the goal outside that 'must' be achieved. They will often point to the fact that their children are no longer babies and so they deserve to be free to make their own choices, or they list the academic achievements of their children as their 'success story'. This is all in pursuit of their quest to be released from their responsibility and to make their child believe that they have 'arrived', when there is still so much to be done to enhance an all-round development of the child. In addition, part of these parents' motive is to fast-track their own 'liberty' and 'freedom' from overseeing the development and training of the child. In most cases this is because of their own shortcomings, as they do not see what else they could offer. As they disappear without a trace, so their children disappear without a trace too. These parents often have no clue where their children are and their children usually have no clue where their parents are. These parents forget that they, as adults, may be able to cover up their tracks, but children can only act as children, and sometimes they will do things that are detrimental to themselves.

They also have no understanding that their children are likely to repeat what they have observed and perceived to be 'normal' in their own union later, causing heartache for their partners and handing the same legacy over to their own offspring. These parents fail to appreciate that they are exposing their children to danger, as they cannot guarantee the character of their children's future partners, who may not tolerate this 'loose cannon' behaviour and can go to any length to deal with it. The basis for law and order in society is the family!

Where children have a 'disappearing' parent, they are likely to, at first, become confused about the particular parent's whereabouts. However, when the pattern continues, children would often see it as 'normal', especially if no one challenges such behaviour. The 'disappearing' parent would have no clue about the fact that, what they are doing is easy and a 'can do', which yields momentary pleasure but causes permanent displeasure. They are likely not to appreciate the impact of their behaviour on their children. By the time they realise that their real dividend would depend on how successful and well behaved their children turn out in the end, it would have been too late. They are also likely not to see anything they had done wrong rather; such parent/s stand ready to blame something or someone else for the way their children turned out. Furthermore, they forget that when a parent has no regard for accountability, their children respond in a similar fashion. No wonder our streets are full of such children doing 'their own thing'. In this modern age, where liberty, choice and freedom without responsibility are the order of the day, if you are the parent who tries to preach family values in order to bring cohesion and orderliness to the family for the benefit of all, particularly the children and are the one trying to promote sound family ethics and values while the other parent remains determined to live a 'street life' by just 'get up and go', you very quickly find yourself looking and sounding like Arsene Wenger (manager of Arsenal Football Club). In football terms who, seeks to bring some level of 'sanity' back into the game and retain the 'values' of football by not breaking the wage structure of his club. He clearly shows that he wants football to win in the game of football, not money. Although he is trying to do what he believes is right for the game and humanity; many people criticise him without a thought on the effects the crazy, outlandish wages and outrageous transfer fees paid to some footballers and their clubs are having on our children. What message are we sending our children, is it that money is everything? Well, money can buy all the best players in this world but one can only put eleven players at a time on the football pitch. The effect of this madness is now being felt as clubs like Rangers and Portsmouth are now facing serious financial crises. The fact that many are against you, does not necessarily mean you are wrong. History will prove Arsene Wenger and any partner condemned for pursuing the right family ethics right in the end. The parent who seeks to do the 'right' thing soon finds out that there are other families where such bad behaviour is similarly rampant, but the way they deal with it is to pretend it is not happening in order to present as a 'normal' family to the outside world.

They do not realise that children are 'copy cats', with no understanding that keeping silent in the face of evil is evil itself, as it encourages evil to multiply. These parents will try to make you feel that you are doing the wrong thing by stressing the need for parents to show a good example. These parents would even try to justify the unjustifiable by pointing at other similar examples of their own simply because they are 'birds of the same feather', therefore they will not see or condemn anything the 'loose cannon' parent is doing. If you are not careful, you will not know that your partner is being recruited as 'a partner in crime', or, as the sayings go, 'there's strength in numbers' and 'birds of a feather flock together'. These parents are quick to advise you not to 'wash your dirty linen in public', and are also quick to minimise every wrong thing your partner is doing. The truth is that dirty linen is best washed at home. However, this can only be done when the dirty linen has not compromised one's health and safety. If it has, then it must be taken out or else you stand the risk of losing your life, and the dirty linen will continue to represent a risk to others that come into contact with it. It must be taken and washed outside so as to get some fresh air into it, and then one might be lucky enough to find others willing to bring a solution to the dirty linen problem, having gone through similar experiences. Those who disclose their illnesses are more likely to be cured of them, and those who hide theirs because of their embarrassment are likely to die from their illnesses.

Even if there is a justifiable reason for leaving your family home for a day or two, your family needs to know where you are and needs to know in advance; in the same way as you need to know or account for where your family members are or are likely to be at any given time. That way, children learn accountability in their relationship with others, and will not dream of leaving the house without saying where they are going or when they are likely to be back. If you are sick and tired of your family, then make plans to leave for whatever place you think will bring you all you desire in life and remain there honourably. Through their actions and inactions these parents give rise to what is going on in our streets today because where parents are not accountable their children are very likely not to be accountable too. These parents, also through their actions and inactions, make the future life of their children 'hell' because, either way, their children suffer the consequences of not being brought up the right way. They either choose a similar partner with whom they produce and bring up children who then reek havoc on humanity, or they choose a partner who views their behaviour as 'out of order' or 'abnormal' leading unfortunately, to perpetual conflict – conflict that could lead to anything, depending on one's temperament, as one partner is at odds with the other partner's stance on life.

Parents who leave their homes without stating their destination are responsible for their children being on the street, as the children copy what they see from an unruly parent. It is virtually impossible for children to leave their family homes unannounced or without stating their destination, if parents set good examples. Parents must and should be, first and foremost, adults before cohabiting, and being an adult means understanding rights and responsibilities. The things we, as parents perceive as liberty, choice and freedom today will cost us dearly tomorrow if we do not engage the reverse gear NOW!

Worst Parenting

With parents who provide the worst parenting, it is usually the case that they are in children mode, as they react to satisfy their immediate needs or desires for pleasure and damn the long-term impacts or consequences of their actions and inactions. They do not know the words 'deferred gratification'. They share their bad habits with their children, for example the consumption of illicit substances and use of bad language. Just like bad parents, these parents go out and come in as they please without accountability or stating where they are going or when they are likely to come back. They abandon their children at any given opportunity and start having other children somewhere else. They usually have the innate belief that nature brings up children and their only responsibility is to perform the act of either impregnating or carrying and bringing the baby into the world. Their actions are usually based on the idea that 'it is a free country' and of course their children follow suit. Where the country is not quite so 'free', such parents pursue money and leave their children in the care of housemaids who themselves require parental guidance. They have no clue that the ability to do anything useful and properly can only be attained through nurturing. Often, these parents derail and in turn their children derail too, as indicated earlier.

These parents actively teach their children how to be bad. They (whether a couple or a single parent) sing from the same hymn sheet in getting their damaging message across to their children. They spend their time teaching their children how to discriminate, giving them messages of hate, teaching them how to dominate and feel superior to others and allowing them to get away with anything. The children replicate what they have learnt from their parents, who could not give what they did not have or failed to learn from other people. They are in an actual sense 'children bringing up children'. They are the sort of parent on the London underground train who, in her ignorant state, swore and racially abused passengers whilst holding her baby, with no knowledge of the impact of her outburst on her child and other children in that carriage. She had no knowledge that she was sowing a dangerous seed and forgetting that if all nations were to send back all foreigners, she might have more people coming into England than are going out. She may also find, to her shock, that she would not be part of the country she claims is her own, if her forefathers happen to have migrated from somewhere else. The lesson for such parents is: before you pollute the mind of your child, ensure you understand what you wish for. If you want everyone from India, for example, to go back to India, you should start with some practical steps by ensuring you do not use any services or products or partake in anything that has been or is sourced from India. When you do this you will understand how no nation, no community and no individual can survive without others. We are simply interdependent: 'no tree ever makes a forest' – that's what you ought to be teaching your child. Who, as a child, has the mindset to ask legitimate questions starting, 'Why this, why that'? If you sow the right seed, you are likely to reap the right fruit and vice versa.

The worst parents are also those who encourage violence and risk taking, just as long as their children make money from it. They turn a blind eye to any wrong thing their children do, and are ready to defend their children in their wrongdoings. They are quick to speak of what they did not do or say to their children, but would never reveal what they failed to say or do.

They minimise the ills of their children, encouraging them to 'get on with it' and guaranteeing support for their children no matter what the issue is. These parents promote the adage that says, 'A child sent by his or her parent to steal uses his or her boots to break down the door.' They are the ones generating children that are causing mayhem on this planet. It is usually from such families that those flooding our streets with illicit drugs emanate from. They are usually the ones to seek out pleasure and self-gratification, leaving their children to grow up on the street, not in their homes where they should be brought up. These parents have no shame and do not feel embarrassed at their children's bad behaviour whether in or outside their homes. Unlike bad parents, the worst parents allow their children to run wild outside and are quick to say, 'It is not your business how I bring up my child,' if one tries to intervene. They have no understanding that tomorrow that child will be someone else's neighbour, partner, son-in-law, daughter-in-law or the one with a knife or gun with an intention to use it against someone. In the end it becomes everyone's business, as the United Kingdom riots of 2011 showed. The worst aspect of such parents is the fact that they are unrelenting in blaming others or providing excuses for any mishaps brought about by their children's behaviour, whilst absolving themselves and their children of any responsibility. They are usually the parents that complain of being 'controlled' by their 'reasonable' partners because no one is sure what they are going to do next, as they create problems in their homes in order to disappear and pursue outside interests. These are the kind of parents who do not see anything wrong in giving an eight-year-old Botox. There is also the example of the fourteen-year-old who took part in the United Kingdom riots (August 2011) and was ordered by the court to bring her parents to the hearing. The fourteen-year-old even had the cheek to say, 'our parents aren't us; we decide what we do; there are times we do what is wrong.' This is an indication of the state of affairs in some of our homes today, when a fourteen-year-old has the boldness to utter such a chilling statement. If one makes the mistake of not verifying the background of children brought up by such parents before marrying or cohabiting with them, the person will experience 'hell on earth', as they are likely to yield what has been sown into them by their parent/s.

CHAPTER FOUR

Personal Encounters

*Story of Ms S Who Cohabited with a Partner Mr P
Brought up by Parents in the Worst Parenting
Category*

Parents who understood and believed in family
etiquette and values brought up Ms S. They instilled
these values into her. Her partner, Mr P was brought
up in an environment where his father went drinking
after work and never believed that having children
involved any hard work or responsibility. His mother
did not bother whether his father came back or not.
She left Mr P and three of his siblings to do as they
pleased. Mr P learnt from his parents how not to
disclose his whereabouts because each time any of
his parents went out of the family home, they only
said 'I am coming'. They would never state where
they are going or when they are likely to come back.
Mr P's parents always argued, used swear words and
fought in the presence of their children. At times, Mr
P's mother would park her belongings and threaten to
leave the family home. This was the life Mr P knew
and he grew up believed it to be normal. Ms S got
involved with him and became pregnant before
meeting Mr P's mother (his father had passed away a
year before they got to know each other). Though Ms
S never met Mr P's father, her mother-in-law and her
partner always told stories about his father. They
would describe him as a powerful man who never
took any nonsense from anyone and of how many
people he had slapped or beaten up. These stories
were adoringly, and Ms S then began to see why her

partner and his siblings were very violent people. She could see why her partner had no communication skills and would rather keep silent or start screaming if anything was not going the way he wanted it. She could also begin to make sense of things when her partner told her that 'fatherhood is merely a natural thing'. She also began to understand that he was only replicating what he had seen as 'normal' behaviour during childhood. But each time she said this, she would get a thorough beating and her partner and mother-in-law would accuse her of insulting someone she had never met. They failed to realise that they had given her this information, and that one does not need to meet someone to know them. Hearing and reading about someone gives one an insight into the individual's character.

Mr P did not believe in any family ethics and values. He would organise outings with single, divorced and men in their second and third marriages. He would have very little in common with married men or men in stable relationships. He would keep all his affairs and connections secret. He would disappear from the family home, sometimes for days, without disclosing where he had been. He would deliberately seek to create problems in the home in order to disappear, with the claim, 'I need to go and clear my head or I need a break.' At times he would claim that Ms S was trying to control him and was **physically, emotionally and psychologically abusing him.** He would also claim that she nagged too much. Her mother-in-law would support and encourage everything Mr P does and says. She does not see anything wrong in her son spending days outside the family home with none of his family members being aware of his whereabouts. Ms S's mother-in-law had told her that if she knew where her partner had been staying she would 'kill' someone, and tried to reassure her that her son would not do anything immoral: and 'he is not that kind of person'. Ms S asked her mother in-law how she came up with the notion that she (Ms S) would 'kill' someone if she got to know the whereabouts of her partner. She also asked her to mention the number of people she (Ms S) had killed in the past to justify such statement, but her mother in-law would not provide any response.

Ms S's mother-in-law would also claim, when talking to other people, that her son's disappearance from his family home is for 'the sake of peace'. However, the contradiction was that her son returned to Ms S without trying to make peace with her, indicating that there was no 'war' going on. Ms S would be left alone with her children, and when her partner returned he would start celebrating his outing by contacting someone on the phone and speaking in a strange language about their outing. He would never say where he had been. Ms S recalls an incident when a nine-year-old schoolmate of her son kept contacting her son at 7am. She would take the call and ask the boy where his parents were and why he was using the phone at such odd times when he ought to be getting ready for school. She tried to bring this to the attention of her partner, who saw nothing wrong with what the boy did. The partner tried to make her realise that the boy was a good boy by pointing him out at a school event and saying to her, 'Does this boy look like a bad boy to you?' to which Ms S replied, 'How do bad boys look?' Realising that he had made a fool of himself by such a statement, he frowned and didn't speak to her. Ms S stated that incidents such as this were usually the reason he gave to have been emotionally abused by her, as he does not like anyone to highlight the real consequences of his utterances even if it threatens the future of the children. He then accused her of damaging his confidence and would use this as justification to seek outside 'pleasures'. Ms S would beg him to stay in because she wanted to keep the family unit together. Ms S stated that she only wished and hoped that her partner would appreciate that all she wanted was for them to share and learn from each other and stop viewing everything said or done as a criticism. Ms S said that her partner and mother-in-law brought 'hell on earth' to her, as she had to try to ensure her children did not copy any of their bad habits. Ms S described her partner and mother-in-law as people who could lie through their teeth in a subtle manner and draw people's sympathy by crying. She stated that they have the ability to give three different versions of an event, to different people and all the versions would seem true, when actually they are lies. She said they would hate with 'passion' anyone who tries to bring the truth to bear on the event.

The Sorrow of A Mother Whose Son Was Stabbed To Death

Ms J lost one of her two sons through a stabbing on the streets of London in 2009. Without narrating every moving statement she made, she agreed I could share them with the world. She wanted to reveal to the world, especially to any child carrying a knife or intending to carry a knife, the far-reaching impact of such evil acts on the primary victim and secondary victims. Ms J broke down and said:

'Since the death of my son, I have lost the will to live. I merely exist, waiting for death to come one day. I have thought about killing myself but couldn't do it

164

because I am a Christian. The scripture says one cannot take life be it someone else's or your own life because no one gives life but God. However, I have had times when I question God but I am always reminded that God allowed His only begotten Son and our Saviour Jesus Christ to die a shameful death for a reason. Therefore I take it that there's a reason why God allowed my son to die the way he did. I have gone through all the possible emotions but I still ask 'why me?' but then again if not me who on earth deserves this type of thing?' Ms J suddenly began to smile and I had to interrupt her by saying, Sorry to interrupt you, Ms J, I noticed you just smiled, what was it about? She replied, 'My dear I just had a thought in my head remembering some of my fellow Christians who continuously say, 'It is not my portion', so each time I ask 'why me?' that is what comes to my mind. I always argue that Christians should not hold such lines as, 'Why me or it is not my portion.' I feel as a Christian that whatsoever is not good for you should not be deserving of someone else. If you say it is not your portion, whose portion is it then? Even your enemy should not deserve it because as a Christian, the one who made us Christians (Jesus Christ) charged us to wish well, pray, love and do good to our enemy and leave vengeance to God.' I thanked her for clarifying that and she then went on, 'Though I know these things, but sometimes as a human being, the whole thing still overwhelms me, especially when I think of the pain my son must have suffered before paramedics arrived. He later died in hospital. The other thing that saddens me is the amount of blame I received from my ex-husband, who said that our son died because I sent him on an errand. As a result we went through a very difficult divorce. Since my son's death our family has been ripped to shreds. I have continuously prayed for forgiveness from God for my ex-husband and me. Sometimes I don't feel like doing anything because I struggle to find pleasure in anything. Sometimes I blame myself, but that was not the only time I sent my son on an errand or his father sent him. If I knew my son would come into harm's way I would keep him in the house forever. That would not even be a choice issue. Though the killer of my son was arrested, prosecuted and convicted, the pain is still heavy.' Ms J made it known that she has forgiven the killer of her son and would prefer repentance for the killer to a prison sentence: 'I would rather have that young man on the street telling others like him or intending to do what he did; that grave consequences are not only for the primary victim but also for the secondary victims. Words alone cannot describe what families in my shoes go through. Not a day passes without me thinking of my son. Sometimes I think of what my son would have been doing now, what he would look like and all the dreams he had for himself. Sometimes I wish my son died of an illness or even an accident, but to think that another human being just did that to my son ... hm. Then I remember the life we used to have as a family, which was torn apart by that singular act of madness. I would never wish my enemy to go through this. It is simply unimaginable and unbearable, but my faith is in the Lord who knows all things and knows why my situation is the way it is right now.'

The Ordeal of a Father Who Physically Removed His Son from Possible Danger

Mr H was at home with his wife and daughter and called for his fourteen-year-old son who had been at home about an hour earlier. His son did not respond and he went upstairs to check his son's room but he was not there. He became worried because he had cautioned his son only a few days earlier about the type of friends he was keeping on the estate. Mr H went out in his car in search of his son. He found him having a chat with some young men wearing hooded tops. He quickly jumped out of his car grabbed and dragged his son by the hand and pushed him back into his car and drove off. Mr H was later surprised when the police turned up at his doorstep and arrested him. He was arrested for assault, having forcibly removed his fourteen-year-old son from associating with those he perceived as young men having a bad influence. He was later released with a caution. This is the sad state of libertarian Great Britain and the reason some parents feel powerless to control their children. The government cannot have it both ways: on one hand blame and fine the parents of unruly children, but on the other hand actively prevent parents from parenting.

The Story of a Woman Whose Son Escaped a Gang Knife Chase

Ms E told of a harrowing story of the day her son had a narrow escape following a chase by a gang of knife-wielding youths operating around the North London area. Ms E said her son recognised one of the three young men chasing him with a knife and so they went and reported the incident to the police. Following a police investigation, the police told Ms E they had identified the young man and that indeed he was notorious and dangerous. They were willing to arrest him but could not guarantee Ms E's safety and that of her son due to the imminent release of the suspect by the granting of bail. Ms E and her son therefore dropped the case. This is currently the state of Great Britain where the wrongdoers have the upper hand and are being shielded by specious claims of human rights.

Interview With a Probation Officer

An interview with a probation officer highlighted the fact that most offenders come from dysfunctional homes. The officer said, 'Amongst the young male offenders, there is a recurring theme, which is the lack of good male role models in their lives.' She went on, 'Many of them who ended up joining the gangs have said (and this is individually, I do not run group therapy) that they joined because it offered them the love, protection, identity and camaraderie they lacked in their homes. They clearly do not see their homes as stimulating or engaging. One of them described his home as only a place to sleep and eat; the rest of his activities are performed outside with no adult supervision and guidance. This is what gives room to the serious crisis produced by peer pressure without moderation. Peer pressure is what causes most of these young adults to act with bravado to satisfy their peers. She noted very importantly that 'the society needs to wake up and understand how some youths of today view the world. She said that 'some youths cannot relate to a world where young people are not meant to carry weapons, take drugs or join gangs for protection. They see violence, drug taking and street life as the norm'.

The probation officer offered some useful advice and solutions to the crisis confronting mainly black families living in London. She said, 'Being a single black female in my late twenties and having been to school, live and now working in London, I can say that the problem facing black people is multi-faceted. My family migrated from Africa when I was just eleven and my younger brother was seven. I can relate to most of the things you are saying because it sounds as though you lived within my household. When we were in Africa, we had a good life. My father is an engineer and was the main provider. My mother was a nurse but my father took care of almost everything financially. I later gathered from my mother that all her salary went into my father's bank account. However, the house we lived in and the two cars were my father's. Anyway, without going into too much detail, things changed when we came to live in England. It was like a reversal of roles, as my mother became the main provider whilst my father struggled to find a job. In the end, as my father could not gain employment within his chosen career (engineering) in this country, due to various complexities I couldn't fully explain to you now (some are his own making and some are structural and systemic problems), he became frustrated and ended up doing all the menial jobs. As children we could notice the change, and it was clear that my mother was the one calling the shots. You see, what people do not realise is the dilemma and interchange at play. When we were in Africa, my father provided everything financially. My mother earned very little but did not have to do an extra job to pay the mortgage, service her car and at the same time look after us. Therefore she was able to play her role as a wife and she always made sure that my father's food was ready before he came back. Here in England, due to all forms and manner of pressures, all this changed. I don't think my mother and father really understood the dilemma. My father could not understand why he no longer had his food ready before his arrival from wherever he had been.

My mother could not appreciate why this man she used to adore had turned into a 'useless' man, as she sadly called him occasionally when they argued. As a child, it was unbearable because the fear and respect we used to have for my father went out of the window. He got so frustrated that four years later they separated. My younger brother was eleven years of age when my father left. It did not quite get up to two years before my brother became very unruly. My mother could not control him. My mother did everything to get my father to help, but to be quite honest, my mother failed to realise that she had already rendered my father (excuse my 'French') 'impotent' before us. The only saving grace that turned my brother around was my uncle, who came and helped shape my brother up.

So for me, the way I see the problem confronting us as black people is, first of all, I think our black men have forgotten what being a man means. Don't get me wrong; I understand that there are structural problems when it comes to employment in this country. I don't know what the figure is, but black men struggle to gain employment in this country. However, some of the problems they create themselves. Though they are disadvantaged in securing employment, they can learn to be creative and also play an active part in the day-to-day running of the home. They need to realise that here women work so very hard, therefore cannot be expected to do all the domestic tasks by themselves. If women can interchange and do those things they never did in Africa, then men should do the same and do those things they never used to do in Africa.

As a child, the worst thing, I would say, that happened was the loss of respect to my father, which my mother was responsible for. I don't know what my brother would have turned into if not for my uncle. No matter how loving a mother is to her son, I believe every male child needs his father. Though some women have made a good job of bringing up male children on their own, I believe it is rare and usually it depends on many other factors in terms of association and extended family impact on those male children, just like in my brother's case. Though my mother now claims to have 'single-handedly' brought him up, I know she's not telling the whole truth because then she was petrified by my brother's unruliness. I agree with you that a lot of black boys are on the street because of this particular problem. My honest advice to all mothers out there is never to demean your husbands in the presence of your children.

You see, as I am, I am happy with my job and I can say I am very comfortable in my single life now. But I must be honest in saying that there are days I get worried because I have many single, black, female working-class friends in their late twenties and thirties, desperate to find suitable and eligible black men to marry, but [they] can't find [them]. I won't lie; I am also one of them. It seems to me that many of our black men who are reasonable and suitable are either taken or married. The number of black young men I see in prison and those I work with scares me. Having heard from you in terms of the number of black men you work with who are in mental health institutions, it seems like all our young men are ending up either in prisons, mental health institutions or in the grave. Now, because our young girls who live in this country are used to the way of life here, it is difficult to marry [men] from Africa because men there, have different orientation and you don't know who is pretending they love you simply because [they] want to come and settle in England. You have really made me see that we are in real trouble the way things are going,'

The probation officer agreed that this crisis has the capacity to force these single women to end up with just having a man to 'father their child', as their biological clock for bearing children does not tick forever. That means that the vicious cycle continues. We need to smell the coffee now because when children (especially boys) born under such circumstances become unruly, the effects will not only be felt by their mothers but by our entire society!

The Story of a Man Excluded from School

Mr A, who is twenty-four years of age, told how his father left the family home when he was nine years old. He said, 'Mum and dad always argued and fought. As a child I was very scared that dad would kill mum. I was so glad when dad left. Thinking about it now, I was not only happy because the arguments and fights had ended, but I was glad because dad was always the one asking me to do my homework, tidy my room and read. He would sometimes take my toys and lock them away if I hadn't done what he said. I felt a sense of freedom when he left because mum was fun. Mum cooked or bought takeaway and tidied my things for me. She took me to McDonalds and bought me games. She was always busy with house chores so I got on with my games. As a child I had a 'great time'. My mum was always tired when she came home from work, so most of the time she came home with takeaway or gave me money to buy takeaway. My mum bought me whatever I wanted. At school I was bored and hated to study. I got into a lot of trouble at school and wanted to stop going. When I got into secondary school I couldn't cope with schooling and studying. I began to miss school by hanging out with other boys. I was very disobedient and got into so many fights. I would come home and lie to my mum. The school would write to mum and I would tell her lies. She believed everything I told her and would go to school to defend me; but in the end I was expelled. My mum was very angry that I was expelled, but I was glad because it gave me time to hang out with friends and play games. At age fourteen, I was dreaming of becoming a football star or a musician, but another friend of mine introduced me to drugs. We began to steal a few little things in order to get cannabis. Though we were just users of drugs, our dream was to find the opportunity to become dealers. As the opportunity to become dealers was not forthcoming, we started breaking into people's cars and houses to steal in order to feed the habit. At age eighteen, I had my first spell in prison following a conviction for burglary and theft. In prison I made friends and got a lot of information about crime and gangs. When I came out I found life outside a bit hard because in prison I was king. Everything was free; the food, accommodation, with no bills to pay. The only punishment was that I couldn't come and go as I pleased. All through my life I have never learnt to cook or do things for myself. Mum always did them. I came out of prison after a brief spell and started stealing again because I have nothing to fall back on and I needed to feed my cannabis cravings. I also joined a gang with two of my friends. One of them got stabbed and died and we planned a revenge attack, but few weeks from his death I lost my mother to cancer. Since then I have suffered from depression, but doctors say I suffer from paranoid schizophrenia. I disagree with the diagnosis. I know that taking drugs worsens my illness, but the drugs relax me. I do not see how I would cope without drugs. I know I do some things that are not right in order to feed the habit but I cannot see any way out.'

Damaged from the Womb-kids

An interview with a neonatal nurse revealed the presentation of babies whose mothers were abusing drugs during their pregnancy. The significant thing is that such babies are different compared to those whose mothers did not abuse substances. The biggest point noted was the babies' inability to respond to 'human touch and comfort'; for example, they have a persistent high-pitched cry and 'no amount of comforting would stop them from crying'. The babies are usually very irritable and display abnormal gesturing compared to 'normal' babies. They suffer from the same withdrawal symptoms as adults and are treated with morphine, whilst their mothers are treated with methadone.

According to *Mail Online* (14.3.12), 'the number of babies born to drug addicted mothers has almost doubled in the last five years, it has been revealed. Last year there were 1,970 women who were addicted to drugs at the time of the birth, compared to 1,057 back in 2003. Of those 1,970 women with a drug dependency, 1,211 babies were born with their mother's addiction as the habit was passed on whilst the baby was still in the womb. It means that every day five drug addict mums give birth to a baby and of those births three babies will suffer the withdrawal symptoms of their mother's addiction. The symptoms associated with babies who are addicted to drugs are a loud, high-pitched crying, sweating and stomach upsets. These babies often need specialised care in hospital before they are allowed home and on occasions are taken from their mothers and placed in care. Last year there were 82 pregnant women addicted to alcohol, a rise from 62 the previous year, and only 22 back in 2003. Pregnant women dependent on heroin or other opioids was up to a staggering 1,059; almost double that of the 535 in 2003. Thirty-two women gave birth whilst hooked on cocaine, 641 were addicted to tobacco and 100 pregnant women gave birth whilst dependent on cannabis.'

Without condemning these babies, one has to ask what chances these babies have in life. It is true that with the right kind of care and support some of these babies may not suffer long-term effects, but the reality is that many will go on to become drug addicts themselves, with dire consequences. Some will not be capable of weighing things up but will grow up to pose a severe risk to both themselves and others. *The brilliant statements made by some 'clever' people in society, such as, 'we need to sit and listen to these children and understand why they are so angry' will not fit in with these children.* These figures will continue to grow unless there is a proper awareness, strong parental control and a collective approach by all of us to fight this menace. If we fail, the consequences will be terrible for our children and future generations. The civil libertarians need to examine their approach to life. Access to drugs is easy, but many a time there is no exit, with huge consequences to one's pocket, health and other people's health and safety. Simply say NO to drugs! It simply is not worth it and it is not cool![4]

---

[4] Read more: Mail Online (2012)
http://www.dailymail.co.uk/health/article-564097/Babies-born-drug-addict-mothers-DOUBLED-years.html#ixzz1p7FWFjo3

My Painful Heart Bleeds

Not being a saint and not coming close to being one, I wish to share this, my heart-breaking story, with the people of the world.

One fateful morning in February 2011, I was driving from Edmonton to Enfield. As I drove along the Hertford Road I noticed a squirrel crossing the road. The squirrel had safely navigated the side of the road I was driving on, but as it tried to navigate to the other side of the road, it was accidentally hit on the legs by an oncoming police vehicle. My heart sank as I saw in my driving mirror the squirrel limping in pain, but still alive. I became confused, and wondered whether I should turn round and stop the pain by ending it for the poor squirrel or whether I should leave it to die in pain. I thought to myself that I would look stupid if I called an ambulance because of this squirrel. In my confused state of mind I continued to drive, as I could not bring myself to feel the guilt of aiding a squirrel in pain to die. Having said that, I still live in pain today because each time I remember the event I question myself, wondering if I prolonged the suffering of that squirrel. I hope someone will advise me on the right thing to do should I find myself (though I am hoping and praying not to) in a similar situation in the future, or reassure me that I am doing the right thing.

Now, contrast that with what happened in the early hours of the morning on Tuesday, 2nd August 2011 in Nigeria, when a bus travelling from Lagos to Abuja was hijacked and robbed by armed robbers. The passengers were forced to disembark and made to lie in the middle of the road; 'all 14 of the passengers, including a child, were killed' (*Metro*, 5.8.11) by an oncoming bus. A survivor of that horrific carnage whose legs were broken when the bus ran over his legs 'told the police that his wife and son were among the dead' (*Metro*, 5.8.11). Those armed robbers were once harmless babies. News like this can easily be swept under the carpet as 'no big deal' because there are so many crises and so much madness in the world today. It is unbelievable that innocent passengers still paid the ultimate price (death) after being robbed. One would have thought that the normal human reaction or tendency would be to chase away an animal about to be run over by a vehicle, or to scream to alert the driver to the fact that they were about to harm the animal. Yet to think, let alone know, that human beings can deliberately force other human beings (even if those people did something wrong) to lie on the road, knowing full well that they would be run over by a vehicle is beyond comprehension. These victims were relatives of living people, who have received a death sentence because for the rest of their lives they will never be able to forget that dark day. Consider the injured man who lost his wife and son. What else is left for him in this world? Oh God! Have mercy! How can a human being generate so much pain for another human being? How can a human being not have empathy for another human being? What joy, what excitement can the perpetrators of this heinous crime be having, and how were these creatures nurtured from innocent babies into deadly monsters? No matter how hard I try, I cannot comprehend this evil. My heart bleeds profusely!

On Wednesday 7th September 2011, a young man who 'was about to start a three-year architecture course was attacked as he walked to a suburban railway station' (*Metro*, 7.9.11). That young man was a former altar boy and described by his father as 'the perfect son; we will miss everything about him'. The young man was 'on his way home from helping his grandmother with weekly food shopping' (*Sun*, 8.9.11). His grandmother was in her 70s. Such a wonderful young man, such an angel and a star, but what was his crime that he had to pay with his life for? His crime was that he told a teenage gang to stop throwing conkers at him. This was his only crime, which led one of the gang members to produce a knife and stab him through the heart. A fifteen-year-old was arrested for the crime. A fifteen-year-old who could have been helping his own grandmother with some shopping. A fifteen-year-old who should still be under parental control, but was on the street with his gang members enjoying their career of inflicting pain on others, while their parents were nowhere to be found and society have become immune to all this madness. The civil libertarians are confusing children by making acting morally a 'situational' thing. They confuse children by saying 'one man's right is one man's wrong' and encourage people to adopt any lifestyle they chose, in the name of freedom, liberty and choice, without responsibility. Many children who are poorly brought up have capitalised on these by using all sorts of flimsy reasons such as 'I stabbed him because he did not show me respect' or 'my father abused me and my mother did not show me love'. The next minute psychological therapy would be prescribed for the perpetrator at huge cost to the taxpayers.

Think for a moment about the pain this young man went through while dying and of a lifetime's psychological impact on the young man's parents, three siblings and his poor grandmother, who was looking forward to having him come and help her with the shopping. The entire family are now condemned to everlasting pain and sorrow by thinking about what might have been and continually soul-searching to try to understand what they could have done to prevent this terrible tragedy. On top of all that, they are likely to be confused as to why this happened to them because of one unruly child.

On 29th July 2008, a medical doctor on her honeymoon in Antigua was murdered and her husband critically injured after their fellow 'human beings' shot them. Without insinuating that anyone's life is less valuable than this woman's, it is so sad that such a young bride who went through the rigours of academia to become a doctor (a qualification that is an asset, with the potential to help save the lives of even those that murdered her, had her life not wasted in such a dreadful fashion. She lost her life not through an illness, accident or natural disaster but by deliberate actions of fellow human beings who were once vulnerable babies.

On 13th June 2010, a neighbour stabbed a woman in her eighth month of pregnancy to death in Israel over a spilt coffee in her doorway.

On 7th February 2011, a woman who was eight months pregnant was stabbed to death and her house set on fire in Newport, England by a fellow 'human being'. On New Year's Day 2012 a girl escaped her 'crazed stepfather as he shot dead three members of her family' (*Daily Mirror*, 3.1.12) before turning the gun on himself. The eighteen-year-old lost her mother, her mother's sister and her twenty-year-old niece. She escaped with 'shotgun pellet wounds to her wrist and shoulder' (*Daily Mirror*, 3.1.12). The following day, a mother of a one-month-old baby was 'killed in knife kidnap horror' according to the same newspaper. The young woman's brother and sister were both injured in the attack, leaving the one-month-old baby motherless. On 12th January a couple described by their daughter as 'the sweetest and kindest people' were 'beaten to death with "horrific" force by a frenzied killer at their home in Handsworth Wood, Birmingham. The ferocity of the attack stunned even the hardened officers' (*The Sun, 13.1.12*). The heartbroken daughter of the victims went on to say, 'Yesterday the light was switched out in our lives.' These are the acts of human beings on other human beings. These may seem like statistics but these are real human beings torn to shreds, heart broken beyond measure and haunted by these acts for the rest of their lives. Many of these acts could have been stopped if we had paid more attention to the perpetrators of these heinous acts when they were children.

The perpetrators of these evil crimes were, at one time, harmless babies! Babies are born neither evil nor good. However, the truth is that nature offers every baby, every child the ability to destroy without coaching. Whilst the ability to build, has to be acquired through persistent observation, learning and teaching. In view of this, one can conclude that, human beings are born to do bad naturally; hence nurture is required in order to get your two year old to say good morning or go and brush their teeth when they wake up.

It is sad that people are quick to conclude that such horrible incidents are borne out of mental disorder, but the fact is that genuine mental health clients carry more threats against themselves than towards others. Where mental health clients have gone on to commit homicide, it is usually the case that illicit drugs and/or alcohol use also played a significant part. Those committing these heinous crimes are very likely to be abusing drugs and/or alcohol and their upbringing and background are suspect and critical.

If, as a society, we cannot allow anyone to breed a wild animal and unleash it on the community, then it is outrageous to allow anyone to breed an unruly child and unleash it on society. As a human being, a child or adult has more potential (as events such as 9/11 in America, 7/7 in United Kingdom and, most recently, July 2011 in Norway and the August 2011 UK riots indicate) to bring mayhem to mankind than all wild animals put together. This is because no matter how wild an animal is, its ability to plan is limited and it has no weapon to deploy or use. Also, we can see dangerous animals, recognise them as such and avoid them. In contrast to animals, human beings' ability to plan is unlimited; we can deploy and use weapons and the degree of our dangerousness is not written on our faces, according to Shakespeare in Macbeth Act Scene 'there is no art to read the mind construction in the face' (though recalling my story) earlier of a father who, pointing at a nine-year-old boy who was making calls to his nine-year-old son at 7am, asked his wife who believed that the boy may not be under proper parental control 'Does this boy look like a bad boy to you?' Of course, we know that there are no designated looks or marks to indicate good or bad people. That's why human beings are more in danger from their fellow human beings than anything else, as the assumption is that everyone is rational, considerate and thoughtful. That is why I say that the bushes may be safer than the streets, so long as human beings are not inhabiting the bushes, as animals can only attack when threatened or in need of food, whereas humans can attack their fellow human beings for 'the fun of it' or for some other weird reason. We all know that in the same way positive thinkers remain creative in thinking out new positive things, for example in the field of technology; in the same way, negative thinkers generate negative thoughts and ideas, develop them and are able to execute them if they are not stopped or caught. Any negative ideas they conceive that gives them the ability to harm others, make profit or excite their fancy they are not likely to be given up easily, no matter how damaging it is to the individuals affected or society at large. What is scarier is the fact that for a child to become unruly and negative no training is required. An unruly child is likely to breed a generation of unruly children because they cannot give what they do not have. It is important that a baby should not be seen as a toy or part of one's accessories. A baby must be handled with the utmost care in view of its potential.

The only thing that could save mankind is our thought process (cognition). Think right and you are likely to do good; think in the wrong way and produce evil; think nothing at all and you are more likely to produce evil because you become like waves, tossed about by any wind that comes your way. And of course to do the wrong thing does not require training, it is usually easy. These are not just hard times but dangerous times! Therefore check your activities. What the world witnessed happening across the United Kingdom in August 2011 was nothing other than 'a state of anarchy' generated by the failings of society as a whole. We might be able to calculate the cost of the physical damages done, but what is incalculable is the psychological damage on people, especially children, whose reactions vary from child to child. No child brought up with discipline, love, respect and consideration for others, no matter how socially deprived or disenfranchised he/she had become would have taken part in setting houses and cars ablaze, running people over with cars, throwing objects at police officers and fire fighters and looting. It borders on psychosis to expect those growing up and being brought up on the streets not to feel in control and take over the streets when the need arises. The breakdown of families, the loss of values and morals, the culture of wants overriding needs, civil libertarianism gone mad, rights galore without responsibility, the substitution of human interaction with gadgets, consumerism and the need to have the latest have come home to haunt everyone. Are we expecting a mango tree to produce an orange? Aren't our chickens coming home to roost? Who is going to pay for all this? What is the punishment? A slap on the wrist? Or are we going to build more luxurious prisons and employ more prison officers, with perpetrators virtually giving the V-sign to the judicial system they are so conversant with? Can we see what we, as a society, have brought upon ourselves? Never make the mistake of thinking that this is a repeat of history, because riots in the past have always been political: people revolting against injustice and their fight to make right what they perceive as wrong. This is carnage of a higher magnitude, different in all its ramifications and very complex in nature. It needs to be fully understood and addressed appropriately. The question is, are we ready to learn and understand it; are we ready and able to begin the process today of laying a new foundation for a better tomorrow for all, because delay may be too late?

CHAPTER FIVE

Governance

As an opposition leader, David Cameron may have touched some nerves when he spoke about 'broken Britain', but he failed to say that it is not just 'broken Britain', there is a broken world, too. Because what he talked about is not only happening in Britain, in fact, many would argue and rightly so that, Britain is 'less broken' compared to many other countries. I wonder what David Cameron would say now he is prime minister? Perhaps Britain is not as 'broken' as he thought whilst he was in opposition. Having said that, take a look at the man-made crisis around the world: economic meltdown, violence, killings, wars, uprisings, riots (to mention but a few) that result in untold suffering for the children of this world. In effect our children are also being conditioned to see these things as 'normal'. Collectively, everyone has played a part, especially those in government. Each of us has made a contribution, either by action or inaction, to this malaise confronting our world. The question is, can each of us, especially those in government around the world, find it in us to work towards bringing some level of sanity into this world, so that the future of our children is not further compromised.

It is an embarrassment to know that there is enough wealth and resources in the world for everyone to live a peaceful and decent life, yet research carried out by 'Wealth 4 Everyone' showed that '80% of the world's population live on less than $10 per day'. Within this, the poorest 40% of the world's population accounts for 5% of global income, and the richest 20%

accounts for 75% of world income. THIS IS SHOCKING!! According to UNICEF, 22,000 children die every day due to poverty. These are children of the world, and by implication these children belong to all of us, as no child elects the family or nation they are born into. The pain felt by a parent who loses a child in 'Bongololo' is the same as that of any parent who loses their child anywhere else in this world. It is fair to say that the few individuals and nations who are greedy and selfish are responsible for this state of affairs on our planet, earth! We ask these few individuals and nations what glory, dream, desire, goal or future are you pursuing that cloud your judgement and cause you to take action, not take action or make decisions that adversely affect the growth and development of our children (the children of this world)? The greatest tragedy is that as human beings we are equipped with the cognition to think and do things better that would make our world a better place for everyone to live in. The only problem is that the status quo is not easy to reverse, and making things better consumes a lot of time, effort, resources and sacrifice. However, the cost of retaining the status quo is huge, and we all stand at risk of bringing disaster onto ourselves if we fail to act. THINK! In this time of economic hardship, millions of families have seen their living standards drop, with many losing their jobs and a lot in fear of losing them. The high cost of living is met with a drop in wages for so many people. Some parents who have lost their jobs, or whose businesses have collapsed are unable to provide for the basic needs of their children, and in some cases some of these parents have now become users of the mental health services due to depression. How else are they going to justify their inability to provide for their families? Some are so depressed they do not see any way out, and as a result feel the only way out is suicide. Amidst all these crises, the chaos and the frustration, the so-called 'fat cats' of this world are rewarding themselves: 'Directors of the UK's largest companies awarded themselves pay rises of 49% in the last financial year', according to research from Income Data Services. 'This includes bonus payments, which have risen by 23% from £737,624 in 2010 to £906,044 in 2011' [5](Moneywise, 28.10.11). While many are being squeezed and crushed, the few greedy ones, who are mainly the ones who have caused this crisis, are still benefiting from the crisis and do not seem to have been punished for their actions. These are human beings who can only see themselves and no one else. They believe that all that matters is 'me, myself and I'. They seek to justify their poor judgement by letting the rest of us know how hard working and intellectually capable they are.

Perhaps the sermon of Rev. Stuart Owen of All Saints, Edmonton can help us all reflect. He said, 'I wonder what you'd list as your achievements in life? What can you look at with pride and say, "I did that"? Perhaps you're proud of your educational achievements, of owning your own home, of the level you've reached in your professional life, proud of the money you have made, the family you've raised.' He went on to say, 'It is true, some people have worked tremendously hard to achieve financial success,' and then he sharply reminded us 'But it is also true that all over the globe there are millions of other people working every bit as hard, if not harder, just to have a few square feet of shelter to live in and a handful of food at the end of the day.' Reverend Owen then

---

[5] http://www.moneywise.co.uk/news/2011-10-28/fat-cats-award-themselves-49%-pay-rises Accessed 3/2/2012.

drove his point home by saying, 'I wonder how you'd feel if I suggested that the largest part of your achievements in life are not in fact down to you, but down to luck, to good fortune? Most of what people achieve is really down to the opportunities they are given through birth and upbringing, down to the country and family they happen to be born into.' He then posed these questions: 'your education: would you have achieved so much if you'd been born into an ordinary family in Mali, where almost 75% of people are illiterate? Would you have become the owner of your own home if you'd been born in North Korea, where officially housing is the property of the state?' Rev. Owen recognises the fact that although this particular sermon may not have been his 'best' sermon and may therefore not be the most deserving sermon to be mentioned in this book, he agrees and appreciates that the mention of his sermon in this book is also down to sheer luck. Many priests may have preached better sermons in the absence of a writer! He said, 'the better way to think about this is to think that what we have we do not possess, but rather they are gifts which have been entrusted to us.' (The sermon was delivered on 13th November 2011.)

Have you also considered that our 'good fortune' extends to good health and life; and these are the two major components behind all of our achievements; but guess what? None of us is in control of any of these. There are many who can write better books, but are on their hospital beds unable to stand or make use of their hands. As everyone knows the very bests of humanity are wasting in the graveyards and crematoriums, awaiting our imminent arrival whether we like it or not. Therefore we must (whilst we are enjoying good health and life) use our gifts for service: service for the less privileged, particularly children, but humanity in general. Any other thing is a waste of time, as we will soon realise in old age if life permits it. Take a look at the 'wonderful' film, *(The Iron Lady)* and see what you make of it!

The so-called fat cats even use a constant threat, by reminding everyone of how competitive their area of work is and how they will move to other parts of the world if they are not adequately rewarded for their 'hard work'. The question is; would they be having such huge bonuses without the efforts of those on the shop floor who are living on the breadline? These individuals, who were all once harmless, vulnerable and needy babies, are now willing to pick up huge bonuses on top of their hefty salaries whilst others in the same establishment are losing their jobs and struggling to put food on the table for their children.

No wonder the anti-capitalist campaigners who are seeking answers from the church, whose silence on this matter is deafening, are using the slogan, 'What would Jesus do?' As they faced the threat of eviction from St Paul's Cathedral, they continued to ask this question. As one of them told me, 'we seek to understand what the church really stands for, because we have nowhere else to turn to. Our governments are in bed with the devil, so their hands are soiled; they stand by and watch all these injustices and outrageously disproportionate distribution of wealth, with the rich getting richer and the poor dying in poverty. The expenses crisis showed that there is very little difference (if any) between these fat cats and some Members of Parliament. The deafening silence of the church in these matters is of great concern to many people, who believe that the church may have lost their true essence of 'serving the needs of the poor and

bringing salvation to mankind'. So, what do we do as individuals and as a government to reverse this awful trend?'
In life, there are things we can do; and things that are right things to do!

Retaining the status quo is easy, but it is far less beneficial, brings low dividends and is more costly to mankind, overall, than doing the right thing. Business as usual is easy, and it is a 'can do', but it leads to crises and difficulties that are unimaginable and sometimes unexpected. Doing what is right (challenging and/or changing the status quo) is difficult, but the right thing to do. Devising the strategy to make the world a safer and just place for all is the biggest challenge facing human beings. It is the right but most difficult thing to do. It would be time consuming, mentally draining and costly, but once achieved, there would be no better benefit known to mankind. It would be just like the experience of good parents, who go through the difficult parts of parenting early on, educating their children in high morals and values, self-respect, respect for others, discipline, taking responsibility as an integral part of their rights/choice and preparing them for independent living. These parents usually reap the benefits and secure high dividends in return for their efforts and hard work, whereas those parents who took the easy way out and offered nothing, or only the wrong things, to their children suffer the consequences later. So it is either pay now and enjoy later, or enjoy now and pay later. Either way one MUST pay.

Well, as the saying goes, 'if the shoe fits, wear it'. There is no governance without the people, just as there is no church without a congregation. In truth, you need the people; the people do not necessarily need you, whether you are leading a government or a religious establishment!

The primary aims of every government should and must be, at all times, to protect the interests of the governed (life and property), to give service to the people and to provide an enabling environment in which citizens can fulfil their potential. It is unjust and unsustainable for any government to negate the interest of the nation and people they are meant to serve; at the same time, it is dreadful for any government to pursue their own national interest by any means possible at the expense of or detriment to other people's national interest. It is unethical and morally reprehensible for any government to devise or pursue a policy (be it by commission or omission) that adversely affects a child anywhere in our world, because that child could so easily be your child. Remember, babies do not choose their parents or the nation they are born into. Every child deserves good health care, education, protection from harm (physically or emotionally), nutrition and stability. This point cannot be overemphasised. As an individual or as a government, any decision, any policy and statement made that deprives any child of these basic human needs (wilfully or otherwise) is an outrage and a shameful act. Focusing on what a person or state perceives as 'my own' only and negating the rest is a shortsighted approach that is creating such mayhem on this planet. One doesn't need to be a rocket scientist to know that the word 'independent' is an illusion, as we all are inter-dependent: nation with nation, community with community and individual with individual. Furthermore, the world is now a 'global village', as the economic crisis in one nation affects other surrounding nations. The mere facts that nobody can feel rich unless there is a poor person around and no nation can feel powerful unless there is a weak nation around show that we need each other. If only governments around this world made policies and decisions after first of all asking, 'How would this policy or decision affect the children or what would this mean to the next generation?' things would begin to change positively. Instead, policies and decisions have been devised without proper consideration for the impact on the recipients, as governments around the world focus more on priorities that ensure second or third terms in office.

Some Governments devise and pursue policies all in the name of freedom, liberty and choice that cripple parents trying to parent, which in turn encourage some unruly children to roam the streets late at night wearing hooded tops and trousers ready to inflict pain on anyone who they perceive as 'disrespecting' them. They empower children and young adults to run their lives independently of their parents. Golding (1954) reminds us of what can happen to children without adult guidance in his book, *Lord Of The Flies*. In it we are told that, 'A plane crashes on a desert and the only survivors, a group of schoolboys, assemble on the beach and wait to be rescued. By day they inhabit a land of bright fantastic birds and dark blue seas, but at night their dreams are haunted by the image of a terrifying beast. As the boys' delicate sense of order fades, so their childish dreams are transformed into something more primitive, and their behaviour starts to take on a murderous, savage significance'. This is because children naturally pick up bad behaviour, and this kind of behaviour does not need to be taught. The reverse is the case if one wants to inculcate good morals into a child. Allowing children to run their lives independent of their parent or guardian is nightmarish. These governments also devise policies or pursue ideologies that stop people from challenging bad behaviour, tying the hands of law enforcement agencies from nipping an impending crisis in the bud and only acting when someone has already been robbed, killed or injured, all in the name of 'civil liberty'. This is woeful! It has turned the police service into a crime solving, not crime preventing force, and brought about a reactive not preventive criminal justice system, thus creating a system that breeds and encourages too many rights, liberties and choices, with limited responsibility. Even when people are convicted of their crimes they are sent to prisons with all manner of luxuries, with no bills to pay and little or no work to do, free food and catering services, and so on and so on. When some of the convicts leave prison, they begin to view life outside as the 'real prison', as they are expected to live an independent life. This prompts and encourages them to find their way back into 'freedom' (prison). Therefore, this provides them with the incentive to commit another crime or even a more serious crime to ensure a longer stay in prison. Such individuals have no regard for the law and treat the judicial system with contempt. Being in front of a magistrate or judge holds no fear for them; rather, they enjoy the experience as it serves as the route to their desired destination.

Such governments also promote the idea that people can and should live any way they like, drink as much as they like, and take illicit drugs in the name of 'recreation'. They also promote the idea that embracing consumerism and capitalism is the only way to exist, and this allows greedy bankers to take ridiculous risks that are responsible for bringing the world's economy to its knees and encouraging our children to become 'want', and not, 'need' driven. The same type of government empowers schoolchildren and/or parents to have rights that are ranked above those of their teachers, making teachers powerless in dealing with badly behaved children. These governments should appreciate that many parents themselves were not parented properly and therefore have no parenting skills to use to bring up their children properly. Such governments fail to ensure that teachers have adequate power and authority to deal with unruly behaviour or that 'morals values' or 'good citizenship' should be a much bigger and an integral part of the curriculum for every primary/secondary school, which would help correct bad behaviour learnt at home. How can a child learn from a teacher they do not respect, and how can any child learn without being disciplined?

One of the contributing factors to the crisis in the United Kingdom, which started in London in August 2011, can be traced back to the mid to late 1980s, when teenagers lacked parental control and saw getting pregnant as a license to acquiring council flats and handsome benefits to go with it, due to government policy. Some of these teenagers became pregnant while under the influence of hard drugs, as their children were already in the womb, and withdrawal symptoms from illicit drugs are manifested on the day of delivery (*see* page 174). The worst aspect of this is the fact that a lot of these teenagers had no parenting skills. Guess what, these children have now become teenagers and adults; do you think any of them took part in the rioting? Today a number of these children end up on the streets where they grow up, in gangs, or in mental health wards, prisons or graveyards/crematoria. Some of the brain

196

development of these 'poor children' has been impeded by poly-substance misuse from the womb. They are 'poor children' because they played little part in what they have become. These children see nothing wrong in putting a knife into someone with no regard to the consequences and no idea what the relatives and associates of the victim will go through. Interestingly some 'clever' people tell us that we need to sit down and find out from such children what is making them behave the way they do. Yes, there are many you can sit down and reason with, but from my experience, there is no reasoning with some of these children, as their view of the world has been clouded by damage from the womb and their upbringing. *It is important to note and understand that the physicians interviewed for this book agreed that poly-substance use during pregnancy can cause all manner of damage to the unborn baby, including possible damage to the limbic system (the central part of the brain that controls emotion, attachment and memory). It is this part of the brain that is mostly tampered with. Often, when criminals commit heinous crimes, many intoxicate themselves with illicit drugs and/or alcohol and temporarily lose all sense of consideration, moderation and reality. These senses could be destroyed in unborn babies sometimes whilst in the womb. They are likely to suffer permanent damage and are unlikely to relate to 'real' human emotions. Putting a knife into someone and inflicting pain on others is of no consequence to them. It would be impossible to fully calculate and appreciate the true cost that the abuse of illicit drugs and alcohol has on individuals, their families and wider society.*

In some developing countries, the reason slates are still used in class rooms, chalks used to make tablets and water is used as drip in some hospitals, is simply because those charged with providing the basic educational and health care needs of the people do not subscribe to them. Once in government, they transfer their health care, as well as that of their relatives, and the educational needs of their children abroad. Conversely, no foreign leader has been known to obtain their health care in Africa, for example; neither has anyone heard of foreign leaders' children obtaining their education in any part of the African continent or owning properties in Africa. In some countries in Africa, the masses are left with no electricity supply or, at best, regular interruptions, which destroy enterprise and the economic development of a nation, whilst the leaders of these countries enjoy a 24-hour, 7-day-a-week, regular supply of electricity, with high KVA generators. This is because they have not subscribed to that which they have provided for their people. In some parts of Africa, ambulance services (if any exist) are for the dead not for the living. The dying and injured victims of road accidents, including women and children, depend on willing (in most cases) medically untrained 'good Samaritans' to ferry them to hospital, whilst those 'elected' or 'selected' and charged with serving the poor masses parade with their fleets of Hummer jeeps and other luxurious vehicles, with their sirens blaring. Their so-called law enforcement agencies collude with them and are willing to ruthlessly deal with anyone attempting to slow the free movement of their entourage. They show total disregard to human life, let alone human rights, and negate the core principle of governance, which is 'protection of life and property'. They become completely oblivious to the needs of their people. They are consumed by their own importance and 'relevance' and get excited at people praising them whilst the rest of the population is perishing in dire suffering as a direct result of their poor and inept leadership. They forget that though they can escape 'human justice' they cannot escape 'natural justice'. These leaders are so shortsighted and lacking in insight that they believe they will be forewarned of an impending illness and then hopefully arrange for their foreign health care trip. They forget that some illnesses require immediate and emergency care. They forget that if they had invested in improving the health care facilities in their own countries their chances of survival and that of their loved ones would increase. Having moved their health care abroad, these leaders provide room for unscrupulous elements, who also are lacking in insight, to flood their country's health care facilities with adulterated and fake medicines. These unscrupulous elements have no interest in the number of people they are sending to an early grave or whose health they are damaging. They have no clue or fail to understand that the fake medicines could be used as treatment for their relatives and loved ones or could fall into their own mouth one day and lead to their own death. They are solely fixated on the weight of their bank balance. This is what happens in nations where the government has not provided proper leadership or helped to focus the minds of citizens in setting the right priorities. In such nations, money becomes everything and is seen as the master rather than the servant it should and must always be. What do you expect, though, when those charged with protecting the health and safety of a nation have no interest in what they have prepared for their own people? The question I ask these African leaders is, what happens if the leaders of the country you go to for your health care decide to do exactly what you have done or failed to correct in your nation? Would you go to the moon then? Don't you feel ashamed and guilty when you board that plane, knowing that you have either provided poison for your people or have allowed the poison to continue destroying your own people, whilst you go elsewhere for your treatment? Do you think you would be a leader without the people who put you there? Isn't this the height of betrayal, and couldn't you say, 'OK, the state of my nation's health care has been left in a terrible state, but I have it is a priority to lay a new foundation for changing it'? *I tell you this, my brothers and sisters who inhabit this planet with me, there can be no president without the people, no clergy without the congregation, no doctor without a patient, no lawyer without a client and, of course, no actor without an audience.* If the agenda is not to see and embrace the truth, but to destroy the truth and those that bring it to you so you cannot face the truth, then be duly reminded and assured that your own time awaits you, for no one, and I mean no one, is immune to answering the call, when it comes and in whatever circumstances. Even if the call does not come, nature will gradually strip off everything that turned you into what you became in between your points of arrival and departure. There will be no escape from that!

Whatever position any human being has and whatever power and privilege they possess is assigned to them by others. One can be the best surgeon, but if everybody decides to boycott them in vain do they then answer to being a surgeon at all, let alone the 'best' surgeon. With this in mind, human beings need to be dedicated to giving service to those who made them what they are! They must desist from oppressing, dehumanising and betraying those that accredit them. Everyone in a position of authority needs to wake up every morning and go to sleep every night with the thought, 'How will the decision I made today and the one I will make tomorrow affect the average person, especially the children and vulnerable people. What will be the likely effect and long-term impact of my decision on these vulnerable groups?' To do the right thing is not easy; therefore leaders must be brave and find ways to convince the structures around them that want to retain the status quo for self-gains. Leaders must also learn to focus on doing the right thing in the interest of the masses not focus on securing a second or third term. Everyone needs to understand that doing the right thing, in the long run benefits everyone: it amounts to 'pay now and enjoy later' not 'enjoy now and suffer later'.

The real achievement and accolade belong to those who succeed in doing hard things and getting them right. Humans have always been nasty to their fellow human beings because those who fail to learn the lessons of history repeat history. Those who maintain the status quo produce the same outcome. Just like a drug addict with cravings, human beings as individuals and nations have cravings to cheat, steal, dominate, subdue and overpower others sometimes in order to control and maintain the status quo. You do not need to fight wars and kill your fellow human beings in order to survive or make history. Terrorising and killing yourself and/or other people cannot secure your future. The future generation is not guaranteed security and prosperity simply because you cheat other people. The fact that you tell your children that they are superior to other children will not immunise your children from the challenges of life; rather, they are likely to make costly mistakes that are likely to put them and others at risk. A case in point currently is President Assad of Syria. The reality is that no matter what President Assad feels, thinks or does, 'by hook or by crook' just like Saddam and Gaddafi; he would be stripped of whatever made him what he became in between arrival and departure. Remember where all the indispensables are, awaiting our imminent arrival whether we like it or not.

In education, most primary and secondary schools in parts of Africa are a health and safety hazard. Some of the higher institutions are unworthy of being called so, with teachers and lecturers often unpaid for months. As a result, strikes are commonplace and teachers and lecturers become so vulnerable that some of them turn to taking bribes from students in exchange for a 'Pass', resulting in the production of 'unbaked or half-baked' graduates, some of whom are unable to write proper sentences. Some universities have become so disorganised and so infested with devious elements that undergraduates who used to be role models in the past turn to prostitution and stealing and join occult movements. Lecturers are becoming market traders, selling handouts and collecting money in exchange for a pass mark; no matter how poorly the students have performed in their academic work. This is because the leaders who are charged with providing excellence in education do not subscribe to the education they provide for the people. Instead, they send their own children to 'super' private schools and/or universities or abroad for their education. They fail to realise that they are destroying one of the major pillars of society, which means that anarchy awaits, as the half-baked/unbaked graduates take up their positions in society. The truth is that 'what goes around comes around', and we cannot escape this. The unbaked or half-baked doctor, teacher, lawyer or pilot will one day (without your desire or design) come into contact with you, your children and loved ones.

Think of the possible consequences! Consider an unqualified and inexperienced mechanic working on your Rolls Royce, or an unbaked doctor operating on your child, wife, husband, parents or siblings. The unbaked/half-baked graduate who is unemployable may be the one that visits you, your relatives or loved ones at night, with a gun to rob you or kill you. Life can throw anything at us without our consent! Therefore, if you are in a position to serve, please take it as a privilege not a right; serve your people and be our hero/heroine. It is fair to say that no leader who subscribes to the provisions they made available to the people would allow them to degenerate to such a pathetic level. No leader would allow fake medicines and poor heath and educational facilities to become the norm in the knowledge that they and their loved ones have a stake in them.

When people are pushed to feel dead already, they hold no fear of the grave. Remember, before you became a leader you were once led, but it is a fact that you won't remain a leader forever; so, my brothers and sisters within this our 'human family', think, and if you can't remember anyone else, please remember Gaddafi of Libya! What type of a human being, indeed what type of a so-called leader resorts to killing the same people who either put them in a position of leadership or allowed them to be there; the same people they are 'supposed' to serve, simply because they are told their service is no longer required? Some leaders are renowned for looting their nation's economy. Those who loot and those who provide or create the environment that protects looters are responsible for and answerable to any woman that dies during childbirth, any malnourished child, deaths on poorly maintained roads, poor infrastructures and the suffering of the country that is looted from. Why are we, and those we are meant to serve, suffering? Why are we destroying ourselves and rendering the future of our children hopeless and useless? Why have we turned into the proverbial snail that sought to extinguish the fire by producing bodily fluids, without knowing that it is hastening its own death in the process? What is the overall gain in all these things? Please open your eyes and minds and see the suffering of our children and your fellow citizens. Your country and our world are crying out for true heroes/heroines that can give selfless service to mankind. The same blood that runs in you is what runs in the other person too. Haven't we heard that Heads of States at the height of their 'earthly power' can die in office? Isn't it enough to inform us that no matter where we find ourselves, we are not immune to the natural forces that can befall any one of us at any time? Don't we know that the legacy we leave and the judgement we get (here and beyond) does not depend on how much wealth we acquired here on earth, but on how we treated the very 'least' in our midst? Those aspiring to be in public office should, and must, demonstrate verbally and practically, as well as in writing, their services to humanity and their intention to continue to serve humanity. It is a calling, and if you are not called, do not volunteer yourself. Our children are suffering dearly, at times, with no hope on the horizon and their future looking very bleak. When one child suffers (whether we realise it or not) the rest of humanity suffers. Remember that an untrained, ill-disciplined, uncultured and uncared-for child can pose a huge danger to you and your loved ones in ways you never imagined. The world we live in is a complex one and sometimes our 'little' minds cannot fully appreciate or understand it! However, once in a while, nature reminds us of how feeble, weak, vulnerable and little we all are, irrespective of our positions. Nature has a way of stopping every human being, no matter what or who we think we are. Just consider the tsunami in Japan (2011), the volcanic eruption in Iceland (2009) and the tsunami in Malaysia (2004), to mention but a few, and remember how helpless we, as human beings, were in spite of all our technology. Visit the graveyards and crematoria and see for yourself those who thought they owned the world, awaiting our eminent arrival. Remember the 'power' you feel and know is conferred on you by others; if life permits it, you will gradually proceed to the gates of old age, when these powers fall from you, and you become vulnerable, weak, needy and helpless, just like when you arrived in the world. The power we feel is not ours to keep; consider Colonel Gaddafi of Libya, for example. Stop viewing the resources meant for serving the people as a cake to be consumed for your own use. Stop being so short-sighted. Use the power people conferred on you to serve, protect, defend and improve the lot of the people that put you there, particularly the children of this world. Do not abuse your power by suppressing and oppressing the people. See any opposition and criticisms as an opportunity to review your policies with a view to making things better. It is those who oppose and criticise that make us better, as they make us look at things we may have not considered or wouldn't have considered at all. Create an enabling environment in which your people can maximise their potential. Our world is acutely ill and requires sound physicians who are dedicated to the diagnosis and treatment of the cancer gripping us today. What type of a human being would resort to killing the people they are meant to serve, simply because the people are saying, 'Thank you very much, but your services are no longer required'? Serving is not easy; therefore a true servant is only too happy to stop serving when those being served say, 'Time is up!' unless their mission is based on something other than service to the people. Remember, as a human being one must be able to reflect and project. If you only act 'on the spur of the moment' then you cannot say you know what you are doing. If you can reflect, you will consider the fact that now you are a 'somebody', you were once 'a nobody' and that there will definitely come a time when all your powers are either stripped from you by those who gave you the power or nature would force it out of your hands. No one has any choice in the matter!

To get things moving in the right direction, every government in this world must devise and pursue policies that are family-orientated which must include, mandatory attendance by parents at parenting classes, in view of the facts, highlighted in this book, that a badly behaved child or a badly nurtured child can go on to create mayhem that all the wild animals put together could not create. The importance of such a policy can never be over-emphasised; it has to be mandatory because a badly behaved child is a danger to everyone, including you and your loved ones. In addition, everyone needs to understand that human beings are the most dangerous weapons known to mankind. The appreciation of this fact makes it essential that, it should not be a matter of 'choice' when it comes to nurturing the child the right way. Some children are mainly being brought up by gadgets these days; gadgets that are full of 'disturbing' images and some parents have no time in finding out what their children are watching and being indoctrinated into. In the olden days the availability of such 'disturbing' gadgets was limited and where the parent fails, the community may succeed. Today, even teachers are struggling to deal with badly behaved children due to government legislations, let alone members of the public.

Parents-to-be need be made aware of their responsibilities and the importance of accountability before they start having babies. When parents understand this, it is likely to cure the problem of 'controlling partner' and lessen domestic violence, which has become endemic in our society. It is fair to say that domestic violence and warring partners are the biggest threats to children's development/welfare which account for the number of unruly children on our streets, psychiatric units, prisons and graveyards.

__In respect to domestic violence, it is vital that the law should and must be blind to gender, race and creed. The law must cut both ways. It must seek to protect the few men and many women affected by it equally. It should not discriminate by giving unfair advantage to either party based on bias or need to boost statistics. Each case has to be treated on its own merit. Couples need to learn and be encouraged to keep their hands to themselves!__

When a parent does not understand accountability and responsibility (due to their associations and/or upbringing) their behaviour becomes at times, childlike and impact adversely on their children. Where separation occurs, each parent must be made to face up to this 'primary' responsibility by law, and any parent that puts an obstacle in the way of the other parent or wilfully refuses to play their part in ensuring the sound upbringing of their child should be made to pay heavily. Think about it: if restaurant owners are required by law to meet certain health and safety standards, then it is irresponsible not to require that parents-to-be are made to learn some basic parenting skills and conduct, especially in this modern age of intense corrupt technological world. Everyone in government, including you, comes from a family, and that's why good parenting is crucial. Isn't it shocking that in most cases parents of badly behaved children have no clue where their children are? This is mostly because the children themselves have no clue where their parents are, and sometimes one parent does not know where the other parent is or when they are likely to come back. This is one of the worst things threatening the health and safety of our children and our entire society today. One cannot run a business like this and succeed, let alone run a family, which is the most important aspect of life.

Every government needs to encourage collective responsibility for correcting bad behaviour, to make instruction about values and morals part of the education curriculum and, above all, whilst allowing people to retain their traditions and culture, have a baseline value standard that foreigners must subscribe to if, they wish to reside in a country other than their own. For example; the idea of having an interpreter service for people who decide to migrate and reside in countries other than their own is absurd. Having worked in public sector in England for more than two decades and seen the amount of resources 'wasted' in the interpreting service, it is no surprise that so much waste, in so many areas has contributed to the economic downturn, as the cumulative effects of these wastes have taken their toll on the economy. People who decide to leave their own country for another country must show respect and study the language of the country they wish to reside in before arrival and work hard on integration upon arrival. Unless a person is forced to go or suddenly has to go to another country through no fault of their own, they should not be entitled to use the interpreter service. Even when someone is forced to go to another country through no fault of their own, there should be a maximum time limit set for such a person to have access to the interpreter service. For those who do not wish to 'respect' the country they are going to move to or have moved to, they should consider going on holiday to that country or visiting it without the intention of residing there.

All governments must pursue policies that ensure 'the right person is for the right job' otherwise society, especially our children, will suffer the consequences. Putting people in posts they are not qualified for or do not merit simply on sentimental grounds or because of an existing friendship, repayment of a favour or as part of a quota system built, for reasons of 'positive discrimination' is doing a disservice to mankind. In the same way, we deprive ourselves and society at large when we deny someone their rightful position on grounds other than their ability to do the job and their supporting qualifications and experience. How many times have we seen 'professionals', charged with providing support, care and treatment to the most vulnerable, who struggle to communicate with fellow professionals? Sometimes, as a fellow professional, you struggle to understand what they are trying to communicate to you. Goodness knows how they manage to communicate with their vulnerable patients. This has become so bad that not so long ago someone lost his life because a foreign doctor, who did not have a proper and effective command of the English language, treated them under a European employment rule that stated that a European doctor who did their training and gained their qualification outside the United Kingdom was free to practice in England. This crazy rule could apply to other things, but should not apply to people's life and liberty. How can a person provide a proper service to someone they cannot understand or receive a proper service from someone they cannot understand, especially when it relates to life and death? It is true indeed that common sense is not quite common!

By the same token, the law must be on the side of those who seek to correct bad behaviour. The law enforcement agencies (through no fault of their own) are not usually on the scene when incidents occur. This is not because they do not want to be there, but because that is just how it is. People must be made to feel safe and secure to collectively challenge and interrupt bad and dangerous acts in our homes or on our streets. We must pursue strategies that actively prevent harm to others and destruction of our properties, not just those that encourage and facilitate detection and resolution of crime. As such, crime prevention must and should be for everyone to participate in, whilst detection and resolution of crime should be for the law enforcement agencies. Very rarely do we hear that the police were present when someone's home was burgled or someone was killed. They usually appear after the event, when people's lives have already been shattered. Government policies and legislation have made it so that the police's primary focus is to respond after a crime has been committed. The criminal's mind should be set in a defensive not offensive mode. The person about to commit a crime should be made to understand that members of the public can stop them with the full backing of the law, and members of the public should not be put in a position where they are confused about what will happen to them if they intervene. It is the criminal/s who should think twice before committing a crime, not those trying to prevent them from committing the crime. Let the public have full rights, and it is then up to them whether they choose to exercise those rights. People in their own houses should not be made to think, 'Oh, I need to have a word with this man who has just broken into my house to find out whether we will be wrestling or boxing' when confronted by someone who has left their own home and is trying to force entry into someone else's home. People should not be made to gauge 'proportionality' when trying to protect their own lives, family and property. Those trying to unlawfully break into other people's residences should be in violation of the homeowner's human rights, and should, at that point, lose their own human rights. Their act is not seeking but forcing entry, therefore it is impossible to know what their intention was at the time. No negotiation should be entered into as to the level of response required or needed from innocent occupants of the home being forced open. What we have now is not working, with criminals having a field day to do as they like in the knowledge that people are scared, confused and unable to intervene, due to legislative restrictions that have put the criminals at any advantage. Remember! Stonycreek Township has become famous today because citizens decided to act, and threw away the idea that one cannot take the law into one's own hands. If the passengers on Flight 93 flying from New Jersey to Pennsylvania, which was hijacked by 9/11 terrorists, had decided not to act but instead to wait for the law enforcement agencies, there may not be the White House as we know it today. Contrast this (though not on the same scale or magnitude) with the incident of 10th October 2011 in South East London where 'A woman stole a 12-inch knife from a butcher's shop then stabbed a Gran to death in a busy high street' *Daily Mirror* (11.10.11). According to the account in the *Metro* (11.10.11), 'The attacker was said to have entered an Asda supermarket in Bexleyheath, Southeast London, and stolen a knife before running to a bus stop and stabbing a 23-year-old woman in the hand. She was disarmed by the victim and a passer-by, but ran into a butcher's, where she took a large steak knife and left. She then attacked a second woman, stabbing her fatally in the neck.' It beggars belief that after the first attack and then being disarmed, someone who had already committed a crime in broad daylight was then allowed to run to a butcher's shop to get another knife. Something is terribly wrong with the human psyche currently which has been emasculated by government policies. It is shocking that this woman could not be held by people for the initial offence until those responsible for resolving crime (the police) arrived. People, however, could not be blamed, as it is likely that they would have been brought before a judge or magistrate to explain inch by inch how much force they used in restraining the woman if they had chosen to stop her. Before you knew it, the person trying to prevent the crime would have become the 'criminal'. Today hearts are broken, bereaved families torn to pieces; colleagues devastated and witnesses live in shock, all because of a stabbing that could have been prevented under normal circumstances. It is not an excuse to note how infrequently such incidents occur or whether the perpetrator suffered from a mental disorder or not. One incident is bad enough, and people should be empowered to intervene in the knowledge that the law will be firmly on their side.

On 19th November 2011 a similar incident occurred in London. One headline said, "'Give me a chopper!" What maniac told butcher before snatching a knife and stabbing four policemen' *Mail Online (*20.11.11). Butchers' shops are now becoming a great source of danger because copycats which, is what human beings are, go to work on copying. This incident confirms the view that 'crime knows no bounds or limits' and that 'an unruly child has the capacity to do more damage to mankind than all the wild animals put together'. Without knowing the background of the perpetrator of this terrible crime, and judging from my experience in mental health work, I can confidently say that two things are obvious here:

This individual has some psychological problem.

His background is likely to include something such as; his parents separated or divorced before he was fifteen, he never had contact with either his father/mother, he was abused when he was young or that he abuses drug/alcohol. The government has a duty to protect the public, therefore health and safety officials now need to go to work to find ways to secure knives and sharp objects in places where they can be legitimately purchased to make certain that they are not easily removed. We cannot wait for another incident to happen, for the victim could be you, a close relative, or, indeed, anyone.

It is true to say that in the case of the incident in October 2011, if the woman had been stopped following the first incident, no one would have known or appreciated that the second incident would result in a fatality. Those who stopped her in the first incident may have faced some questioning by the police and the possibility of being cautioned at best or being prosecuted at worst. Therefore it seems that someone has to be seriously injured or killed before action can be taken against criminals carrying weapons. In the same way no one can fully appreciate what the brave United States citizens on Flight 93 did for us when they intervened. Must we always wait for the worst to happen, so that our forensic wizards can put their expertise to the test and provide us with the evidence that may lead to conviction; but will never bring our loved ones back?

In view of all this, people should and must be empowered to be able to (at the very least) act to limit the damage. Evil should and must not be allowed to be **BOLD**. Those committing crimes against their fellow human beings must be made to think twice and know that the public are empowered to stop them before the arrival of the police. As a police sergeant (Shaun Goodchild) put it, 'It is a moral, social and civic responsibility for members of the public to be at the fore front of crime prevention.' This is because, it takes a second to save or take a life, but it takes at least five minutes for law enforcement agencies to arrive. This issue of 'never take the law into your own hands' as a blanket rule needs a proper review, as it is empowering criminals to create a climate of fear for law-abiding citizens. These are not just hard times, but dangerous times! People should be fearless in trying to prevent crime and should not be treated like criminals when they do. The climate has changed and we must and should respond accordingly. When the drumbeater changes the beat, the dancer must adjust their dancing in order not to dance out of rhythm. If the bird continues to fly without perching, then the hunter must shoot randomly without aiming. The die is cast!

Governments around the world have a huge responsibility on their hands, and they should, and must, realise it and do something about it. They need to realise that although one is expected to have the cognition to think and act positively in adulthood, one cannot act out what one hasn't learnt. Asking a father who has never heard or spoken Mandarin to start speaking Mandarin is like asking an iron bar to produce water: can we squeeze blood out of a stone? People who were not parented properly are likely to struggle as parents (in most cases) through no fault of their own because they can only give what they have. Therefore all governments need to clearly and (in a practical manner) devise the baseline requirement or expectation for parents in relation to their babies. They would then make it mandatory for all 'parents-to-be' to not only attend the relevant classes but to participate too. This point cannot be overemphasised; if we are not allowed to drive without first being taught and without acquiring a driving licence, then it becomes ridiculous not to prepare and equip potential bearers or agents that could turn the car into a hazardous object and possibly bring more mayhem to fellow human beings than any other creature on this planet could. It should also be everyone's responsibility to correct bad behaviour irrespective of where or when it occurs. It may be chaotic at first, and opponents to the idea may say it would encourage 'vigilante' groups, but if the parameters were set correctly, people would understand the expectations required of them. Remember that this idea automatically puts the criminal on the back foot even without people taking up the offer.

Yes, it is everybody's right to have a baby, but society must demand that every parent who exercises their right to have a baby takes responsibility for giving it a proper upbringing. A baby's potential knows no bounds; one minute of pleasure for one individual can lead to a lifetime of hell for innocent others.

I repeat, business as usual will earn very little or no dividends as we walk through paths already established by others before us. Those in government, the media and voluntary and private sectors who now work towards and devise ways to achieve fairness, equality and justice for all, especially the children of this world, will produce a resounding and invaluable dividend. This is the new challenge and the great invention as yet not invented. This is the most important history awaiting mankind! At the same time, everyone should and must know and realise that it is rare for any government to introduce positive changes for the benefit of the people without pressure from the governed, because only responsible fellowship can produce responsible leadership. Unfortunately, people in government are usually the last to catch up with the true feelings of the people. Power not only corrupts, but can make one lose a true sense of reality. It is the brain not the bullet that will bring mankind to the 'promised land' where fairness, harmony, justice and true freedom reside. This is not advocating socialism, because that is as bad as capitalism (they are two extremes). Socialism is responsible for rendering people useless, with no adequate reward linked to input, whereas capitalism is the mother of greed and selfishness, as we can all see. What is required is a middle ground:

'capitalism with moderation' based on sound moral values. Let us all go to work now and save our children and the future generation by inculcating in them self-respect and love, respect and love for others, a sense of moderation and an appreciation that whether black or white, big or small, rich or poor, low or high and irrespective of our creed, gender, colour of skin, family or the nation we were born into, we need each other in order for the world to go round. When every individual, family, community and nation does this, our world will change for the better. Do unto others as you would like them do unto you!

The Role Of The Mass Media

The impact of information passing from the media to society as a whole, especially to our children, can never be measured, estimated or qualified. In my previous book I said that 'the power of the mass media in society today is so enormous, it is unimaginable. It has been suggested that the media have the power to control how society thinks, perceives and reacts to any particular situation' (*Nacho*, 2010, page 40).

The media mechanism can make or break a person; group or community and can bring down a government. No wonder politicians and celebrities pander to the media when it suits them and criticise them when they do their real job in the 'public interest'. People seek the instrumentality of the media to get their messages across, but when the media become 'really interested'; the same people start seeking privacy and accuse the media of going 'too far'. My suggestion is that, it is better to call 'a spade a spade' from the start. If you are a footballer, make it clear that, your area of specialism is football and that you are only a role model for those wanting to play football the way you do. Let it be known that, you are not a reverend, pastor or saint. Even reverends and pastors are afflicted as well. The reality is that we are all afflicted, and remember that being a doctor does not mean you won't become ill or in need of medical assistance yourself. This story from Ven. Dr. Onundu Amatu Christian-Iwuagwu (the Vicar at St Marys The Virgin Church, Harmondsworth, England) illustrates this fact. According to the story, *'a Catchiest died and went to hell. When he arrived in hell, he was shocked to see his vicar, who died a year before. He could not believe his eyes because, that was the last place he expected his vicar who, lived a 'holier than thou' life whilst on earth. Therefore in his shocked state of mind, he screamed, 'Oh, my vicar, what the hell are you doing...?' Before he could finish the sentence, the vicar quickly rebuked him and with his finger fixed on his lips, he said to the Catchiest, 'Shush! Keep quiet! The bishop is coming behind me.'* Whether we want to believe, accept it or not, we are all like fish inside the river, none of us can deny having tasted the water.

However, whether we love them or hate them, we cannot imagine a world without the mass media. They provide us with 'checks and balances' but they are by no means saints either, as we can all see from the closure of the *News of the World* in relation to the hacking scandal, and the case of an elite member of the media who sought a 'super injunction'. Having said that, without the mass media would we ever have known of the abuse of expenses by Members of Parliament, for example? The free and independent media in the West have brought so much good. However, there needs to be improvement of the images and branding of products on show for our children. Society is craving for real role models, by which I mean the unsung heroes/heroines: the brilliant teachers, doctors, nurses, 'Good Samaritans', inventors and entrepreneurs. Able people and healthy body images should be shown, not the images of skinny people, naked and half-naked people that currently cover our screens, magazines and newspapers, inducing our children to copy what they see. Though peoples' excitement grows with bad news and inappropriate images, feeding society with good news is what is required now more than ever. Insisting on and rewarding good behaviour and frowning at and discouraging bad behaviour is very necessary for our children. Though having talent can be very rewarding, individuals born with it still have to work hard in order to achieve excellence. However, more credit goes to individuals without natural talent who work extremely hard to achieve the same or higher levels of excellence. The promotion and advertisement of how much some of our footballers earn per week is sowing some dangerous seeds for our children, some of whom play truant from school in the belief that they too could become the next £100,000-a-week footballer. The promotion and advertisement of violence, inappropriate sexual images on our screens is destroying our children. The images of 'celebrities' on drugs and alcohol send very negative messages to our children, who in turn possibly think that without their poly-substances use they cannot perform well. They need to be reminded and made to understand that it is debatable whether someone like Michael Jackson was taking drugs at the age when he started singing; yet he performed extremely well and pulled in the crowds. The images on brand products that persuade our children to want those products, even though they may not necessarily need them, need to be reviewed. Some of these images are so sensationalised that some children value these products and gadgets more than their fellow human beings. One can observe this in action, as some of these children would ignore the world around them, as they are fixated on their gadgets and violent screens. It is understandable that these are the forces of capitalism in action, where money, making a profit and amassing as much wealth as possible are the main aims. That is why we need 'capitalism with moderation/consideration'. Therefore, it is important for editors and those responsible for bringing us information, to always consider the possible impact of their stories, pictures and information on our children. The media world needs to realise that in this highly demanding and pressurised 21st century world, many parents are fixated on making 'ends meet' that they allow the screens to parent their children. As such, the media world has a great responsibility to ensure that images and information on the screens and broadsheets are not inappropriate for children. It cannot be over emphasised that children, indeed human beings in general are 'copy cats'. Two cases in point are the horror news of 'a boy of 14 who beat his mum to death in a hammer attack copied from Coronation Street'. He 'was locked up for a minimum of 16 years' on 2nd April 2012 according to Parker A *(The Sun,* 3.4.12) and 'A gunman opened fire at a Christian college in California on Monday (2.4.12), killing at least seven people and wounding three after telling former classmates: "Get in line and I'm going to kill you all" according to Randewich N and Nayak M *(Reuter* 3.4.12).

The 14 year old was said to have 'repeatedly battered Jacqueline's (his mother) face and head before setting her body alight'. People can debate until the 'cows come home' on whether violent films, games or images make human beings violent. The truth is that human beings copy bad things easily and good things are usually hard to learn. Yes, violent images would not turn everybody into a violent person, however there are individuals who have the notion to commit evil but are not able to plan and execute it. Such individuals are likely to copy an act seen on the screen and execute it. Furthermore, there are a lot of people whose mind are unstable and made worse by abuse of illicit substances. People in this category are more than likely to copy violent images and re-enact them in real life. The stories of 'feral children' confirm that children are 'copy cats'. The media needs to fully appreciate that the world has enormously changed, therefore our approach need to change as well. Children seldom committed such deliberate heinous crimes in the past. A lot of children are being brought up today by the screens, as their parents are busy either fighting amongst themselves or 'trying to make ends meet' due to huge demands on human life orchestrated by capitalism gone mad. This is coupled with the culture or climate of wants outstripping needs, as most children want to have what their peers have, whether they need it or not. Many children are destroyed from the womb due to abuse of drugs and/or alcohol by their pregnant mothers. The culture of extreme freedom, liberty and choice has led to a lot of family breakups, as parents seek out individualised 'carefree lifestyle' and society in general has abandoned its children to the devices of nature. The media need to take on board the fact that bad news can be attractive to a lot of people and so easy to copy because much training is not required. They need to adopt a strategy that aims at spreading more of good news, no matter how boring. It would remain arguable whether the 14 year old, (no matter how bad or dangerous he had become) would have been able to have this idea in his psyche, had he not seen it acted on Coronation Street. There are many of such individuals around plotting their strategies. The media has a great responsibility in moderating and influencing positively the thoughts of these children and adults alike. It is true that what we watch does not (on its own) make us violent; however what we watch can give us ideas and impetus to act out our ideas. We must at all times bear in mind that the dangerous weapons out there are human beings because; no hammer, gun, knife, stick, stone has ever used itself. These items become dangerous only when they come in contact with human beings intent on using them. The media need to be mindful about what they feed the psyche of human beings, particularly children with and understand the possible implications and interpretations that could apply to various individuals. Most importantly, it is crucial to appreciate (irrespective of whether it is right or wrong) that the media, screens and gadgets manufacturers are playing a key role in parenting children in our modern world due to severe pressures put on parenting. As such parents and media need to be sure and aware of what the children are watching! The next chapter will explore how the changing norms and values of society can impact on children either positively or negatively with a focus on Igbo people.

CHAPTER SIX

The Igbo people

The best and most valuable asset and resource of a community, ethnic group or nation is its citizens. Any ethnic group or nation that fails to recognise this is doomed, as it might seek to eliminate those best placed to save it. When this becomes a norm, children copy and easily would replicate it, resulting in a broken society, as the good is replaced by the bad, inducing a state of anarchy.

My beloved people of Igbo land, the land of the rising sun, east of the Niger: it is my hope, desire and dream that we will one day realise the special gifts, talents and attributes of Igbo people and use them in a positive way to benefit ourselves, our neighbours and the entire society. Most of the issues raised here are applicable to a lot of the minority ethnic groups in Africa. However, Igbo people need to pay attention to their great attributes and acknowledge their peculiarities with a view to understanding, accepting and addressing them, with immediate effects due to the adverse impact on their children and future generations. This will surely not be easy, because old habits die-hard. However, addressing their peculiar issues would hold the key to their aspirations as a people, and when they start and complete this task; they will occupy a special place in the history of Africa and will shine as a beacon to other minority ethnic groups around the world. Nigeria as a nation and the entire world would benefit enormously, if Igbo people can stop, reflect, project, work hard and accomplish this. Igbo people cannot be rivalled when they work positively together in pursuit of a noble goal.

There is no other venue available to highlight these issues, because in our meetings everyone seems to know what our problems are. In our villages, it is difficult for someone's views to count unless they have plenty of money to go round or old enough for people to want to listen to them (as highlighted below). Even old age counts for nothing these days if there is no money to back it up. There are also too many kings and chiefs, and each of them is autonomous, with views and counter-views. As a result, it is virtually impossible to find a medium to explore, acknowledge and address our issues collectively, as a people. I would not have bothered but for the sake of our children and future generation, we really must be brave in tackling our problems, as we cannot afford to maintain the status quo. Let us reflect and project now before it is too late, if it is not already! Igbo people are suffering severely due to our collective failings and the untold suffering of our people can never be fully quantified.

Remember, the future belongs to those who prepare for it today. Those who only focus on material things have no place in history, because history belongs to those who manufacture and invent things, not those who consume and use them.

It is crucial to note that doomed is a community, an ethnic group or nation that fails to recognise that, what brings the best out of mankind is opposition, controversy and criticism. Without these, people are bound to stagnate and degenerate. Therefore we must embrace these in order to see things we might ignore or condone which are harmful to our existence.

To all African nations and minority ethnic groups where, people are still performing rituals, with 'strong' belief in 'witches and wizards', places where people are carrying out beatings and killing both children and adults for all sorts of unjustifiable reasons based on superstitious beliefs, I wish to highlight that the civilised parts of our world had indulged in similar activities and practices in the past, but they eventually rejected these evil practices based on well-informed evidence, following a careful review of these practices. Subsequently, they consigned these practices to history books, storybooks and movies, for entertainment and information only. They began to lead a new life based on 'reality'. They knew that, even if, these practices had substance; the fact that they cannot be measured or understood meant that they were put to one side. They also appreciated the fact that, they had no control over these practices and pursuing them could only make their society deteriorate. Though they rejected these evil practices, they used these concepts to bring us things like 'the haunted house' for entertainment purposes. Of course a lot of Africans believe that 'the haunted house' is real. By departing from these negative practices, the advanced Western Scientists were able to bring the positive things we all enjoy today and are killing ourselves for such as; cars, aircraft, supermarkets, sophisticated advances in healthcare and educational equipment, high tech phones, and the guns we are using to destroy ourselves. The civilised parts of our world have led the way, and through our actions, we have voted with our feet that, we prefer the way they have organised their societies. This is why many African leaders have their bank accounts abroad, get their healthcare and their children's education abroad and shop abroad. When we contrast this with our frivolous, primitive and 'shadow chasing' lifestyles, we have to ask whether anyone has heard of or seen any foreign leader getting their healthcare, bank account, owning properties or obtaining their children's education in any part of the African continent. Then we must call to mind, the adverse impact of our lifestyle on our children who can only copy what they see in us. Do we really want this 'dark' vicious circle to continue? Would it surprise anyone to note that, if Fabrice Muamba's cardiac arrest happened on the African continent, he would have died? It would not have been different from what happened to Sam Oparaji who suffered the same fate but died playing for Nigeria against Angola in 1990. In our bizarre and convoluted thinking some Africans claimed that another player who played in the same position was responsible by using 'black magic' on him, so that he would always feature. Our belief system has damaged us and continues to damage us as we pass this nonsense over to our children.

It is embarrassing and shocking to note that, just recently a fifteen-year-old boy of African descent (from Congo) was tortured to death (in England) with hammer and chisels on Christmas day (2010) because relatives thought he was a witch. (*Mail Online*, 1.3.12). Further investigations carried out revealed the extent of such practices in Congo. A 'haggard looking' woman who claimed and believed she had powers to cast out demons was seen slapping and beating up children.

It can be categorically stated that, if there is anything useful in these deadly and unacceptable practices, the Africans, won't be the first to adopt it. They won't be 'the champions' in them and won't win the trophies that go with it! As they are far behind in terms of technological advancement, so they would have been in this area too. Africans need to be assured that; the civilised world would not have abandoned these practices if there was anything beneficial in them. What is stopping the Africans from analysing these customs and practises in order to see whether they are advancing or setting them back?

Igbo people generally are wonderful, determined, resilient, hard working and intelligent. However, the few who are dedicated to committing evil are spoiling it for the many, and the few are rapidly increasing in number. This is down to our negatively changing values and belief system, which revolves around acquisition of wealth.

Belief systems, norms, culture and tradition are the ingredients that define a person or a community. Therefore as individuals, families or communities it is crucial to develop ideologies, norms, traditions and culture that are forward looking and beneficial to all for the emotional, physical and spiritual growth of the populace. These ideologies are meant to serve the best interest of the people, with particular focus on the impact of such practices and norms on children who are not only the future but the present also. They should also be reviewed periodically to ensure that the actual purpose for which they were established is being realised. If we fail to organise our lives, we would automatically live a disorganised life. We do have some good cultures, which we must treasure and sustain.

One of the good practices the Igbo people have is the belief that everyone must play a part in nurturing a child. Although children are allowed to act like children, anyone can caution a child behaving badly.

The child does not only belong to their parent/s but to the entire community.

Children in traditional Igbo communities have little opportunity to use drugs and/or alcohol, let alone abuse them. This is part of the reasons; it is a rare event for children to deliberately harm other children. This culture needs to be nurtured and encouraged worldwide. Criminal activities are usually adult affairs that are strongly associated with poly-substance abuse and the conversion of moral values into MONEY. Having said that, when it comes to adult crimes, our situation as Igbo people can be described as worse than that of a child with a big abscess that is generating unbearable and excruciating pain. Though the child would like to be relieved of the pain and cannot wait to go back to the playground, the child does not want anyone to come close, let alone touch the boil, to get rid of the abscess. The child is trapped between a rock and a hard place. On one hand, if no one touches the boil, the abscess will remain, the pain will persist and there could be a lasting damage, which may include the death of the child. On the other hand, if treatment is sought the pain will disappear as healing takes place and then the child can be happy again and forget about the pain s/he has endured. In the same way, every 'realistic' Igbo person knows our peculiar problem and that we are in great danger of destroying ourselves (if we haven't already done so), but at the same time feels afraid of confronting those issues, let alone bringing them out into the open. This is not just because we may not have appreciated the huge dimensions of our problems; it could also be that we are simply in denial. However, just like the child with a big abscess, treatment is the only solution. We cannot afford to keep enduring this unbearable and excruciating pain for much longer when we could instead face up to our demons, endure a sharp pain once and for all and deal with it so as to enable the healing process to commence. The impact of our situation on our children must be paramount in our thoughts, coupled with the long-term consequences of inaction. Minimisation of the problem, avoiding it, not confronting it, denying it, ignoring it or misrepresenting it will hurt us more than facing up to it. What are we afraid of that we are not already experiencing at present? Is it crisis or is it death? It is crucial that we think about the future of our innocent children, who had no choice about being born to us.

Every 'well-meaning' Igbo person must adopt the position of the hen and reject that of the cock. In the Igbo mythology, the hen, as every Igbo person knows, screams and shouts to the heavens when a force beyond her control, such as a hawk, preys on any of her chicks. In doing so the hen is saying that although she's aware that her chick will not be brought back, she wants to tell the world that the demise of her chick was caused by forces beyond her control and it wasn't her that ate her chick. The position of the cock is different, and can be illustrated by the story that follows. The cock, one day, was so busy trying to catch up with the hens that he told other birds on the day of an important meeting, *'my fellow birds, I am very busy today and I am even feeling a little sick and the doctor is on his way to see me. Therefore I can't attend the meeting today. However, I want to make it clear that I am in support of whatever decision you reach at the meeting. I will abide by it and will be there with you in spirit'*. The birds accepted the cock's apologies for non-attendance and departed for the meeting. At the meeting, when it came to nominating the bird that was to be slaughtered for sacrifice, to be eaten for Christmas dinner, all the birds voted for the cock to be used. In the cock's absence, he was voted to be the sacrificial bird. This is why everyone in Igbo land should adopt the hen's disposition instead of that of the cock's.

The lesson that can be learned from the above story is that, if a person thinks they are too 'decent', 'important', 'busy' or 'comfortable' to get involved, and as a result decides to withdraw from any business that would end up affecting them, their children, their loved ones and community then this person has voted in support of what those who have become involved decide to do with their lives. Don't let others who might be 'less capable' decide your future and the future of the society you find yourself in. To make a difference one has to be involved: never has anyone made a real difference in absentia. Making a difference does not necessarily mean winning the argument or securing the votes but can be by registering one's protest, opposition or objection to an unworthy course or decision as history vindicates. If one does not get involved, those that one condemns will not only set but regulate the pace of things around them, their loved ones and the community in general.

Umunnem na umunnam, anyị bu ndị Igbo natu ilu si 'akpachapu anya ko uko otule ya akwusi. Agba oria oshi y'ala. Ihe negbu okenye bu ahu ekpuchie ma ihe nke n'egbu nwata wu ekwuwe ma anughi. Obukwa ndi Igbo n'ekwu si na nwakego.'

The above means, 'my sisters and brothers, we the Igbo people have idioms that say 'deliberate scratching of a rash stops it from itching. Exposure of an illness gets rid of the illness. What destroys old people is seeing without talking but what destroys younger people is ignoring or not heeding advice. It is also Igbo people who say a child is worth more than money'. Yes, all creeds, races and gender value money, but not at the expense of everything else, the way some of us would have it. From the look of things it seems some of us have made money our master not our servant. How come some of us have placed money above the individuals that acquired it? What are the factors that have brought us to this terrible situation and what can be done to reverse the trend? There is need for some considerations to be given to the impact of our current lifestyle on our children. We also need to appreciate the dangerous batons we are handing over to our children, one of which is the message that money is everything! Children can only copy what they see, hear or perceive from others'. Yes, everyone acknowledges that not all of us are mad about money, but some of us are; but the few have become the many and the good ones have become the few and far in between. Hear the words of Chief Charles Chibo, my younger brother's father in-law: 'Our love for money is so bad that when you ask some local traders what 5+6 is, they struggle to work out the answer but when you change the question to what is 5 Naira + 6 Naira you have your answer within seconds.'

I am compelled to use this book to speak directly to Igbo people, where, through no fault or design of mine, my roots are. I look at the past and compare it with the present and my heart bleeds excruciatingly. If it were not for the human cost, the pain and suffering of real people, the generational impact as a result of what we are handing over to our children coupled with the fact that I know, silence of the graveyard in the face of evil is evil in itself, I would have remained silent, like most of us who think silence makes us 'good people'. The lessons about silence have been learnt and everyone now knows that though silence is said to be golden, it is immoral, futile and deadly when it cohabits with evil. Those who say that evil strives when 'good' people stand aside and do nothing are completely wrong. Those who stand aside and do nothing encourage evil to spread. Therefore, they are co-participators in the evil and cannot be considered good people. A good person does not stand aside and do or say nothing in the face of evil. To those of us who may argue that 'dirty linen is best washed at home', I say this: our dirty linen has been washed at home for a very long time, but it has not yielded any positive outcome; rather, the poisonous smell of the linen has killed a lot of us and threatens to wipe all of us off the surface of this planet. Therefore, I suggest that the dirty linen be taken outside so we can have some fresh air and other good-natured human beings can teach us or help us to do the washing. Remember, a good parent is one that acknowledges when their child is ill and seeks medical intervention and does not pretend that 'all is well' by trying to hide the illness due to shame. Of course the child is very likely to die from that undisclosed and untreated illness. Any parent who loves his or her child will never neglect or conceal an illness, let alone one that has the potential to kill the child. If you love Igbo people then join us in this diagnostic work in order to provide the right prognosis.

It is evidently clear that the Igbo people from the land of the rising sun, east of the Niger are industrious, hard working, intellectually sound, capable and full of adventure. They are egalitarian by nature, with huge emphasis on the 'self'. It is my take that our people are so 'blessed' that when we work together in a positive manner we cannot be rivalled, but, to our cost, the same applies when we work negatively. Our exploits, despite all the odds, during the Nigerian/Biafran War, from 1967 to 1970, highlighted the true potential and ingenuity of the Igbo people. "... a country that is not yet two months old that can manufacture Ogbunigwe (Monster Bombs) and rockets must be feared ..." (*Soviet Union Government Official cited in Ezeani, 2012, back page*). The war also, sadly, highlighted our weaknesses, which we have not corrected and which are therefore being exploited by others. In recent years one has seen the true potential of the Igbo people when they work together selflessly for good. Using a football analogy, consider the Nigerian national team (the Super Eagles), assembled for the first time, in the knowledge that only talent not ethnicity, quota system or geographical location of an individual player qualified them to put on the national jersey and play football matches for their country. A team without political interference was put together by Clemens Westerhof, made up primarily of young men from the east such as; Jay Jay Okocha, Kanu Nwankwo, Daniel Amokachi, Sunday Oliseh, Emmanuel Amunike, Finidi George, Ben Iroha, Victor Ikpeba, Taribo West, Uche Okechukwu, etc. Only players such as Rashidi Yekini, Samson Siasia, Peter Rufai, Celestine Babanyaro and a few others, judging by their surnames, were not from the east. It was this team that conquered African football by beating Zambia to win the Nations Cup in 1994 and in the same year ending up at the top (in spite of it being their first outing) of their World Cup group which included Argentina, Bulgaria and Greece, and in the process perhaps became the first African side to achieve such a feat. The same team conquered the world in the Olympic games in Atlanta, Georgia in 1996, defeating Brazil from 1-3 down in the semi-final and Argentina from 1-2 down in the final. Their fighting spirit, their 'never say die' approach and their determination, poise and skills were there for everyone to see.

The true Igbo spirit is described above; these are the people as we know them, when they work for each other and are their brother's keepers and sing from the same hymn sheet; there is no rival. It is this spirit that we require in order to influence the growth of ourselves and by extension our country Nigeria.

Unfortunately, we advance to the same heights when we become negative, and that is where we are at present, with shocking consequences and terrible impact on the entire society, especially our children. Prior to the civil war and immediately after it, Igbo people had a spirit of oneness and togetherness. They trusted themselves, and all an Igbo man or woman who travelled out of Igbo land needed was the relevant language to enable another Igbo person to accept them whether it was within or outside Nigeria. During my primary school days, as pupils we always looked forward to having guest speakers, who came once in a while to inspire us with their achievements, particularly academic achievements. They usually reminded us that hard work pays, and as a child I just wanted to work hard and be like them. It is clear from everything we know about children that they are 'copy cats', therefore as adults we must ensure that what they are copying are the right, not the wrong things. The question is; who are our children copying today? Who are their guest speakers at school today, who are their heroes and heroines? Today our children are seeing material things displayed and celebrated without any illustration as to how they are gathered or made. As a child, I couldn't bring home a pencil or anything that had not been bought by my parents without an explanation. I knew I would get a smack and would have to return the item in shame to the rightful owner (unless the owner had lost it and the general advice then was to give it to a teacher as a 'lost and found' item). My parents would hand any of their children that stole over to the authorities to ensure that whatever the punishment for committing such an act was accorded to that child. They made us know where they stood on most issues; therefore they were our first consideration before we considered the legal consequences. My grandfather went down in history as one of those that handed over his son, who had violated the law of the land, back to the community where he had to face the music. He was given a rare opportunity to intervene on behalf of his son, due to his position as the Warrant Chief of Ogwa community. However, my grandfather, being a principled man, stated that they must take him back and accord him whatever punishment people who committed such acts usually received. Today some people in authority pay bribes to get their children and relatives, who have raped, killed, kidnapped and destroyed lives, out of prison and release them back into society. When I was a child one could not even buy a bicycle without showing proof of how they were able to afford it. The fear of being unable to demonstrate to your parents how you managed to afford it was enough to stop you from thinking of having what you could not afford. Parents then never wanted to be associated with anything illegitimately obtained due to shame.

In those days people were happy receiving relatives who had returned from a long distance travels, especially those who travelled abroad. Just the mere sight of them gave people joy, but today, in some cases, people do not want to see anyone returning from a long distance away unless they have material goods to offer. In some cases one stands the risk of upsetting people if they visit empty handed. In the early to mid 1980's this trend began to emerge. With the introduction of a business called 'clearing and forwarding', Igbo land and its people began to change. This business ushered in all sorts of dubious activities, as people, including those who had no genuine means of livelihood, would set up a business as a smokescreen when the real business was armed robbery; they would rob people at gun point, steal all their belongings and come home with cars, justifying this by saying, 'I am a business man.' When asked what type of business, the response would be 'I am into Clearing & Forwarding.' Parents who used to be petrified when their children came home with a bicycle now celebrated their children's homecoming with cars in the name of 'I do business', to the envy of other parents whose children were at home doing nothing or doing legitimate but poorly paid jobs. The celebration did not just end there, as some of these 'businessmen' would not only use the stolen money to buy traditional titles (reserved for people of integrity and honour) from corrupt traditional rulers, but would also buy knighthoods and other titles from some churches. This brand of businessmen began to corrupt everyone they came into contact with. The older people at home, who used to speak openly and honestly, began to keep silent or pervert the course of justice because they had been bought over. Historically in Igbo land the position of 'Eze' is reserved for honest, decent, traditionally prudent and wise people capable of leading their communities and delivering justice at a local level. It was a non-political position, traditionally inherited and usually given to the oldest son of the Eze. Those with titles such as Nze and Ozo got their titles because of their honesty, integrity and full understanding of Igbo traditions and their application. The position of Chief was conferred on the basis that the individual understood the tradition, was honourable and had made outstanding contributions to their community, although the word or title 'Chief' historically had nothing to do with Igbo people. The Nzes, Ozos and Chiefs form part of the Eze's Cabinet. In times past, if there was a dispute and any of these was called, they would only say 'I don't know' when they truly did not know. But today, many of our Ezes, Nzes, Ozos and Chiefs cannot be called upon or relied on to say the 'truth and nothing but the truth'. Today, these titles, including titles in our churches, have all become commercialised and once someone has 'enough' money they can wangle and buy themselves into any of these positions. If anyone has 'enough' money they can start a campaign to carve out an autonomous community, local government and (in some cases even in our churches) diocese in order to become an Eze, a local government chairman or a bishop. The fabric of our society is decaying before our very eyes and we pretend or delude ourselves that it is not happening. Those who have worked hard, led exemplary lives and have given genuine service to their communities before obtaining their titles by merit are now forced to share the same platforms with bandits. For parents whose children are at home doing nothing, the desire to drive their children away so they can compete and achieve what others are 'achieving' becomes great and irresistible. These criminals gradually became the mouthpiece of not only their communities but in some cases the churches, as some preachers do not want to say anything that would offend the main source of funding for their churches. This is because the system suddenly corrupts all its values and morals to a focus on money. Money becomes the all-important subject matter. The subject of money is so important to some of us that even in some of the churches the brand of preaching revolves around 'you can't be poor if you are serving the Most High God; for you are sons and daughters of The King above all Kings, therefore you have to live like Princes and Princesses with the best things of life, the best cars and the best housing'. Some preachers categorically make it clear that 'poverty is sin'. In other words, wealth is righteousness. The only example known to man which reveals 'life after death' is the story of Lazarus (the poor beggar) and the rich man, as highlighted in the Holy Bible. These Christians and their preachers fail to see how all these perishables, including the best cars, houses and aircraft were swept away during the Tsunami in Japan 2011, and they also forget where Jesus Christ said treasures should be stored. They forget that it was Christ who said it would be easier for a camel to pass through the eye of a needle than a rich man to enter into the Kingdom of God. If money and earthly riches were important to God, Jesus Christ would have been conceived by the richest woman on the planet and would have been delivered in the best hospital known to mankind. Those Christians whose faith is feeble and not deep-rooted forget that their preachers are fellow strugglers in the faith, as afflicted as anyone else and unsure of their final destination when death calls. Due to this brand of preaching and brain washing, noted above, many people, including the educated, literally believe that once they have money, irrespective of how they got it, they are righteous; and of course they get all the titles and praises that go with this money, from their pastor, who also assures them of their 'guaranteed' seat in Heaven for their donations and 'service to God' even though the blood of innocent people may have been shed in order to make such donations. In some of these churches the 'widow's mite', favoured by Jesus Christ, is frowned upon.

As Igbo people, we went from the menace of clearing and forwarding to the scam of '419' and now, the cancer of kidnappings, which were rife in Abia and Imo States in particular and which have taken and wasted the lives of too many prominent, wealthy and talented Igbo citizens, for examlple; doctors, lawyers, judges, industrialists. Kidnapping psychologically damaged those released from captivity, destroyed lives, enterprise and economic development. It shattered families and communities but above all, because this is a peculiar case of Igbo people targetting Igbo people, the little trust between our people has evaporated, as no one knows who would betray them. This is the worst carnage that can befall any community. How on earth can we prosper, develop, advance, fellowship and do business without trust? It seems as though we are committed and destined to self-distruct by wasting and destroying anyone or anything that would have offered us hope, instead of nurturing and preserving it. Such a waste was highlighted when kidnappers killed a Chief Medical Officer of a Specialist Hospital. The Chief Medical Officer was just one of the many doctors kidnapped and sometimes killed by fellow Igbo people in the name of kidnapping. These are doctors charged with saving lives, including those of kidnappers. The question is, do these kidnappers know how long and what it takes for one to become a doctor? Do they know that they are not just denying themselves their own medical care, they are denying others and, more importantly, they are destroying institutions, as these doctors train other doctors by passing on their knowledge and skills? Another case in point is the kidnapping of an Abuja-based business man, Mr Hyacinth Ibe from Inyishi in Ikeduru Local Government Area on 27th December 2011. Mr Ibe had returned with his wife and two children to his home town in preparation to open his newly completed house scheduled to take place on 30th December 2011. However, on 27th December the kidnappers descended at his residence and in the process killed his wife (Alice) and shot his two daughters who were taken to the intensive care unit of the Federal Medical Centre, Owerri. On top of this despicable act, the kidnappers were demanding 10 million naira ransom for the release of Mr Ibe. This man has lost everything, his wife and was unsure whether his children would survive. There are numerous cases where these kidnappers, kidnap women and not only collect ransoms but rape them at the same time. These could be your wife, mother, sister, cousin, aunty or friend. How sad and how revolting in this 21st century? Are we going to continue playing games or sweeping this evil under the carpet whilst it damages all of us? How come as Igbo people we are shooting ourselves in the foot? This is an outrage and goes a long way to highlight what can happen to a society in which

money becomes the all-important thing; a society in which children are left under the supervision of maids (who need parental guidance themselves) whilst parents pursue money. Many parents believe that the way to train their children and resolve any problem is by throwing money at them. Education has lost its value, moral values have been consigned to the dustbin and abuse of illicit drugs and alcohol amongst our children is blossoming into something we cannot define, as parents and leaders continue to chase shadows. The crises in some parts of Igbo land have led to many Igbo people in the diaspora deciding to have their remains buried abroad, against our tradition of being buried in our homeland, because no one wants to put their family through the nightmare and agony of not knowing what some evil relatives or associates are planning. It has to be re-emphasised: it is only by accident or insanity that a total stranger would harm you. A stranger avoids you as much as you avoid them. It is usually a person who knows you that sends strangers after you or mask his or herself to harm you! This issue of kidnapping is the worst evil to befall Igbo people, and we are destroying ourselves with it (Igbo people on Igbo people). How can someone eat of his own flesh and steal from his own pocket? These kidnappings and killings in Igbo land need to stop with immediate effect. Igbo people need to rebuild trust and foster co-operation amongst themselves, for posterity.

Be warned! The worst risk to take in life is taking part in killing someone you consider your enemy. This is because no one can tell what really happens after death. Therefore sending your enemy first, to a place you are destined to go yourself is the height of risk taking. Your enemy may be the one to 'welcome' you on arrival and could determine your punishment for eternity. Don't take the risk.

On 2nd March 2012, as he was returning from the burial of Dim Chukwuemeka Odimegwu Ojukwu, 'the Anglican Bishop of Okigwe South, Rt. Rev. David Onuoha, narrowly cheated death in the hands of armed gangsters operating in Imo. It was not clear at press time if his attackers were armed robbers or kidnappers.The hoodlums shot eleven times at the Bishop's Toyota Sequoia Jeep with number plate Abuja FU 513 ABC. The bullet that would have hit him in his spine was miraculously stuck in his seat.

Bishop's ordeal: Narrating his ordeal to Crime Alert, Bishop Onuoha said: "I was coming back home from Nnewi, Anambra State. On getting to Eziachi, Orlu local council area of Imo State, we started hearing sporadic gun shots from behind us.We also saw that the black Murano Jeep coming behind us appeared very desperate to overtake us and I asked the driver, Mr. Oliver Okeke, to allow them to pass. As soon as the driver stopped, the armed men rushed at us and ordered the driver to get out of the car.

The spirit of God descended heavily on me and I greeted them and they looked at me. One of them said 'oh, he is a reverend, please leave him.' The other said, 'he is a man of God, don't touch him' and the third said 'he is a Bishop. Let him go.' The last one picked my phone and asked if he could go with it and I obliged."

The Anglican cleric was slightly downcast when he could not continue with his journey as the hoodlums had shattered the two back tyres of his vehicle. The driver equally informed him that the exhaust pot and the gas pot of the air conditioning unit were all blown open' Nkwopara (Gbooza news 15.3.12).

My dear good people of Igbo land, how are we destroying the cream of our society and replacing it with hoodlums? How long and what does it take to produce a Bishop? All that would have been wasted in a second by someone who only knows how to pull the trigger but cannot manufacture a bullet, let alone a gun. Had that bullet that lodged in the back seat hit the Bishop, we would have been talking about something else. 'Oh, he is a reverend' wouldn't have saved the situation. We need to compile a list consisting of the calibre of individuals rendered useless or killed due to this evil 'kidnapping' by Igbo people on Igbo people and contrast it with the hoodlums that are roaming our streets. This would help us appreciate the need to do whatever it takes and by all means necessary to, not only stop this madness but to ensure it would never rear its head in our society again. There is no darker age than this one we are currently witnessing in our society. Are we going to continue to keep quiet, condone, ignore, pretend or hope that one day this evil would run its course and stop? Do we really understand the true nature of this cancer?

We must not be content with the reduction of this evil 'oh everywhere has been quiet in the last two months, there was only one incident and that one was politically motivated'. There must be a consistent proactive moves by the Government, religious and traditional leaders and the public to hault this menace. We must all understand that, so long as there are people who now see kidnapping as a 'lucrative trade' that makes them 'money' they can never stop. We cannot treat this evil that threatens all of us, especially the future of our children the same way we treat other crimes. Children can only copy what they see, therefore this evil is being 'normalised' in the eyes of our children.

The worry is that the Igbo people brand of kidnapping seeks to eliminate the pillars of our society. This trend, if not checked would surely lead to monsters walking and occuping our streets, as those who would have helped our society to develop are either destroyed or in exile.[6]

Every Igbo person, especially our leaders, must realise that this is a cancer that is spreading like wildfire, and it has the capacity to destroy all of us, including those who delude themselves by thinking they are benefiting from it. Every kidnapping 'success' creates more kidnapping cells as people break away to form their own cell in order to increase their profit margins. Remember, when it comes to doing bad things there is often no training and not much hard work involved. Once someone crosses that threshold and becomes a kidnapper or killer, repeating the action then becomes easy or easier. Kidnappers are very likely to remain kidnappers because they may be scared of investing the money due to fears of becoming the target of another kidnapping group; though at the onset some aspiring kidnappers may think otherwise (see below).

The number of young idle Igbo men and women aspiring to become kidnappers in Igbo land would shock the world if proper data were collected. I have been privy to a discussion by two youths who made it clear that they wished a kidnapping gang could recruit them. 'All we need is a gun and with just one clean deal our hardship would end. A fraction of the money we can make would help us start up a genuine business and we won't need to do kidnapping any more'. When asked if they had considered that they could die from that single attempt, one of them

---

[6] Read more:http://www.gbooza.com/page.html#ixzz456
http://www.gbooza.com/group/crime/forum/topics/apprehension-in-imo-state#ixzz1rLy5WokD Accessed 3/4/2012.

sharply reminded me 'Oga, the kind suffer weh I dey suffer now, dey worse than death oh! Anything weh go get me out of this wahalah weh I dey now; I go do am,' meaning 'Sir, the kind of suffering I am going through now is worse than death. Anything that would stop this suffering that I am going through now, I would do it.' This is chilling, and yet this is the current state of mind of some young people now. If we fail as individuals and communities to fully appreciate what is upon us and rid ourselves of this highly destructive cancer, the vicious cycle will continue and one day engulf all of us. Already we are all suffering the consequences of this cancer. Many Igbo citizens are now afraid of investing in their homeland, and many who live abroad travel back but stay in other parts of Nigeria with their families, depriving Igbo land of the benefits that foreign exchange, vibrant business activities and building projects can bring. Similarly, many of us who believe our children would benefit from the experience of living in Nigeria for a while and might consider sending our children to school in Igbo land are now likely not to. Of course, I had to withdraw two of my own children from their school in Nigeria following the kidnapping of two of my cousins in Imo State and some other school children in Abia State in 2010. The withdrawal of two of my children automatically deprived that school of some revenue for paying teachers and the effective running of the school. The cost of this cancer, kidnapping, is incalculable; that's why it is shocking when people minimise it or see it as a laughing matter. You hear things like, 'Look, don't upset me or else I will kidnap you' or 'Oh, you know Mr B? Ah, they came and carried him yesterday,' which in Igbo language means 'ha biara kuru ya echi garaga.' Others seek to give reasons why it happened to a particular person, and would say, 'Well, that one was to do with politics' or 'well, it is his or her own people who organised it.' Some ex-government officials gave reasons such as, 'It is happening to those who want to eat everything they have on their own.' We also shouldn't be interested in the opinions of those who try to minimise the importance of it by saying things such as, 'Well, in the last two months we have only heard of one incident' or 'in my state it has only happened twice.' These are some of the utterances minimising, glorifying and almost legitimising this shameful act of the kidnapping of Igbo people by Igbo people. The issue now is not why or how often it happens. No one wants to know why someone was kidnapped, though it is useful to understand why things happen and who the likely perpetrators are, but in the case of kidnapping there is no justification! IT JUST SHOULD NOT HAPPEN AT ALL, AND ONE IS BAD ENOUGH! WE SHOULD NOT BE DESTROYING OURSELVES BY TAKING AWAY THOSE WHO CREATE JOBS, HELP IN GETTING US WELL WHEN WE ARE ILL AND DEFEND OUR INTERESTS IN COURT, TEACH OUR CHILDREN AND REPLACING THEM WITH HOODLUMS, THEREBY BREEDING A STATE OF ANARCHY! KIDNAPPING SHOULD BE MADE A FEDERAL CRIME! When the case of Abia State became a federal issue it was stamped out. Thanks to President Goodluck Jonathan for sending the military to reduce or stop kidnapping in Abia State and thank you too for the efforts of the current government of Imo State under the governorship of Owelle Rochas Okorocha, who is now holding each traditional rulers accountable for any such crime in their area. However, all hands must be on deck, and even the kidnappers and those who think they are benefiting from these monstrous acts need to be saved from themselves, as they are like boxers who do not know when they are beaten or what damage they are doing to themselves by fighting on when they are already in trouble; the referee must intervene.

A young Igbo man recalls being summoned to a family meeting on his first return from London after seven years. He was told that a number of people, who travelled abroad after him, had come back and made some investments at home. He began to appreciate how families back home can put pressure on their relatives abroad and lead them to make commitments that force them to get involved in fraudulent acts, in their quest to 'meet up'. Consequently, most times, they end up giving not only themselves but also their families and country a bad name in the process. The young man intelligently asked the members of his family who were gathered to remind him of the names of those that had made those investments that attracted their fancy. He noted that none of the names they mentioned was his, and stated that even if there was similarity in names, personalities differed. By saying this he was telling members of his family that he had his own agenda and cannot follow someone else's agenda. He made it clear that he was not in competition with anyone and would go about things In his own way. He summarised by telling them to go and challenge those they wanted him to compete with and warned them not to expect him to live out their own dreams. He stressed that this kind of pressure is what is making a lot of feeble-minded young people get into trouble and bring a bad name to themselves and their country.

Talking about giving a bad name, another Igbo man who had lived in the United States of America for six years, combining work and studies there, had similar pressure from his father, who queried what he had been doing in the United States 'all this while', when other young men who had travelled at a later date had been sending cars and lots of goodies home to their parents. The young man tried to inform his father that the circumstances of those his father was comparing him with may be different from his. He further told his father that he did not want to do anything that would damage or bring their family's name into disrepute. On hearing this, his father replied, 'Shut up! You are talking rubbish. Go on, damage and bring the family's name into disrepute, if that is what it would take for you to do what your mates are doing. Please– "damage the family name"? Nonsense!' This is the kind of hostility and pressure from some families in Igbo land that lead a lot of feeble-minded relatives abroad into lives of crime. Suddenly the Igbo adage, *'ezi aha ka ego'*, meaning 'a good name is better than wealth' is ripped to shreds, and the belief now is that money cleanses a rotten image. One good thing, which is clear from the examples given, is that there are still plenty of principled, well-meaning Igbo people around, and to them I say, 'Hold on to your principles, hold on to your values and never give in or give up!' Never subscribe to the "if you can't beat them, join them" attitude. Take a stance that unequivocally affirms your position, making it impossible for you to shift from your position rather, convince others to join you. Even when they don't, simply remember the hen story, and stick with the hen not the cock. Seek for like minds and share your ideas and ideals. It might not be you that would implement those invaluable ideas but some other person who wants to see the right thing done. *After all one of the best managers in football (Jose Mourinho) never was a high profile player and the best boxers are never the best boxing coaches.*

Reasons why Igbo People must act NOW!

1. In Igbo land, as well as in the lands of many African societies, each Sunday many people mainly Christians carry their Bible to church, proclaiming their love for Christ, their love for one another, sharing in the peace of God and stating their belief in God Almighty. Very rarely would one find someone in Igbo land who would say, 'I am not a Christian' or 'I don't believe in God.' Those who may say that are usually very old and not physically capable of taking part in criminal activities, even if they so desired. It is then, a matter of surprise, shock and wonder to witness the level of armed robbery, kidnappings, ritualistic killings and atrocities being committed by some Igbo people on fellow Igbo people. Everyone's home ought to be a refuge, and a person should not have to 'pay their way' before having their home as a refuge. Too many reasons and excuses have been given as to why some of us are besieged in our own homes. No reason or excuse is good enough. As an Igbo person, be honest; do you feel that your home is a refuge?

2. In Igbo land, as in most developing countries, very rarely do people die a 'natural death', no matter how old or ill they are. It is always someone else that is responsible for the death of another. A mother who was ill for nearly three years was brainwashed by her son-in-law and daughter to believe that her late husband's brother caused her illness. She was warned not to go to hospital, as the attack was 'spiritual' and must be fought 'spiritually'. The woman was told to confront the perpetrator and that when she does so, the perpetrator would die. She was given a date when her late husband's brother would die. In the end, all the native and spiritual approaches

to curing her illness failed and at the eleventh hour, she decided to go to hospital but it was too late. She sadly passed away in 2005 and the man accused of causing the illness is still alive in 2012. The most shocking element to this event is that, those that brainwashed the dead woman are today eating from the same pot as the accused innocent man. The reason for this type of brainwashing is money, as the one doing the brainwashing receives a percentage of the money that has been paid to the 'prophet or voodoo man', as the person that brought the customer. Once anyone succumbs to this madness, they might as well consider themselves as 'finished', because the 'prophet or voodoo man' will continue to see and forecast doom and gloom for him or her and list out all that have to be provided (money and items) in order to avert an impending 'disaster'. Just like a predator, these voodoo men and prophets would first of all inject fear into their prey before going for the kill.

Just imagine, if the children of the dead woman believed (as some Igbo people would) that their uncle was responsible for their mother's death, the level of enemity, which would have ensued in that family. As the children to the late woman would seek to eliminate their uncle using any means possible; and then war would break out between cousins, all caused by the love of money, greed and false prophesy.

A couple came home from America to bury the wife's father. The husband left for America a few days before his wife. He did not realise that in one of his bags was his wife's passport. The man got to America and, as some men do, left his bags unpacked and went about his business. Three days before his wife's return to America, she began to look for her passport. As she was in a completely frantic state, in the belief that someone had stolen her passport, a child came running to her and said, 'Auntie, Auntie don't worry, there is a prophet who can come and tell you who stole your passport.' Auntie, in her desperation, only wanted answers; she couldn't wait for an answer and was not interested in how she got the answer. All she wanted was her passport by 'any means possible'. Therefore she begged the boy to bring the prophet as soon as possible.

On arrival, the prophet met with the woman. No one was privy to their discussion, so it was not possible to know whether the prophet asked her if she suspected anyone in the family in particular. However, it was certain that money exchanged hands. The prophet, who dressed up in a long white robe, went into action and paraded the compound, walking from one end of the wall to the other, chanting away. In full view of the villagers, who were interested in finding out who was in possession of the missing passport, the prophet spoke some words as though he was speaking in tongues, and charged himself up before pointing at one middle aged man as the one who stole the passport. The prophet said that the man was not only responsible for the missing passport but also responsible for all the bad things happening in the compound. The man lifted a chair and wanted to smash it on the prophet's head, but people held him back and saw him as merely reacting in denial of an act he had committed. The prophet warned him that if he weren't careful he would deal with him and make him 'vanish from the face of this earth'. The poor man was beaten up by the crowd, and the only reason he was not killed was because killing him would have meant the possible loss of the passport forever.

Therefore the woman paid the local police to torture the man until he produced the passport. The woman did not want to inform her husband, possibly because she did not want to be reminded about the number of times she had been careless with her valuables, but in the end, she summoned the courage and contacted her husband, who went through his bags and found her passport.

The above incident is a drop in the ocean compared to the true extent of this madness. People are going through pain, lives are lost and enemies are being made on a daily basis, due to false prophets and prophesy. This is total madness, people basing reality on fiction! This is the unjust and unnecessary suffering and death that make it impossible for silence to win the argument. This cannot be minimised, swept under the carpet, laughed off or condoned in any way, shape or form. Igbo people need help now, if it is not already late. The children are watching and copying. Igbo children are being handed dangerous batons and they can only take from what they see, perceive and feel. Why are Africans generally and Igbo people in particular, mistaking fiction for fact? Yes, it would border on insanity to believe there is good and deny there is bad, or believe that God exists and deny that Satan exists. However, there is too much credence given to the work of evil and believe in fiction. To the extent that, every good thing done by an individual is credited to God and every bad thing credited to Satan. The individual therefore loses all responsibility in their wilful action or inaction. In the developed, 'civilised' world, these concepts were thoroughly explored and researched before they were discarded and are used now strictly as fiction only. For anything to have credence in a 'civilised' world it should and must be evidence-based and scientifically proven. Yes, we accept that the things of the spirit have nothing to do with science. But I maintain that if there is anything useful in this shadow-chasing business of the Igbo and Africans in general, we would have been the last to know.

The question 'Why have mermaids swapped the Pacific and Atlantic Oceans and all the massive seas around the world for the little rivers and ponds in the third world?' was asked deliberately. Mermaids, from what we see of them in films, are beautiful creatures that enjoy space and freedom to express themselves. It is a surprise that none of the ships that frequent all these massive oceans and seas has ever reported seeing them, while on a regular basis some people in Igbo land claim to see them. A respected Igbo elder, who is one of their traditional ruler's advisers, once told me how his 'evil in-law' stopped his usual communication with his late brother by planting something beside his late brother's grave. He was unable to state how he got to know this, and could not answer my question, 'so do you mean this in-law of yours has the power to control both the dead and the living? 'Without doubting whether a human being can control the dead and the living, people claim to be able to spiritually see the future, visit and have meetings with God or Satan (depending on their persuasions), call out people who are somewhere else in the mirror or send a remote-controlled poison to someone wherever they may be. I just want to state what I would do if I could do any of these things, and I urge all people with these apparent skills, that I will call 'technology', to please, please, please do us a favour and mimic what I would do if I were in the shoes of the people who claim that they can do the things described above.

I would start by calling out from the mirror all our leaders and commanding them to subscribe to all the provisions and services they have laid out for the citizens of Nigeria, for example health care and education, and tell them that if they did not do this, then when I called them out again, they would not like the type of discussion I would have with them. I would remind all our leaders that, to date, I have not seen or heard that any foreign leader had come to Nigeria for their health care needs or sent any of their children here for their educational needs, so why must our leaders be different? If that failed, before I summoned them again, I would call out all the influential world leaders and tell them what they must do to better the lot of the children of this world and that if they did not do what I asked then they would not like the contents of my chat with them when next I call them out. If I had such power, I would rule the world and no one would ever know where I was ruling the world from. If we had all these 'technologies', why are so many cases in court waiting for evidence when we have people who can see the past and the future? I would ask for a fraction of the huge amount of money paid to lawyers and supply evidence to every difficult case in court.

Why isn't someone winning the lottery or the football pools every week, if some people can see the future? Wouldn't those who claim to be capable of doing these things benefit more from using it positively than deceiving the vulnerable and the children in our midst? What propels all these gimmicks is money, and I wonder why the people with these 'technologies' could not collect the $50 million bounty the Americans had for anyone who could provide them with the information leading to the capture of Osama Bin Laden. Well, they may not have heard about that opportunity and so lost out on it, so let us bring them more good news from which they stand to make a lot of money. There is at least £10 million on offer, and I am happy to add another £2,000, for information leading to the finding of Madeleine McCann (dead or alive), the little girl who went missing in Portugal in 2007. Why are we deceiving ourselves? When are we going to carry out a review to see whether the road upon which we travel leads anywhere, let alone our intended destination? Is the word 'review' only for theoretical, not practical, use in Africa in general and Igbo land in particular? Yes, there is evil, but no human being can act as God. All human beings are mere mortals destined to die irrespective of what position they occupy.

I want to categorically state that there are only two ways your fellow human being can harm you. These can happen through poisoning or violence. I challenge whosoever can do it any other way to come forth and display their wonders for the world to see. I maintain that if there is anything in this shadow we continue to pursue, we won't be the first to reach it. The 'first world' would occupy that position, and of course they have explored all these things and found there's nothing in them. That's why they only use them in films, for entertainment, but we have them as our reality.

As an ex-seminarian who did not get the calling and couldn't call or send myself, I say this to you with a total guarantee: every miracle and healing by Jesus Christ and all His disciples, as detailed in the Bible, were performed free of charge and Christ commanded all of us to do the same by saying, 'freely you received and freely you must give'. Even in the Old Testament of the Holy Bible, the story of Neman

257

and Elijah stands out to demonstrate that any healing from God is free. That's why, when anyone, irrespective of who they tell you they are, asks you for anything, including 'holy water' in order to heal or perform a miracle for you, rest assured that the person is not doing God's work. This does not mean you should not show gratitude or give thanks, but it is a matter of choice. Remember when Jesus Christ healed ten lepers and only one came to thank Him and He asked, 'Where are the remaining nine?' Although the one that came to thank Him did not present any gifts, Jesus was pleased with his appreciation.

Neman presented gifts to Elijah but Elijah refused the gifts, and we all know what happened to the servant of Elijah who ran after Neman and lied, saying that Elijah had changed his mind and wanted the gifts. So to offer any appreciation when you receive healing from God, whether by presenting a gift of any sort or by just offering thanks, is a matter of choice. Anyone commanding you to give them something or requesting even a candle from you in order to heal you is not a servant of God. As a Christian, that's one of the signs you look for in order to know who is a 'wolf in sheep's clothing'.

Our mistaking fiction for reality knows no bounds or limit, that's why, no matter how honestly and genuinely an Igbo man's wealth was obtained through hard work, there would still be some envious and lazy people who would say 'o gworo ogwu ego', meaning 'he obtained his wealth by ritualistic means'. If you happen by be a successful woman in your chosen career as a lawyer, engineer, broadcaster, doctor or banker, for example, then those who are envious of your achievements and find themselves unable to work hard, would claim you got where you are by sleeping with all the 'powerful men'. They would not consider that they could sleep with all the powerful men on this planet but that would never give them the qualifications needed to do any of these jobs.

This category of people also do not believe that there is no evidence anywhere in the world that a dead person can produce money rather, if proper analysis and a detailed autopsy is carried out after a suspicious death, especially those where the head or private parts have been removed, it can be scientifically proven that there are other factors at play other than a dead body producing money. The problem is that life in itself has lost its meaning to those charged with protecting it. Therefore, 'wasting money' on the dead in terms of the cost of autopsy and so on, is certainly not part of the agenda. Of course, the human mind never tolerates a vacuum; therefore seeing a dead person in any part of Africa whose private part have been removed can only be classified as a 'ritual' act, if there is no scientific proof of what really took place.

The time people spend talking about material things, fictitious things and other people, neglecting their own needs and discussing and sharing ideas are at the root of our backwardness. The time they spend discussing others, they could invest in doing something useful for themselves, their family and society. They live a life of lies, fiction and deception and pass this nonsensical way of life to their children for further replication.

3. In Igbo land, as in some other African societies, a lot of people cannot wait to tell you about their achievements in life, and attribute all their successes

primarily to themselves. The same people, in the same breath, will point at someone else as being responsible for anything that goes wrong in their lives, absolving themselves of any responsibility for their own failings. Remember blaming of others on issues relevant to you, means you have failed on whatever the issue is, as you never attributed your success to anyone.

4. Take a look at your local primary school and ask whether you would send your dog there, in view of the risks posed to health and safety by the structural damage. Look at the children, past and present, in your locality and see how uncultured they have become, due to our collective failure. Think about how this may worsen in future for our children. They lack moral values and ethics and have not been exposed to proper academic foundation. Parents, the government and our society, at large, continue to abandon substance in favour of chasing shadows. Children have only seen and copied what adults have shown them, that is that our 'values and morals' revolve solely around money. Therefore they are not interested in education anymore, and even the proper facilities to educate them are non-existent. What is at fault? Is it the unpaid or poorly paid, half -baked teachers? Is it the poor educational materials and equipment or the dilapidated structures that threaten their health and safety? Many generations would prop up from these children, who will only hand over what they have received.

5. Nothing in life reminds us of our mortality than the death of someone. This is reflected in the Igbo sayings, 'okuko lee aka eji abo ukwa' and 'nga madu na akwa ozu, ka ona'kwa onwe ya', meaning, 'the home chicken should observe how the bush chicken

is being cut to pieces, as it will receive the same when it gets to its turn' and 'where one is mourning someone, they are mourning themselves.'

So, despite these wise sayings, how come in Igbo land today some of us now see events such as death as an 'opportunity' to commit heinous crimes against the bereaved, who need our support and sympathy? In some cases the corpse is kidnapped for a ransom. There are numerous examples of these terrible and terrifying incidents, and it is so close to home that almost everyone has been affected directly or indirectly.

On 10th September 2005, following the burial of my mother, armed robbers laid an ambush and gave me the chase of my life. It was only a miracle that I, with four of my siblings escaped unhurt; it was even more of a miracle because during the chase the vehicle I was driving broke down. But the Hands of the Almighty God kept us safe, as He brought confusion to the people who were chasing me. When one lives in England, or another developed country, where everything seems to work, it is harder to notice or realise when miracles occur.

On 13th October 2010, as the remains of my cousin and best friend Kingsley, to whom I dedicated this book, arrived at Port-Harcourt International Airport from London, two of my cousins, who had come back home from Abuja for his funeral, were kidnapped for a ransom. There are numerous sad stories like these in our society today, some leading to fatalities as armed robbers descend on the bereaved and sometimes kill someone or people in the process. These incidents send shock waves through the sane mind, and show the level of moral decadence in Igbo land today.

Nothing is more shocking than the fact that one can no longer bury one's loved ones in peace. It is even more shocking that today people have become immune to these evil actions, and not only expect but prepare for them. This preparation means that the whole area close to the bereaved family is flooded with armed police and security operatives.

6. In most places where there is kidnapping for ransom, one is usually made aware of a particular course of action that is being pursued by those committing the crime (though nothing can justify such outrageous acts of evil against humanity), even in the Niger Delta area where kidnapping started in Nigeria; they say why they are doing it, and in the process draw some sympathy from certain sections of society. Everyone is waiting to hear the course of action that the Igbo people who copy these acts are pursuing as they are committing such acts against their own people, dehumanising and destroying lives, preventing and destroying enterprise, ruining the economic prospects of Igbo land and shattering trust, which is the key ingredient for progress. The poorest people in Africa are not the Igbo, so the cause cannot be poverty. If that theory were to stand, then it would apply to any other people as poor, or poorer than the Igbo people.

7. Looking at the three major ethnic groups in Nigeria, the Igbo people are peculiar in our approach to life these days. No Hausa person would ever think of killing another Hausa person. Their religion alone prevents such an act, and it is only when someone has gone against their religious doctrines and traditions that the person is punished by the Hausa people collectively. When a Yoruba person kills another Yoruba person, one will find that they had

been fighting over something, for example a land dispute. But what does it take for an Igbo person to kill a fellow Igbo person? Can greed, envy or jealousy be enough? It is important to appreciate that the deliberate killing of an individual is usually done by or through someone who, is either related or close to the victim. It is a well-known fact that only by accident or insanity would a total stranger harm someone. People are known to have lost their lives just by trying to assist their uncles who become jealous that it is not their own child but their brother's child that is coming to the rescue.

To date in Igbo land, Nigeria and many African countries, people cannot see the merits of opposition, constructive criticism and the benefits of controversy. How can anyone broaden their horizons, learn more, see 'beyond their nose', develop and improve themselves without seeing what they need to improve on? The civilised world has developed the way it is today because of how it nurtures and encourages constructive opposition, criticism and debate on issues. Because Igbo people, Nigerians and Africans in general are not encouraging these things, we continue to go round in circles chasing shadows and focusing only on materials things. We seek to destroy any opposition in our quest to retain the status quo that favours us. We think that it is more important and relevant to ask questions such as, 'Nnah what type of car do you drive and what type of house do you live in?' People are known to have paid a terrible price for saying what they truly believe is the truth. This led me to state in my local church that although we know the story of the death of Jesus Christ so well, and everyone seems to condemn those that killed Christ, if the same scenario were to be repeated in my home town and most places in the African continent, so long as Christ's father remained a carpenter and we knew when and where He was born, we would kill Him quicker than those we condemn did. Considering his poor background and age, once He started telling us what we are doing wrong, we would surely repeat 'ten fold' what those we condemn did. He would NEVER have lived to anywhere near the age of thirty-three. *The good thing about the mysteries surrounding death is, we must all die! But what you don't know is whether the person you paid someone to kill or you killed yourself would be the person to welcome you, when you arrive at the destination you sent them. Think!*

Here lie the true causes of Igbo people's problem

1. The renunciation of our forefather's rules, sayings and guiding principles. For example, there are adages like *'nwata nganga ka okenye isi awo ihe mara, nwanne ka enyi, Okenye anaghi ano n'ulo ewu a muo n'obu, nwak'ego, aru gba'fo ya awuo omen'ala'*, meaning, 'a child that has travelled far and wide is more knowledgeable than a grey-haired old person, a sibling is better than a friend, an old person cannot be at home and watch a pregnant she-goat delivered tied to a stake, a child is more valuable than money, evil practised for a year becomes the tradition.'

In the Holy Bible, there are ample examples to show us that wisdom is not synonymous with old age. In fact there is an indication that God chose and used the younger more than the older person. Take a look at Kane and Abel, Esau and Jacob; Joseph was the second youngest amongst Jacob's children, David the last of Jesse's children and Samuel was only between twelve and thirteen years of age when God called him. Above all, our Lord and Saviour Jesus Christ was between thirty and thirty-three years of age when He performed all His miracles. Even in our world today, most 'real leaders' are chosen based on their ability, not age or how much money they have.

Bill Clinton was thirty-two when he became governor and forty-six when he became president of the United States of America in 1993. Tony Blair was just forty-three when he swept into office as British prime minister in 1997. Dmitry Medvedev was forty-two when he took office as Russian president in 2008. Barrack Obama was forty-seven when he became president of the United States of America in 2009, and David Cameron was only forty-three years of age when he assumed office as prime minister of the UK in 2010.

In Igbo land these days, no matter how much wisdom one has; it would have no relevance if there is no wealth and/or old age to go with it. One's wisdom can be dismissed by comments like, 'He or she is only a small boy or girl of yesterday. How can a child from that retched family tell us what to do?' This means that either the retired, redundant 'old brain' or the empty head with a pocket full of money will provide the way forward. This is as good as riding in an aircraft piloted by a blind person.

In Igbo land once a child, always a child. No wonder I was not nominated a father when I needed one. No one bothered at that time whether I returned to school as a hard-up student or not. But when I started working, left for England, became a father of four children, was older than David Cameron when he became leader of the Conservative Party and when I had almost become an old man myself, a father was assigned and imposed on me. People suddenly became interested in my arrival and departure, to the extent that they complained if my itinerary was not disclosed to them. I wonder why? I am interested in knowing what has changed and what we are teaching our children by this our approach to life? I would argue that it is a life devoid of reality, decency, integrity, honour, principles, dignity and logic. Why do people want to reap where they have not sown?

2. There is a lack of humility, and this gives rise to a problem with using our God-given gifts and/or talent to oppress and intimidate instead of, for service.

3. Our inability to reflect and project that is, to be reflective and try to plan for the future based on our analysis of what we see happening today. This, forces us to act based on 'here and now, get-rich-quick syndrome' which leads us to be irrational and do things that destroy the fabric of our society and trust on one another. This is the reason why, when it comes to business of any kind, Igbo people are likely to fear their own people because everyone tries to conceal an agenda based on individualised 'selfish' ideas in order to 'outwit' the other. In our self-centred way of looking at life we begin to plot without focusing on the overall purpose, principle and objective of what we want to achieve. A young, successful Igbo businessman who was based in Lagos returned to his home town and decided to take his cousin, who was at home doing nothing, back with him. When they got back to Lagos, the businessman introduced his cousin into his business and gradually integrated him into it. The cousin very quickly mastered the business, and without the knowledge of the young businessman the cousin informed his suppliers that

he could offer them a better deal, compared to what the young business man was offering them. To the awful shock of the businessman, his cousin broke away and robbed him of his business. This is the type of behaviour that makes it hard for Igbo people who are successful to bring their own people into what they are doing. And those in need of help feel that their relatives who are in good positions are not willing to help them, and this situation becomes a 'double-edged sword'. This is what some Igbo people call being 'clever' or 'sharp', but at what cost?

4. An immense love of money above any- and everything else, to such a level that our contemporaries say, 'The only way one can be sure that an Igbo man is truly dead is if you present money and he refuses to get up.' Others have said, to my annoyance, that 'If one is looking to make money and visits a country but does not see an Igbo person there, then one must vacate that country because not seeing an Igbo person means there is no money to be made there.' If this is true then it means that for an average Igbo person anything is possible so long as the price is right. I would love to be able to beg to differ, but not when we hear of stories such as what happened in Ihitte-Uboma local government area in Imo State in 2009, when a young man killed his mother and cut off her breast. When he was caught, he said, 'I have suffered enough.' It soon became known that a native doctor had told him that getting his mother's breast was all he needed in order to end his hardship and turn round his fortune in life.

Of all our problems noted above, the main source of our problem is a lack of humility

It is a lack of humility that generates the level of madness we have witnessed in our Igbo society today. It is a lack of humility that forces some church leaders in Igbo land to fight for a diocese because they want to become a bishop. This is the main cancer that is about to wipe us off the face of the earth if we fail to understand it and take action against it now! The baseline is that we are human beings: nothing more, nothing less. We come in and go out as human beings. Everything acquired in between is either stripped off by others or by forces of nature. Saddam Hussein and Muammar Gaddafi, the late leaders of Iraq and Libya respectively, could attest to this fact if they were here with us today. In fact, Hosni Mubarak of Egypt can attest to this. Everything that makes us what we become, be it wealth, education or title is either acquired or conferred on us, as such; they are not ours for keeps. Therefore, whether we acquired them or they are conferred on us by hook or by crook, we must learn to use these acquisitions to serve not to oppress.

It is mainly in Igbo land that division of labour is only taught in theory, but not applied in practice. An Igbo person could be the first person to notice a dirty environment and say, 'Oh, this place is too dirty', but would not want anything to do with the person that cleans the place. The same person is likely to be the first to say, Come on, get out of here, 'ordinary cleaner!' This is the way we Igbo people treat our fellow brothers and sisters who are not 'wealthy' Showing too much reverence to the 'rich' simply forces some of the younger ones to do whatever it takes, including, kidnapping, stealing and killing, to get money so they can earn some respect, as respect only comes with money according to the Igbo people's convoluted philosophy.

This lack of humility is truly big for us, and if we can understand, appreciate and do something positive about it then our lives will begin to take on a new shape.

It is this lack of humility that forces the Igbo people to fight and kill each other in their quest for money and power. Ask the Igbo people to produce a presidential candidate and you will see everyone wanting to argue about whether they are capable or not, because they all know what they would do, which is not different from what the other person would do. The reason behind all this is that an Igbo person uses anything they acquire to oppress. Consider two classmates who had been friends from school and know each other by their first names. Once one of them becomes something as 'important' as a local government chairman the schoolmate can count his or herself lucky if the now local government chairman remembers their name, let alone has anything in common with him again. This is just a local government chairman, not a governor or president. Contrast this with our contemporaries. No matter the height that an Hausa or a Yoruba person attains, when they get back to their roots they remain the same person. They prostrate to their elders, sit on the floor and eat with their people. Money and/or power will never make them outgrow their culture or tradition. That's why they can collectively send one person to represent them in the knowledge that they won't be oppressed; they use their position to serve.

In Igbo land, people pursue careers and interests, not necessarily to serve or achieve the set objectives of the career or interest they are pursuing but for selfish purposes. For example, a young man may decide to join the Nigerian armed forces; however, his first consideration may not have anything to do with the protection and defending of his country but is because he wants to put on the uniform in order to be able to intimidate people or carry out 'jump like nwa awo' (military drills) on his uncle, who is having a land dispute with his father. The use of what we acquire to oppress is the reason why, when a neighbour pretends to be sorry for the theft of your car you are not only sad that you lost your car but depressed that the thieves did not take your neighbour's car as well. As your neighbour secretly rejoices and your depression increases, the thieves are encouraged to do more. For a 'rational' person, the pain one feels for such a loss should make one do whatever it takes to stop the thieves so that no one else should be made to feel this way. For example, speaking on BBC Radio 5 on 16th February 2012, Gabrielle Brown (a rape victim), who had fought tirelessly to get her attacker (who had also attacked many other women) deported, made it clear that the victory was for all the women who could now walk free in the knowledge that this man can no longer attack them in this country. She fought so that no one else here will go through the pain she went through. In our own case, when we suffer a mishap, we 'subconsciously' want everyone to suffer the same.

What is it an Igbo person acquires that they won't use to oppress? Is it money, is it education or power? Once an Igbo man or woman has any of these or a combination of these they are more likely to use them negatively against their fellow Igbo people, saying, 'Do you know who I am? I will show you.' The same person will suddenly turn into a jelly once a little headache strikes or their bladder full and they cannot find where to ease themselves. The same person may have been on a plane with me, flying from Port-Harcourt to Lagos in 2010, when the turbulence was so bad that the aircraft turned into a 'prayer' house, and the true vulnerability of man was shown on everyone's faces. Well, I was so moved by the experience that when the plane landed I said to all the passengers, 'I don't blame you all, because even our president would have felt the way we did on this flight, vulnerable and helpless. However, I guess now we have landed it is time for us to start feeling all-powerful and mighty again.'

Many Igbo people find it difficult to appreciate how lucky they are; if for nothing else, they should remember and give thanks that the life and good health they enjoyed whilst gaining whatever they perceive as their achievements. Had their health or life (which they have no control over) failed them, their achievements would have been guaranteed to remain a dream that never materialised.

There will always be some exceptions to the rules, but our people generally look at things subjectively and are 'here-and-now' orientated rather than looking at life objectively with the overall interest and long-term gain for all being no part of their consideration. That's why, in most cases, our competitions are very unhealthy. Have we not heard of or seen situations in which people eliminate others by assassination or other methods if they feel that the other person is doing better or attracting more customers than them, in order to make 'second best' best? Have we not seen situations where people, due to envy, decapitate someone in order to render them useless at the expense of everyone else? A case in point was when Doctor Mbuko was shot in both eyes at Aba, in Abia State. Without going through all of the different theories that emerged as to what must have led to this terrible episode, it was highly likely that envy, jealousy and wickedness were at the root of that shameful act, because blinding him in two eyes made him work less effectively as a doctor. However, the real losers were his patients (you and I) and our society at large. Remember, not everyone can save life and saving life is one of life's most difficult things, but everyone can destroy life because it is one of the easiest things to do. In some parts of our society, people in all walks of life, including trading, do all sorts of unhealthy things to prevent their rivals from attracting customers, seeking to make the 'second best' best through the process of elimination. With this type of attitude, it is virtually impossible for us to progress as a people. Why are we destroying and wasting our own and each other's lives? The other two prominent ethnic groups in Nigeria, the Yoruba and Hausa, are not the reason why the Igbo people cannot trust each other. They are not the reason why some Igbo people abroad cannot give information about when they are coming or going back; they are not the ones making the Igbo people play 'hide and seek' with one another. There is no way we can progress and reach our potential as a people if we cannot trust each other. People have gone from being 'their brother's keepers' to being 'their own keepers'. We cannot be brothers and sisters only when in crisis and then after the crisis we go back to destroying ourselves. A kingdom divided against itself can never stand! We cannot continue to blame others for our own woes. Yes, others may have played a part in destroying the bonds and traditions we had that kept us together, but we have had enough lessons and enough independence to know what we should and shouldn't do. When we kidnap our own brother, steal from them, trade in one another for money and treat each other with contempt, it is not our colonial masters, the Hausas or Yorubas that are responsible but ourselves. To deal with our issues properly we must fully appreciate the depth of our problem, lest we treat this 'malaria' with 'pain killer'. The Yorubas and Hausas are our brothers and sisters in one sovereign nation, Nigeria. They would rather have us work positively with them, as a united front with sound ideologies to make Nigeria a better place for its citizens, instead of making a mockery of ourselves by trading in one another for money. We must rip to shreds the picture we have now and quickly go back to the drawing board! According to Billy Graham 'when wealth is lost, nothing is lost; when health is lost, something is lot; when character is lost, all is lost.'

The saying, 'He who knows not and knows not that, he knows not is a fool' indicates that you shouldn't waste your time in teaching this kind of person. However, 'He who knows not and knows that he knows not is a wise man' indicates that you could teach this kind of person and h/she would learn. This is all so critical at this stage for all Igbo people at home and abroad. We need to be wise and tackle all these things that are setting us back. Otherwise we will continue to justify, condone and tolerate destroying ourselves by chasing shadows, minimising our ills or using sweeping statements like 'these things are not only happening in Igbo land'. The fact remains that those that brought kidnapping for example in Nigeria were pursuing a course (whether right or wrong) but we are kidnapping and killing ourselves! By implication, we are destroying the prospects of our children and future generation. He who has ears let them hear, BE HONEST AND SHAME THE DEVIL.

Our traditions must be beneficial to those they are meant to serve! We must revert back to our forefather's objectives in setting the guiding traditions around death, marriage, conferring of titles and how wealth is dealt with. We have sustained bad customs for more than is necessary and bad customs have now become our tradition, as Igbo adage has it '*aru gbaa afo ya aburu omenala*'.

Death

In the past, the death of someone automatically brought about sadness and sympathy for the bereaved. Igbo people looked out for each other and tried to alleviate the burden on the bereaved by cooking, bringing drinks and giving financial support. Today, some Igbo people see death as the time to make demands and demonstrate wealth, and people lose sight of the grieving involved for the bereaved. Some individuals, groups, associates and extended family members even make demands of the bereaved. Some people will be ready to fight if their demands are not met. Following the death, the bereaved is already burdened by the cost of the funeral and the pain of losing their loved one(s). We must therefore ensure that we do not add to their burden but rather find ways to alleviate it.

Marriage

In the past, everything to do with marriage was traditional. Things that were not traditionally made did not usually feature. Today everything is involved, including 'love *nwantit*' (little motorbike). It is widely believed that a young man who sets out to get married is in the process of starting a huge project. No project will be too big for such a young man. Therefore it is proper to have a tradition geared towards helping the couple build a foundation by not draining their pocket; but the reality is that the bride's family insists on a high bride prize and an elaborate ceremony.

In our traditional marriages, we need to have a standard mode of execution based on each community's traditions, with nothing foreign included. We do not need to increase the burden but should find ways to assist the couple as they face civil and/or church wedding costs. We must refrain from seeing the traditional rites as a moneymaking venture or a test to prove how ready the groom is. Readiness to marry has very little to do with money. Some men who were financially poor become rich after marriage.

Traditional Titles

Traditional titles used to be inherited or conferred based on an astute knowledge of tradition, uprightness and service to one's community. In those days, as stated earlier, the title 'Nze', for example, was only conferred on people whose yes was yes and no was no. Today it is all about money, in most cases. A person can be as upright as they like, but they still won't be given a title; in fact the more upright a person is today, the more they become an 'outcast' and are in danger of losing everything, including their lives, as they are perceived as an obstacle that prevents wrongdoings flourishing. Many people with chieftaincy titles struggle to perform the simple traditional presentation and breaking of cola nuts? How many Chiefs today are not involved in kidnapping and the various atrocities going on in Igbo land? How many of them have not stood on the fence or given false testimony that led to an innocent person being punished for what they did not do? How many of them would not say one thing to a person and another thing to another person on a particular issue? How many of them understand 'integrity, dignity, etiquette and principle' and show these attributes themselves?

Solutions To Igbo People's Crisis

We must begin by asking ourselves the question, what psychological damage are we doing to our children with our 'money is all and fictionalised' approach to life? What evil seeds are we sowing in our children and what dreadful future are we designing for them and the future generation? Are we not invoking anarchy by walking along these paths? We have led them to believe that money is all they need and it doesn't matter how they acquire it. We have led them to believe that when good thing happens to them, it is their own making but when bad thing happens, one of their relatives is responsible. This has created a climate of distrust amongst our people. We have used every gift and achievement to oppress instead of give service, sending wrong and negative messages to our children. We have left our children 'uncultured' in pursuit of academic excellence and financial acquisition, forgetting that an uncultured child, no matter how educated (academically) is an empty vessel and not fit for purpose. The biggest threat to humanity!

From our religious leaders to our political leaders, these are the messages we passing and sending out to our children. We have made them have no respect for anyone who is poor or even hate themselves and their parents if they are not rich. They have been led to believe that if they do not have money their views will not count and they will be treated like outcasts. In turn, this has led some of them to adopt 'I must have money at all costs and by all means possible' attitude.

For a positive change to occur in Igbo land there must be an acknowledgement that we have got our priorities wrong. This cannot be done by minimising, denying, generalising and ignoring our crisis. A full and honest understanding of our problems must happen; otherwise it will be as if paracetamol is being used to treat cancer. If a person who has lost the way is to find their destination they must locate their starting point first; not knowing where they started from makes it impossible to know, let alone find, where they want to be.

All efforts to find solutions to our particular problems should primarily be geared towards the youths and children, because changing an adult's personality or behaviour is one of life's most difficult tasks. In fact, psychologists inform us that, it would be easier to change the stripes of a zebra than change an adult's personality. Having said that, it is a well-known fact that nothing in life is absolute. There will always be exceptions to the rule; for example there will be some adults whose personality can be altered. But for this to happen, in the first instance, our churches should return to God and rededicate themselves to the service of God and man and not the service of money. They must take a leaf from the Archbishop of the Catholic Archdiocese of Owerri (The Most Rev. Anthony J.V. Obinna), who seems to be a lone voice in the wilderness in pursuit of salvation for Imo and Igbo people by instituting an annual Igbo cultural event called Odenigbo.

Another important example of Archbishop Obinna's moral commitment occurred on the day of the burial of his mother. On that day there were cows and all manner of presents from friends, well-wishers and the congregations of churches under his stewardship. The Archbishop told those who had come to commiserate with him at the burial of his mother that now he is motherless, that all those gifts and presents, like, cows, goats, money should be sent to the motherless babies homes. This true apostle of our Lord Jesus Christ has been unrelenting in his pursuit of peace, equity and justice for all mankind and seeking out of the 'least' amongst us, as Christ instructed. And in doing so he is storing up his treasures above, where moth and rust do not destroy and where thieves do not break in and steal.

The Bible makes it clear that if the salt loses its taste it must be thrown away and cannot be used for anything else. Our church leaders must stop glorifying money and start preaching the gospel and letting God's words do their job. Church is for the salvation of man, not a fund-raising organisation or a place to seek out the 'highest bidder'. Yes! It is better to give than to receive, and it is good to give generously; but the widow's mite should still count. Let your congregation know the reward for honest givers without heaping praises on the person that gave the most; for only God knows the true means from which they had given, and the God who rewards in secret would reward everyone according to their deeds in secret. If the money has been obtained through devious means and you are praising the individual, then you are encouraging them to continue in their immoral acts and inspiring others to do whatever it takes so long as they donate to your church. If that person is a kidnapper, killer or thief you are indirectly playing a part by encouraging them. Jesus Christ never acknowledged those donors who gave a lot, but recognised the widow. If you lead, be a servant as Christ was and as he instructed us to be. He demonstrated this by washing His Disciples' feet.

For our politicians in Eastern Nigeria, an example of what good stewardship is about has been shown by the current Governor of Imo State Owelle Rochas Okorocha, who built a school for financially deprived children even before becoming governor. Here is a man who understands that the test of a civilised society is solely based on how the vulnerable, especially children, are catered for. As governor, he has made the healthcare of the Imo people his priority in the knowledge that without good health one cannot achieve anything. For the first time in Imo State the ambulance service could become a service for the living not the dead. The governor has seen the inhuman situation accident victims face on a day-to-day basis in Imo State and other parts of Nigeria, where the dying depend on 'good Samaritans' with no medical training to ferry them to hospital. This governor has also given free education to the children of Imo State. The challenge confronting this governor and all the governors in the east is huge due to decades of neglect, embezzlement of state funds and abuse of power. Yes, there will always be those critics, but we must be patient and rally around this man who is like a breath of fresh air. So long as he carries on along this path, Imo State will become a better place to live and to do business in.

Both primary and secondary schools in Igbo land need to have Igbo culture built into the curriculums. The education system must not only teach students how to add and subtract, it must teach them how to share. It must teach them how to be considerate, build trust and value human life. It must teach students that the greatest asset and treasure of any society is human beings. Furthermore, the education system must inculcate in students the idea that invention, creativity and ability to manufacture goods and products is not only where the wealth is, but also where legacy is made. Students must learn that being consumers alone is an empty way of life. Academic education without sound moral base and cultural identity is like flying an aircraft blind. **An 'uncultured' child poses the biggest danger to humanity, irrespective of how academically educated s/he is**!

The crucial thing I hope to see is all the Igbo-speaking states electing at least one person per state forming a think-tank committee to review our culture and traditions with a view to harmonising and standardising them. The traditions and culture should lay more emphasis on community rather than individualistic lifestyle. When the community is healthy, individuals within it become healthy. The community emphasis must be geared towards embedding sound cultural and moral ethics in our children. Our children need to learn how to be good citizens and be their sister's and brother's keeper; there need to be set stages when every Igbo child must undertake a particular cultural activity geared toward shared values, irrespective of where the child is born or lives or the status of their parents. For example, it could be made mandatory that every Igbo person needs to observe something like a 'new yam festival', and there would be learning objectives set for that day which every Igbo child would hear and learn about. It is the tradition, culture and norms of society that shape the individuals within it. The chaos we have today is because each individual does his or her own thing. Ask ten people how to boil an egg and see what answers come back. We must place the needs of the community above the needs of the individual and learn to value and respect one another simply as 'human beings', irrespective of how much money we have, how educated we are or how 'good-looking' we are. We must learn to be grateful for whatever we have acquired and use it to serve God and man, not to oppress others.

THOSE WHO MASK OR COVER UP EVIL, ARE EVIL THEMSELVES. THOSE WHO SAY THIS IS NOT THE RIGHT PLACE TO RAISE THESE MATTERS SHOULD TELL THE WORLD WHERE THEY HAVE RAISED IT AND WHAT THEY ARE DOING ABOUT IT, AS THE CARNAGE CONTINUES. THOSE WHO SAY WE SHOULD PRETEND OR WE SHOULD KEEP SILENT IN THE FACE OF THIS EVIL NEED TO TAKE A GOOD LOOK AT THEMSELVES IN THE MIRROR. OUR CHILDREN NEED AND DESERVE A BETTER FUTURE; A KINDRED, VILLAGE, TOWN, LOCAL GOVERNMENT, STATE AND COUNTRY THEY CAN BE PROUD OF. WE CANNOT CONTINUE TO LET THEM DOWN.

'The history of human civilization is replete with contributions made by intellectuals of various disciplines in the form of critique, analyses and recommendations that have given rise to remarkable social, economic, cultural and attitudinal reforms. *Men and women of ideas usually converge in times of social and political upheavals to be acolytes in a march to a new order'* (Simon Okafor in Ezeani, Emefiena 2012, *emphasis added*). It is then fair to say that, civilization would be far fetched in any society where this is not applicable. In life, it is the case that people who face more challenges and are determined to deal with their challenges, achieve more but those who have everything led out for them achieve little or nothing; hence necessity is the mother of all inventions. This very fact lies at the heart of Africa backwardness in general and that of the Igbo people in particular.

All the governments in Igbo land and its citizens (men, women and children) at home or abroad, must make ridding of themselves of this cancer called kidnapping their sole, singular and only priority. How can a human being be sleeping with a deadly cobra? The Maslow's hierarchy of needs must apply. We must have our psychological needs (life) and feel safe before anything else. There is no need for building roads, hospitals, schools and other infrastructures when, the people that would use these amenities would either be kidnappers or kidnapped. We must concentrate fully and sort this evil out because even the kidnappers themselves risk being kidnapped one day and their children and loved ones would suffer the same faith, if this trend is allowed to continue. This evil cannot be treated like any other because; it threatens to destroy our very existence.

My Nigerian Child

One does not need to be a rocket scientist to know that problems accumulated for decades cannot be solved overnight. If a problem is not nipped in the bud it is likely to become deep-rooted; and when it becomes deep-rooted, uprooting it becomes difficult and hazardous. Problems abound in every sphere of life, in the home and the community, the state, the nation and the world at large. These problems can be man-made or natural. In terms of problems confronting a nation like Nigeria, one can say they are mainly man-made. Take, for instance, the much talked about corruption said to be bedevilling the country. Corruption rears its head in every country of the world, but the way it is handled or perceived can be different. The only peculiarity of Nigeria's corruption is that whereas corruption is usually underground in many other nations, it is bold and brazen in Nigeria. This is because corruption in Nigeria can go unpunished, while in most countries the reverse is the case. The other alarming aspect of it is that one is likely to get into trouble by trying to be upright and not corruptible, as one is then seen as being in the way of those who 'benefit' from corruption. That is why you hear terms such as, 'chop I chop' 'man know man' in Nigeria.

As a Nigerian, I feel deeply concerned about what we are handing down to our children, who are potentially our future leaders. In our quest to occupy the best houses and drive the best cars we have negated true life values and become very short-sighted, with dire consequences for our children's prospects in life. The pursuit of power, materialism and vanity have made a lot of Nigerian parents neglect their duties and responsibilities by abdicating their roles as parents to 'house maids' who themselves are in desperate need of being parented. The pursuit of materialism and power has made a lot of Nigerian parents abandon their fundamental role of impressing sound moral values on their children. Nigeria is a country blessed with all manner of human talents and material resources: it is the 'giant of Africa'. What has become of us, that we view our country as a CAKE, with everyone rushing forward with a big knife and a container to cut out their own share, and in the process destroying our lives and those of our children? Even if our country has, metaphorically, become a cake, then it is fair to say that someone or a group of people made that cake, and if another cake is not made the one already made is bound to be finished one day. The question is, who is or who will be making the next cake?

My heart sinks when I see so many people queuing up for political and public office who have no interest in serving the people, but who are totally fixated on how wealthy they would become. Some of these people have no proof of anything they have done in the past by way of a service to the community. It is my contention that the average Nigerian lacks vision. If there is not a lack of vision, how can one justify a person looting billions of naira, sometimes dollars or even pounds from the coffers of the nation? This is money that could provide basic amenities for our hospitals and schools – funds that could be used to ensure the welfare of our children and safe childbirth for our pregnant mothers. This lack of insight and vision is magnified when an individual looting the money makes it clear that the reason for the looting is to ensure that his or her children and their children's children will not suffer. But guess what, the reality is that in some cases no family member knows where these monies are kept, as the looter keeps it a secret. Some of the looters believe that writing a will would mean inviting death, so they don't have any will prepared. Furthermore, the looters sometimes subconsciously believe that death would give plenty of notice and 'a week or two before I die I will tell my wife or children where the money is'. Having interviewed some Nigerian bankers, I learnt that a lot of dormant accounts with very large balances exist and no one makes any claims of ownership of the money because the owners have passed on without a trace. Who knows what is happening with foreign accounts owned by such people? Just imagine, these are the same individuals who claim that the reason for looting is 'I don't want my children or family to suffer the way I did.' They have forgotten that in spite of what they perceived as suffering, they still worked hard and got to where they were before starting to loot. Furthermore, they have forgotten that those born with silver spoons in their mouths usually lack the ability to work hard and achieve. As my late father put it, 'Those born with silver spoons in their mouths are more likely not to have the skills and discipline to work hard and are likely to use shovels in wasting the wealth their parents toiled to acquire with spoons' (Nacho, 2010) or see a tribute to an awesome father on page 102. A lot of people who acquire wealth because they do not want any of their descendants to suffer seem to think that, despite being dead they will somehow be present to observe how the wealth is being utilised. Some, whilst still alive, will be doing certain things subconsciously in the 'deluded' belief that they will be able to observe the number of people that would gather at their funeral.

In Nigeria, some parents are not ashamed to use money to secure their children's places at university and/or to buy their degree certificates. Our nation, as a result, has a lot of half and un-baked graduates, though many of these have been produced as a result of regular strikes due to the non-payment of lecturers. The truth is, in any civilised world (discussed below) those who become millionaires due to their own endeavours don't usually throw money at their children, use money to buy certificates or secure their children places in higher institutions. The quality and standard of education is not compromised by anything, no matter how wealthy one's parents are. Even in the royal family they ensure that every child born within it passes through every milestone and maintains as normal a life-style as possible. They insist on ensuring that every child's life is well structured in accordance with the traditions, which is set to ensure the good and wellbeing of citizens.

Just as with Jews, there are stages and set objectives for every stage in a child's life, male and female. These objectives and stages must be fulfilled in a structured way whether your parents are millionaires or paupers. They understand that any uncultured soul is likely to present a serious risk to themselves and/or others and are likely to operate outside the norms of society. It is a well-accepted fact that nothing guarantees a crime-free society, but in societies where there are proper structures in place and effective law enforcement and judicial systems, crime is usually low.

All Nigerian parents need to know that the best and fastest way to damage a child is to stop the child from learning the day-to-day chores of life (independent living skills), and letting the maids do their work and depriving them of moral values. Why is it that once the average Nigerian finds some money in their pocket or gets into any position of power, they become more likely to sever their family bonds by dispatching their children abroad? Some of these children never return, and when they do, they hide or travel with escorts in fear, and end up becoming strangers in their own nation. In my position as an approved mental health professional, I have sadly taken part in the detention of many young Nigerian men and women whose background history often included the following: 'parents live in Nigeria, came to England to study, started to abuse drugs, used Facebook and the internet, lived with a guardian'. It would be very interesting to even know the exact date when the underpants bomber (Umar Farouq Abdulmutallab) started living on his own in the United Kingdom, in order to appreciate the conditions he may have found himself in.

As Nigerians, we know that the way in which most 'rich' parents bring up their children, that is, 'wrapped in cotton wool', means that even at the age of twenty-two many of their children are not emotionally mature and can only be classified as adults due to their age not their level of maturity. The 'guardians' these children are handed over to are burdened by the pressures of a mortgage, having bills to pay, holding down their jobs, fighting to make ends meet and at the same time even struggling to be parents to their own children. What time do these parents in Nigeria think the guardian in London has to pay attention to a child posted from Nigeria? My heart bleeds when I see such children, who had such promising prospects, ending up in mental health institutions due to the inadequacies of parents and society at large.

Some parents posted their children abroad not because they have found a school or work for them but simply to shy away from their responsibility and gamble that the child my get 'lucky' and run into money. This is because to an average Nigerian, success is defined by how rich one is and nothing else. It often does not matter how the riches came about.

As leaders, adults and parents in this, our nation (Nigeria), we need to begin the process of turning things around for posterity. We need to stop passing dangerous batons to our children by making them believe money is the all-important thing in this world. We need to refocus our minds on the important things in life and stop chasing shadows, remembering at all times the tsunami in Japan in 2011, which serves as proof that all the best houses, cars and aircraft can be swept away as they are perishables. The accolade of legacy and fame belongs to those who manufacture, invent and design the things that excite human beings and preserve life. Consumers of goods and products can gain only momentary enjoyment and pleasure. We must get away from 'abi what car you de drive now' and move to 'what car you de manufacture'. Our leaders need to create an enabling environment that would safeguard the lives and property of all Nigerians, encourage enterprise, bring in indigenous and foreign investments which would automatically create employment, reduce crime and encourage all Nigerians to maximise their potential. Without a strong private sector employment would continue to be a problem in our nation and crime would continue to increase. However no serious private enterprise, especially foreign owned, would invest in a country where there is no security for life and property, and steady electricity supply. Investors are reluctant to invest when they know that people would say one thing now and say another on the same issue. Trust is what drives business, nothing else. We must begin now to work together, with diligence and rid ourselves of this cancer that is eating us and setting our nation backward. Let us aim now to actualise the 'Giant of Africa' we call our nation, Nigeria. **IT IS DOABLE!**

Our leaders also need to encourage the unity of all Nigerians irrespective of class, ethnicity or creed. One of the things required to foster unity for Nigerians is the ability to speak each other's language. As the Nigeria's Deputy High Commissioner for Britain Ambassador Dozie Nwanna (OON) noted, nothing has created more separation between different ethnic groups than 'pidgin English'. In the past people were keen to interact, and the only way a person could interact with his or her brother or sister from the east, west, north or south was to learn their language. Speaking another local dialect creates a psychological bond and can turn a potential foe into a good friend. It would serve our nation's interest for it to be mandatory for school children to study one of the three predominant languages in Nigeria, including their own. We must learn the words 'social engineering'. If our leaders fail to structure, manage and organise the people of Nigeria by studying what is happening now, reflect on it and plan for what the state of the nation could be like in ten, twenty or thirty years time (i.e. having vision) then society is likely to go into turmoil.

Most Nigerians love America. It is believed that one out of two Nigerians want to go to America. If such an interest exists then it means we need to mimic a bit of what the Americans do. If we can only mimic one thing, I suggest we mimic how America values and protects its citizens. I cannot say this enough; **life is worth more than what is used to nourish it.** Every Nigerian child's life should be valued and protected whether inside or outside the country. It should worry every reasonable Nigerian that a person as highly placed as the Attorney General (Bola Ige) was murdered in December 2001 and ten years later and counting, there is still no one held accountable for his murder. The question then is, if this can happen to the Attorney General of the Federation, what fate do 'ordinary' Nigerians have? What is the value of a Nigerian life? The growth of any nation is dependent on its citizenry. Therefore any nation that does not value, defend and protect the lives of its citizens must surely fail.

In a Nation were Ambulance Service is mainly for carrying the dead not the living, yet people in it are classified as the 'happiest' in the world. This is as good as laughing whilst being strangled or roasting inside an oven. If our hospitals are not good enough for you then they shouldn't be viewed as good enough for any Nigerian child. If our educational establishments are not good enough for your children then they cannot be good enough for any Nigerian child. The ambulance service must be for the living, not the dead, and without a steady electricity supply we can wave goodbye to any dream of real advancement as a people no matter what angle we want to look at it from. These are simply must do's and the only basis for change.

To our brothers and sisters who are bombing and taking other people's lives for whatsoever purpose in the name of Boka Haram, I say this: God – Allah– is Love! God –Allah – is Great! He does not discriminate in the distribution of rain, sunshine and wind. These

He ensures for both the sinner and the righteous. He is very powerful and has the capacity to send destruction through natural disasters and other means unknown to man if He so wishes. Therefore He can fight His own war. Therefore, if there is sin, let God –Allah –the Almighty to whom we all pray, to whom you bow your forehead down to and plead, who can send rain, thunder or even death to anyone, deal with it. Any Boko Haram member who takes part in instigating any killing or killing any person is not a true believer in Allah, because true believers of Allah know that Allah is more than capable of self-defence. Indeed true believers look up to Allah for their own defence. The real message of peace and love, the real message of salvation revolves around 'praying for and loving your enemy'; for vengeance is the Lord's not ours. So if there is a crime, let the law deal with it.

It is important to read and understand the Bible very well if one is a Christian; the same applies to the Koran, if one is a Muslim. However, the central focus must be on the life and doctrines of Jesus Christ for Christians and the life and doctrines of Prophet Mohammed (peace be unto him) for Muslims. The question is, did Jesus Christ kill anyone? Did Prophet Mohammed (peace be unto him) kill or bomb anyone? The answer is that Jesus Christ reversed the Old Testament Law of Moses of 'an eye for an eye' to 'turning the other cheek' and 'loving, praying for one's enemy and leaving vengeance to God'. He even cautioned Peter, who became violent and cut someone's ear. There are two versions when it comes to Prophet Mohammed (peace be unto him). Some accounts state that he physically killed and some say that he didn't physically kill anyone, but because he was the supreme commander of the armed forces he had to lead the army in battle and that naturally led to deaths. He was also the supreme ruler of the Muslim state of Medina and had to pass judgement on criminals whose sentences were capital punishment.

The most important thing for all of us is to search our souls and minds and if there is anything that makes us ashamed or leads us to try to conceal anything about our faith then that thing must be wrong; anything that makes us uncomfortable with our religion must be wrong. All other aspects of it we must have out in the open so that we can celebrate our religion. The slaughter of someone else's child is the slaughter of one's own child irrespective of our creed, culture or colour. The truth is that none of us has died and come back to life to testify as to whether all the promises about killing someone else due to 'religious' beliefs are actually facts or not. Those who set out to bomb and kill others are not true Muslims because bombs do not discriminate. If a person throws a bomb that kills people indiscriminately then that person cannot claim to be a person of faith, because it is a sin for a brother or sister to kill a brother or sister. Therefore those that throw bombs are terrorists and we have to offer prayers for their repentance. All killings, especially killings of innocent souls, are sinful to God –Allah – and are crimes against humanity. We have enough illnesses, natural disasters, accidents and all manner of hazards, poor healthcare facilities and natural deaths threatening us on a daily basis. We do not need to inflict more deaths on ourselves for we are brothers and sisters within this nation called Nigeria and outside it, irrespective of our gender, creed, ethnicity or religion, 'though tongue and tribe may differ in brotherhood we stand' according to our previous national anthem.

Echoing the last stanza of that great anthem, we all must pray, 'Oh God of creation, grant this our one request. Help us to build a nation where no man is oppressed. And so with peace and plenty, Nigeria may be blessed.' Let us rally around our President (Goodluck Jonathan) and with one accord begin to right the wrongs of our past for our own benefit, but most importantly with a view to securing the future of our children, keeping in mind that the true test of a civilised society is how it treats the vulnerable within it. Let us build a nation where no man, woman or child is oppressed!

All Nigerians need to appreciate that wrong things are really easy to do and copy, whereas doing the right things are really difficult. Think of how difficult it is to save life: sometimes operations will last for hours on end and the healing process can take an indeterminate period. This is just one side of the equation. Now consider how long it takes to train a doctor, who requires the training in order to carry out such operations. Combine the two, and that's how long it takes to be in a position to medically save lives; but how long does it take to end a life, what training is required and who can do it? The answer is that it takes seconds to end life, no training is required and anybody could do it. This is the reason criminal activities spread like wildfire because often no training is required, hence the need to get a handle on deviant acts.

We have planted and continue to plant dangerous seeds and hand our children dangerous batons by making money the central issue in our lives. Life should and must be worth more than what is used to nourish it, for without life there will be no basis for nourishment. Nigeria had been described as 'the happiest nation'. I suggest we reject this description because there is nothing useful in being happy when you are in terrible pain. It is called the masking of an illness and there is nothing that is more futile; it is what happens mainly when one is psychotic. We cannot be chasing shadows when our house is on fire! Only when a problem is recognised can it be dealt with. Our children need us to nurture them properly now more than ever.

Nigerians working in the more 'civilised' parts of the world have demonstrated their competence and shown how effectively and productively they can perform in a structured system. This is an indication that if our leaders could put in the structures, the manpower to match would not be in short supply. The only concern is that big 'if', because though one wants to remain optimistic, one can't fail to notice the difficulties involved in having a 'proper' structure in Nigeria. This is because we as a people seem programmed to disable and destabilise structures. We seem to take pleasure in putting obstacles where there are none, so when a person jumps over an obstacle they will feel the need to say 'thank you' for jumping over a hurdle that shouldn't have been there in the first place. Take, for instance, a place like England, where the postal system run by non-Nigerians is second to none in terms of efficiency and effectiveness. It is so efficient that if one wants a letter to get to its destination and signed for the next day, there is a guarantee that this can be done by registered or recorded delivery. One can also pay for the item to be returned by enclosing a pre-paid, self-addressed envelope. Keep in mind that this is a system run by non-Nigerians. The question then is why is it that Nigerians in England and those that live in Scotland cannot interact with their embassy by post? Most Nigerians would prefer to pay more to do this than have to spend a whole day (sometimes days and weeks) not only risking their lives travelling but risking losing their jobs (from which they get the money to fulfil their civic responsibility). In fact the money Nigerians use to travel could be spent on employing extra staff to deal with postal enquiries. In this digitalised world, where most things are done online, by fax or on the phone, people are still queuing up like 'lambs going to the slaughter' in London's cold weather. Nigerians who are also British citizens do not need to visit anywhere to sort out their British passport. Everything is done by post. Now, if we can disable an already existing structure here in London, England, how on earth can we facilitate the formation of structures and implement them at home? If someone is thirsty amidst plenty of water, tell me what becomes of them when they are in a desert?

I HAVE NO IDEA WHO WROTE THIS BUT IT MAKES INTERESTING READING AND GOOD FOOD FOR THOUGHT FOR ALL NIGERIAN PARENTS AND THEIR CHILDREN. THIS WAS SENT TO TOPAZ CLUB MEMBERS BY JOHN MOZIE ON 28.6.11

Friends,
Let me add the benefit of my time as a student and then resident in the United Kingdom – I live in Lagos now. The first thing that I discovered about UK-born, white, English undergraduates including the children of millionaires amongst them that all of them did holiday or weekend jobs to support themselves. It is the norm over there –regardless of how wealthy their parents are. And I soon discovered that virtually all other foreign students did the same – the exception being those of us status-conscious Nigerians.

I also watched Richard Branson (owner of Virgin Airline) speaking on the Biography Channel and, to my amazement he said that his young children travel in the economy class –even when the parents (he and his wife) are in upper class. Richard Branson is a billionaire in Pounds Sterling. A quick survey would show you that only children from Nigeria fly business or upper class to commence their studies as students in the United Kingdom. No other foreign students do this. There is no aircraft attached to the office of the Prime Minister in the UK – he travels on British Airways. And the same goes for the Royals. The Queen does not have an aircraft for her exclusive use.

These practices simply become the culture, which the next generation carries forward. Have you seen the car that Kate Middleton the lady married to Prince William drives? VW Golf or something close to it. But there's one core difference between them and us (generally speaking). They – the billionaires among them work for their money, we steal ours!

If we want our children to bring about the desired change we have been praying for on behalf of our dear country, then please let us begin now and teach them to work hard so that they can stand on their own legs and most importantly be content, and not have to "steal".

"30 is the new 18", which seems to be the new age for testing out the world in Nigeria now. That seems to be an unspoken but widely accepted mindset among the last 2 generations of parents in Nigeria.

At age 18 years, a typical young adult in the UK leaves the clutches of his or her parents for the University. Chances are, that is the last time those parents will ever play "landlord" to their son or daughter, except of course on the occasional home visits during the academic year.

At 21 years and above or below, the now fully grown and independent minded adult graduates from University, searches for employment, gets a job and shares a flat with other young people on a journey into becoming fully-fledged adults.

I can hear the echo of parents saying, well, that is because the United Kingdom economy is thriving, safe, well structured and jobs are everywhere? I beg to differ and I ask that you kindly hear me out. I am a United Kingdom trained Recruitment Consultant and I have been practising for the past 10 years in Nigeria. I have a broad range of experience from recruiting graduates to executive director level of large corporations. In addition, I talk from the point of view of someone with [a] relatively privileged upbringing.

I was Driven to school every day, had my clothes washed for me, I was barred from taking any part-time job during my A-levels so that I could concentrate on studying for my exams? BUT, I got the opportunity to live apart from my parents from age 18 and the only time I came back home to stay was for 3 months before I got married!

Am I saying that every parent should wash their hands off their children at age 18? No, not at all, I enjoyed the savings that I made from living on and off at my parent's house in London – indeed that is the primary reason for my being able to buy myself a 3 bedroom flat in London at age 25 with absolutely no direct financial help from my parents!

For me, pocket money stopped at age 22, not that it was ever enough for my lifestyle to compete with Paris Hilton's or Victoria Beckham's. Meanwhile today, we have Nigerian children who have never worked for 5 minutes in their lives, insisting on flying "only" first or business class, carrying the latest Louis Vuitton ensemble, Victoria's Secret underwear and wearing Jimmy Choo's, fully paid for by their "loving" parents.

I often get calls from anxious parents: my son graduated 2 years ago and is still looking for a job, can you please assist? Oh really! So where exactly is this "child", is my usual question. Why are you the one making this call, dad or mum?

I am yet to get a satisfactory answer, but between you and me, chances are that big boy is cruising around Lagos with a babe dressed to the nines, in his dad's spanking new SUV with enough "pocket money" to put your salary to shame. It is not at all strange to have a 28-year-old who has NEVER worked for a day in his or her life in Nigeria but "earns" a six figure "salary" from parents for doing absolutely nothing.

I see them in my office once in a while, 26 years old with absolutely no skills to sell, apart from a shiny CV, written by his dad's secretary in the office. Of course, he has a driver at his beck and call and he is driven to the job interview. We have a fairly decent conversation and we get to the inevitable question – so, what salary are you looking to earn? Answer comes straight out ₦250,000. I ask if that is per month or per annum.

Of course it is per month. Oh, why do you think you should be earning that much on your first job? Well, because my current pocket money is ₦200,000 and I feel that an employer should be able to pay me more than my parents. I try very hard to compose myself. Over-parenting is in my opinion the greatest evil handicapping the Nigerian youth today. It is at the root of our national malaise.

We have a youth population of tens of millions, many of whom are being "breastfed and diapered" well into their 30s. Even though the examples I have given above are from parents of considerable affluence, similar patterns can be observed from Abeokuta to Adamawa! Wake up mum! Wake up dad! You are practically loving your children to death! No wonder corruption continues to thrive. We have a society of young people who have been brought up to expect something for nothing, as if it were a birth right.

I want to encourage you to send your young men and women (anyone over 20 can hardly be called a child!) out into the world, maybe even consider reducing or stopping the pocket money to encourage them to think, explore and strive. Let them know that it is possible for them to succeed without your "help".

Take a moment to think back to your own time as a young man or woman, what if someone had kept spoon-feeding you, would you be where you are today? No tree grows well under another tree; children that are not exposed to challenges don't cook well. That is why you see adults complaining, "My parents didn't buy clothes for me this Christmas."

Ask him or her how old are you? The answer is 30 years +. Because of the challenges we faced in our youth, we are where and what we are today. This syndrome of my children will not suffer what I suffered is destroying our tomorrow.

Deliberately reduce their allowance or, mum, don't cook on Saturday till late afternoon or evening –do as occasion demands.

I learnt that the children of a former Nigerian head of state with all the stolen (billions) monies in their custody still go about with security escort as wrecks. They are on drugs; several times because of the drug they collapse in public places. The escort will quickly pack them and off they go. What a life! No one wants to marry them. For your information, anyone who stops learning is old, whether at twenty or eighty. Anyone who keeps learning stays young. The greatest thing in life is to keep your mind young (Henry Ford). Hard work does not kill; everything in Nigeria is going down, including family settings and values. It is time to cook our children, preparing them for tomorrow. We are approaching the season in Nigeria where only the RUGGED will survive. How will your ward fare?

If the present generation of Nigerian pilots retire, will you fly a plane flown by a young Nigerian pilot, if trained in Nigeria? People now have first class [sic], who cannot spell GRADUATE or read an article without "bomb blast" [sic] tense mistakes! Which Way Nigeria? Which Way Nigerians!! Is this how we will ALL sit and watch this country SINK?

Please forward this to as many Nigerian parents, as you know.

Minor changes have been made to the original text due to some typing errors.

The author of this article couldn't have written better, touching on the core cancer affecting our nation, Nigeria, and the way parenting is carried out these days. The psychotic notion of some of our Nigerian parents is that love for their children means storing up wealth, surrounding them with housemaids, drivers, gardeners, dressing them up for parade, sending them to the best schools known to man and making them 'happy'. Some do not even see their children for days and weeks, let alone spend quality time with them. They leave them to the devices of maids (who need parental guidance themselves) because of their weird notion that 'there is plenty of money to deal with any issues my children have.' These parents genuinely believe that money is the answer to all problems, and this is why they neglect their first priority (children) in pursuit of making more money 'by all means possible and necessary'. I invite such parents to take a good look at the section of this book titled, 'Good, bad and worst parenting' starting at page 142. If possible, check out '*See* 'A Tribute to an Awesome Father', page 102; there you will hopefully appreciate the damage you are doing to your children (and to yourself and society at large) and see that even birds let their little ones learn to fly independently.

This is my message to all Nigerians: please let our attitude, especially when it comes to education, be like that of a young Nigerian man by the name of Nnanyere Ekenna, a supervisor and invigilator who oversees the conduct of both invigilators and students in any particular examination area he is assigned, who said to me, 'Oga Eze, no matter the temptation that comes my way to pass someone who on merit has failed, I would always ask myself one question, which is, if this person wangles his or her way in and becomes a doctor, for instance, what chance would my daughter have if her life were to depend on this person? Based on this I will never accept anything to pass someone who has failed. The half-baked doctor, teacher, pilot or driver might one day come into contact with you or your loved ones. Evil knows no bounds and does not recognise demarcating lines. Just like air, it filters through everyone's nose and spreads like wildfire because a lot of training is not required. Therefore don't let momentary pleasure and satisfaction cloud your judgement and make you forget about the long-term pain and misery you will inflict by letting the cat in amongst the pigeons. Let's learn to do the right thing and follow due process for our own benefit and the benefit of our children and all future generations.

CHAPTER SEVEN

Conclusion

When we are children, it is natural for us to think and act like children. It is natural for us to notice our differences. This is proper and normal. However, we need to progress, through nurtured learning, to appreciate our differences. Without appreciating our differences it will be virtually impossible to celebrate our differences. If an adult or a parent fails to progress and appreciate our differences, then that person is quite simply stuck in a child's mode, because a person will never know they are tall unless they saw a short person, know they are rich unless they saw a poor person or know they are a doctor unless they have a patient by this I mean that we are all different, and without our differences life would lose its meaning and we could not function as a society. It then becomes crucial that we value that which makes us feel the way we do.

If anyone summarises, praises or condemns another person's actions based on how they look, their creed or ethnicity, that person is still thinking and reasoning like a child. The fact that I am 'white', you are 'black', I am male, you are female, I am a Christian and you are a Muslim has no bearing on the good or bad behaviour we display as human beings. On a daily basis we are reminded that there are good and bad amongst all races, genders and creeds. Whether we like it or not and whether we understand it or choose to ignore it; as human beings, we will continue to need each other, individuals needing other individuals, families needing other families, communities needing other communities and nations needing other nations. The word 'independent' is and will remain an illusion because we are interdependent. Failing to understand, appreciate and celebrate our differences is the height of ignorance! The greatest gift to mankind is differences because without it, there would be no value to life. The differences we see in race, gender, creed, ethnicity, status is the only thing that adds value to our existence. So I repeat, we as human beings must learn to value, respect and celebrate the differences that add value to us. Not understanding this is as good as not understanding the value of various parts of our body or suggesting that the only important part of the body is the eye, when we know that the eye cannot do the work meant for the hand. More importantly, how would the eye know it is the eye, if every part of the body becomes an eye?

Ladies and Gentlemen, boys and girls: as stated earlier, babies do not choose which families or nations they are born into or their gender or skin colour. However, no matter what families or nations they find themselves in, there are the likes of them somewhere else on the globe. If all nations were to return what they perceive as not theirs, we might have more people coming into wherever we claim to be our own than people going out.

We are people of the world; we all belong to this world, belong to each other and depend on each other for our survival. No matter who we are, what family or nation we are born into, whether we like it or not all of us will return to a 'common' place (the grave or be turned into ashes). This is not a matter of if but a matter of when. We must learn to love ourselves, one another and treat others as we would like them treat us. We must desist from contaminating our unborn children with drugs and/or alcohol. We need to teach our children from an early age about the dangers of poly-substance (drugs and alcohol) abuse and getting into an emotional relationship at a young age. We need to teach our children how to structure their lives and have set boundaries but a less fixed lifestyle. However, if a person must use alcohol and/or drugs or get involved in an emotional relationship they should aim to do so in adulthood when they can financially afford them and can cope emotionally with the by-products of these activities, in order not to derail or have a life infested with crime against humanity. We need to get our facts right and understand that there's enough space in this world for everyone. The world also has enough resources for everyone to have the basic things of life, if managed properly. There is no need for any child anywhere in this world to be dying due to malnutrition in a world full of plenty where food is being wasted on a daily basis. As human beings we have more than enough illnesses, accidents and natural disasters destroying us and inflicting pain and suffering on us. We need not deliberately inflict more pain and misery on ourselves. We do not need to kill ourselves or others in order to survive. We need to stop sowing the seeds of hatred and violence in our children. Instead we need to nurture love, sharing, respect and peace by seeing ourselves in others and others in us, irrespective of our differences. By freeing others, we free ourselves. By loving others, we love ourselves. And by valuing others, we value ourselves. There is great value in our differences and greater value when we focus on our similarities. Let's understand this in order to celebrate it. We cannot share anything if we all have the same thing, hence the need for differences. We come in vulnerable and leave as vulnerable, hence the value for our similarities. Let's make this world a better place for all of us to live and coexist in. Let's get to work, and deviate from a status quo that leads us to believe that we can cheat others, live in our little bubbles and fight and kill others in order to survive. As nature takes care of our arrival so nature also has more than enough capacity to take care of our time on this earth and our departure. The 'new invention' is the ability to use the cognition we have as human beings to find out how we can better manage the space and resources our world offers, without endangering any of the children within it. This has to start by looking at the man or woman in the mirror, as Michael Jackson tells us! To all those reading this book I say this: find yourselves in the characters described herein; if you have characteristics and behaviour that are described as 'right', then carry on living your life in the spirit of continuous improvement, because no matter how good we are there is always room for improvement. If you find yourself wanting, please challenge yourself and change today. Don't leave it until tomorrow or for somebody else to note. Think positively and your actions will begin to become positive; this will lead to a better tomorrow for you, your family and the rest of humanity. Remember, where we find ourselves as we begin our lives is just a matter of 'fortune or misfortune', but we must learn to give thanks. Go on, be brave and courageous! Be one of those heroes and heroines our world is craving for, and as you become such a person may Almighty God, Allah, Jehovah, Obasi in heaven, whether or not you believe, bless you and your efforts, in Jesus' name, Amen!

However, be warned that if we fail to act now evil would continue to multiply, to the extent that it will locate your 'little bubbles' one day. If we fail to deal with evil or condone it, it will catch up with us or someone we care about because we will either find it or it will find us. It may come to where you live, stay, work or visit. No one is immune to it and it knows no bounds. Keep in mind that evil has multiplied and continues to multiply because we did not fully comprehend and appreciate the true nature of it. Therefore some of us have stood idly by in silence, and by virtue of keeping silent, contributed to the evil. We have all contributed to the unleashing of mayhem on this world, thereby endangering the lives of our children and future generations. Both your child and my child, after all said and done, are *our* children. Let's help them grow into well-rounded adults/individuals that would bring joy not sorrow to humanity. We are all in this together and together we can do it. Yes, we can!

We all need to seek to do the right thing for the harmonisation of this world, as I have been duly informed that 'none of us would get out of this world alive' whether we like it or not. Life should be viewed as a staircase; we must learn to work hard and summon the energy to climb the staircase when people at the same level decide to react negatively to us. We must not be like them and do the 'easy thing' by remaining at the same level or going downstairs with them. Always seek the hard option by going up the staircase, thereby rising above the issue. Hopefully you would have taught those people how to climb the staircase when faced with similar problem. Life can also be viewed as a tree, with everyone trying to climb as high as their ability can take them. No one start from the top, everyone starts at the bottom. Everyone at one point or another would have opportunity to overtake and be overtaken as they climb. The higher one climbs, the more they can

'lord it' over those who are under. There is no guarantee that everyone would reach his or her desired height. The only guarantee is that, no one stays on the tree forever. Everyone must climb down. The climbing down could be safely done, with difficulty or it could be a crash down. The higher one is on the tree, the harder the climb down and the easier a crash, can lead to fatality. Those who are at the bottom have no fear of falling but would suffer most from the mess, those at the top generate. The advice is; when at the top, be mindful of the 'mess' you generate, be mindful of those you passed on your way to the top and those at the bottom, as they are very likely to hold the key to whether you crash or have a soft landing. But most importantly, remember that the treetops cannot feed or survive without the root but the root can survive even when the branches have been cut off.

Whatever we call our superiority, dominance, power, craftiness, cleverness and intelligence, beneath all there is blood and water running through every human being. The blood and water make us mortals destined to the graves and crematoriums under 'normal' circumstances. The unlucky few would die and disappear without a trace. We will never know the hour, means or manner of the final call. So be good to one another and look after that child. Decency is not located on the clothes or smiles we wear but in the heart upon which they are worn and our actions. The value of criticism, controversy and opposition is immeasurable, unquantifiable and incalculable. Think! How would my decision today affect your child, my child and our children... the children of this world? Keep in mind that, if your children are well behaved and orderly and your neighbour's are not; then both you and your children are at risk. How safe is your Rolls Royce amidst vehicles without brakes? For there to be relative peace in this world, the welfare of every child must be paramount. Not just your biological child but every child anywhere and everywhere! This is one global human family; when one suffers, the rest of society should feel the pain, otherwise something is wrong somewhere. Being detached, pretending it is not happening or keeping silent in the face of evil is another way of taking part by encouraging and condoning it! The 'them and us' attitude is key to the mayhem we see in our world today. Let us rip to shreds the *status quo* and do things better. It can be done!

It might be bitter, unsettling, threatening, uncomfortable, frustrating, challenging and upsetting. It can also hurt, but, ladies and gentlemen, boys and girls: the ONLY WAY IS THE TRUTH. Therefore we must learn to embrace it.

References

Attewill F., *Metro*, 7 September 2011.

Candland D., (1993) *Feral Children and Clever Animals.* Oxford: University Press.
 http://www.dailymail.co.uk/health/article-564097/Babies-born-drug-addict-mothers-DOUBLED-years.html#ixzz1p7FWFjo3

Cassin S., (1999) *Your Child and Drugs.* Veritas Publications

Covey S., (1997) *The Seven Habits of Highly Effective Families.* Simon & Schuster Ltd

Cunningham H., (2005) *Children and Childhood in Western Society Since 1500 (2nd edition).* Harlow: Pearson Education Limited.

Daily Mirror, 11 October 2011.

Daily Mirror, 3 January 2012.

Ezeani, E. (2012) *In Biafra Africa Died, The Diplomatic Plot,* London: Veritas Lumen Publishers.

Ezeani, E. (2012) *Philosophy of Education for African Nations - Recovering from the Negative Effects of Colonial Education*, London: Veritas Luman Publishers.

Golding W, (1954) *Lord of the Flies, Faber* and Faber Limited

Gregory A. *Daily Mirror,* 11 October 2011

Greenwood C. (2012) *Mail Online* 1 March 2012,

Human Rights Act, (1998)

MailOnline, 14 March 2012.
http://www.dailymail.co.uk/health/article-564097/Babies-born-drug-addict-mothers-DOUBLED-years.html#ixzz1p7FWFjo3

Metro, 11 October 2011.

Mayhew H (1985) *London Labour & The London Poor.* Penguin Classics

Mill J.S., (1975) *Representative* Government. Oxford: University Press.

Moneywise, 28 October 2011.
http://www.moneywise.co.uk/news/2011-10-28/fat-cats-award-themselves-49%-pay-rises

Nacho, E. (2010) *Hard Hitting (The Real Truth About Men, Marriage & Infidelity),* Central Milton Keynes: AuthorHouse Publishers.

Nkwopara, C. (2012) *Gbooza Internet News Community:* News Blogs and Forums

Orjiako C.L PhD (2009) *Jurisprudence of Jurgen Habermas: In Defence of Human Rights & a Search for Legitimacy, Truth & Validity,* Central Milton Keynes: AuthorHouse UK Ltd.

Parker A (2012) *The Sun*, 13 January 2012

Parker A (2012) *The Sun,* 3 April 2012

Randewich N and Nayak M (2012) *Reuter,* 3 April 2012.

Sumner G (2009) *Body Intelligence: Creating a New Environment,* Singing Dragon

Sky News, 7 February 2011

The Sun, 8 September 2011.

The Sun, 13 January 2012.

Taylor J. *Metro,* 5 August 2011.

Walsh et al (2003) *Prevalence of Violent Victimisation In Severe Mental Illness,* British Journal of Psychiatry Volume 183

Watson, J. (1930) *Behaviourism,* Chicago: University of Chicago Press.

The Author

The Author, who is an approved mental health professional, is as 'afflicted' as everyone else. However he was highly motivated to write this informative book which would be beneficial to everyone.

The author has drawn from a huge wealth of experience from being parented by two teachers, having four children of his own, growing up in a massive family as his grandfather had 32 wives. He was a seminarian who aborted because; he felt he did not get the calling to become a priest. He also has experience in Marriage Counselling, and has worked in homes for children in care, as well as older people's. He performs on a regular basis as an active Master of Ceremonies in State events, Weddings and had drawn so much from entertaining children during Christening/Birthday Parties.

The Author is multi-faceted with hobbies like, boxing, singing; harmonica playing, table and lawn tennis playing. He won the 'Group One' of Haringey Tennis Leagues in 2010, and has the ability to lift people up using his teeth alone; a breath taking skill he used to get a lot out of children for this book (*see* page 44). He is an 'ordinary' human being like everyone else, but strongly believes that 'ordinary people can do extra-ordinary things' simply by putting themselves to the test.

Notes

www.ingramcontent.com/pod-product-compliance
Lightning Source LLC
Chambersburg PA
CBHW020538020726
47494CB00006B/1817